DANIA VOSS

EVERNIGHT PUBLISHING ®

www.evernightpublishing.com

Copyright© 2019

Dania Voss

Editor: Audrey Bobak

Cover Art: Jay Aheer

Model: Luca Pantini

Photographer: Alessandro Frezza

ISBN: 978-1-77339-933-1

DANIA VOSS

DEDICATION

I'd like to thank Stacey, and everyone at Evernight Publishing. It's always such a pleasure to work with you. I'd like to acknowledge the Evernight author community for their assistance, creativity, and suggestions when I needed them. You're all amazing.

I want to thank Erin M. Leaf and Laura M. Baird for their patience with me as I agonized over ideas for the book cover.

And speaking of Erin M. Leaf, thank you for allowing the ladies of the Twisted Tea Society to discuss your book *Dawn.*

I could never have anticipated when I conceived of this storyline that Italian fashion photographer Alessandro Frezza, who has taken photographs for magazines and Italian designers including Elle, Sposabella, Gianni Calignano, Urbano della Scala, and others, would end up shooting the cover for Hannah's Bliss. Then he went a step further and created a beautiful video of the photo shoot. I'm both honored and humbled. *Grazie mille,* Alessandro.

Lastly, many thanks to Italian model Luca Pantini—my Rocco. What an unexpected and wonderful surprise it was "meeting" you. Not only did you help me with the Italian translations from thousands of miles away, but you literally brought the character Rocco Moretti to life. It's been fantastic working with you and getting to know you these last several months. *Abbracci dall'America.*

DANIA VOSS

#

Windy City Nights, 2

Dania Voss

Copyright © 2019

Chapter One

Hannah Hailey threw her hands up in disbelief after she'd parked her car in Grace of God Lutheran Church's parking lot. Was her mother kidding? What the hell? She punched at her passenger seat three times and took a deep breath. *Don't blow a gasket, Hannah. She's your mother.*

It was a beautiful June afternoon in Elmhurst, Illinois. The perfect day for a wedding. A wedding she and her best friend and assistant Joe had planned and organized down to the last cornflower-blue rose petal. And her mother, Patricia Hailey, founder of Hailey's Events, the *premier* event planners in Chicagoland, seemed to suggest Hannah wasn't performing up to her exacting standards.

It wasn't true, but her mother's reservations about her abilities still stung. Hannah was an outstanding Senior Event Planner and had received hundreds of positive testimonials from delighted clients to prove it. Nothing was ever good enough for her mother, though, and she was sick and tired of it.

"If you didn't think I was up to the task, shouldn't you have said something *before* Jake and Cassie's wedding day?" Hannah leaned her head back against her seat's headrest and closed her eyes while taking a deep breath. She willed her mind to calm. *Don't let her get to you.*

"I wasn't saying you're not up to the task." Her mother had the nerve to reply in an exasperated tone in Hannah's Bluetooth. "I'm just saying we need to make sure everything is executed perfectly for Darren Stryker. You know how important he is to this firm."

She smiled at the mention of Darren Stryker, owner of the Chicago Cobras major league baseball team. She'd met him when she was only fourteen and her mother had just begun her event planning career. He'd given Hailey's Events their first major event to plan, a fundraiser for the Cobras' Children Foundation fifteen years ago. And the rest was history.

"I know he is. But the firm doesn't rely on business from Darren and the Cobras' organization to stay afloat, and you know it. The firm thrives regardless of Darren's business." What was Patty, as her friends called her mother, so worried about?

Hailey's Events had built a reputation as Chicagoland's best event planners and had been named as the Top Event Planner in the country twice. Not to mention the national recognition they'd received in publications such as *The Knot*, *Brides*, *Chicago Magazine*, *Martha Stewart Weddings*, and *Modern Luxury Brides Chicago*.

"I know and I thank God *and* Darren for that. He took a chance on me in the beginning. I owe him and he considers Jake and Cassie *family*, so this wedding is especially important," her mother reminded her. Hannah didn't need to be reminded of how Darren valued family. The Cobras' star pitcher, Luke, was Darren's nephew and had been his ward since the age of ten when Darren's brother and sister-in-law were killed in a car wreck.

Hannah rolled her eyes. Every wedding was important, at least to her. Weddings were her favorite event to plan and coordinate. *Probably because I want to design bridal gowns. Design school is all you get. Be happy with your sketches.*

She rubbed her temples, hoping to stave off the usual headache she got when going a few rounds with her mother. When was she ever going to be good enough for the woman? Christ, even perfection wasn't good enough, especially when it came to her.

"I assure you, Darren, the bride, groom, *and* you will be pleased today. Now if that's all, I need to get out of the church parking lot and inside the actual church." She didn't wait for a reply and exited her car, retrieving her everything-but-the-kitchen-sink-is-in-here emergency bag from the trunk.

"No need to get snippy. I'll be there soon and then I'll meet with the bride and bridesmaids at the Fairchild Hotel. Richard should be at Grace of God by now. Isn't it time for the two of you to—"

Hannah slammed the truck shut with all her might.

No. No. No. She was *not* having this conversation. Not now, not later—hopefully not ever.

"Okay, well, I'm headed inside. See you soon." She disconnected her mother, slumped against her car, and sighed. It was going to be a long day. She'd make sure it was perfect, but it would be long nonetheless.

Looking up, letting the warmth of the summer

sun soothe her, she squared shoulders, ready for the day's events to unfold. She strode to the church entrance with purpose, wishing her mother would relax on what she considered professional attire for an event. Hannah had many lovely summer dresses she considered appropriate but was wearing a navy-blue business suit and had her hair up in a loose bun—*Patty*-appropriate. One of these days, she would break free. One of these days ... but not today.

She proceeded through the church's vestibule doors and down the aisle and relaxed immediately when she spotted Joe Burke. Patty-appropriate in a gray, slim-fit suit with his dark locks perfectly coiffed. He was much more than her assistant and right-hand man. He'd been her best friend since the day they'd met when they were five years old. They were twenty-nine now, nearly a quarter of a century of true friendship.

He walked toward her with two clipboards in his hand and a frown on his handsome face. "You've got that Patty face on, hon." He hugged her tight and handed her the day's clipboard. Not that she needed it. She and Joe had memorized everything down to the last detail, having planned and organized dozens of weddings together over the years.

Glancing down at the details she had helped to prepare, she sighed. "We had a little chat in the parking lot just after I got here. I'm fine." She would be once she shook off her mother's doubts of her abilities and got to work.

Joe grimaced. "What the ... heck is wrong with that woman? You are one of the best planners she's got and we're one of the best teams at the firm. You can't take her ramblings too seriously. Even after all these years, she's still trying to prove herself. It's sad, actually. She'll never be satisfied and it's a shame."

Hannah agreed, but there was no time to ponder the inner workings of Patty's mind at the moment. They had work to do, which took precedence over concerns about her mother.

For a moment, she allowed herself the luxury of admiring the church's domed ceiling. She loved this church. Whoever conceived the vision was an incredible artist. The painted artwork covering the entire ceiling with various biblical scenes was spiritual, inspirational, and soothing.

She took a deep cleansing breath and felt re-energized. Ready to give Jake and Cassie the wedding of their dreams and please Hailey's Events most prestigious client, Darren Stryker.

With a renewed sense of purpose, Hannah felt ready to tackle the day ahead. Holding her clipboard in one hand, and her utility bag in the other, she proceeded up the aisle with Joe following close behind.

"The florists and caterers should be here soon. Let's take a look at Fellowship Hall and make sure the tables are set up the way we want them." She marched out the side door to the right of the altar toward her destination, her respectable Patty-appropriate heels clicking against the tile floors.

"I did a quick check before you got here. They followed our diagram," Joe assured her.

She nodded. "Great. Then we're off to a good start." She rounded the corner that led to the large auditorium-style room the church used for events.

As she and Joe stepped inside Fellowship Hall's entry doors, she heard a woman giggle from behind the left door. Hannah put a finger on her lips, indicating to Joe not to say anything.

"Stop," the woman behind the door said with little conviction in her voice.

"Come on, baby. Let me get a good look at those ripe tits of yours before I have to work," Richard Hayes coaxed.

Hannah's stomach churned slightly. Not as much as it had in the past where Richard and his behavior were concerned, for which she was grateful. She nearly laughed out loud. *This* was who her mother and his were trying so hard to encourage a love match with. What a joke. Even sadder was she'd actually tried—for a little while. Mostly to appease her mother. She should've known better. The two of them together had been and would always be a fiasco. But their mothers were still pushing a union between them. *Never gonna happen, ladies.*

Joe yanked the door open, exposing Richard with his hand down the top of the church's cantor Jennifer's pretty, flowered, button-down dress. "Nice to see you, Dick. Hope we're not interrupting." Joe snarled.

"Joe," Hannah warned. Now was not the time for a throw-down. Though she couldn't help feeling loved by her best friend's anger on her behalf, it wasn't necessary.

Jennifer had the grace to blush and shoved Richard away, tucking herself back into her dress top and buttoning it back up. Tears welled in her pretty blue eyes. Jennifer was exactly Richard's type—blonde-haired and blue-eyed, just like him, a size two, and big-chested. She'd seen him ogle other women just like Jennifer enough times to know.

His wandering eyes and dick were among the many reasons they'd never be together. If she could only make their mothers understand without outing his dismal treatment of her, she'd feel less unease in his presence.

Jennifer wiped a tear away from her beautiful face and frowned. "I'm so sorry, Hannah. I didn't know you were with Richard."

Joe scoffed. "Don't worry, Jennifer, they're not together. Not anymore. Thank God for that. He's all yours, dear. You'll just need to pick up where you left off somewhere else. We'll be setting up in here soon."

Richard's eyes narrowed and his nostrils flared. Hannah dreaded yet another blowup between the two.

"Mind your own business, *Joey*. Don't you have some flowers to arrange or altar boys to grope?"

She and Jennifer both gasped. That was low, even for Richard. Not to mention so incredibly unprofessional. Hayes Studios and Hailey's Events worked many events together and since their mothers concocted their harebrained idea of the two of them together, there was always unwelcomed hostility between Richard and Joe.

Joe got in Richard's face, hands fisted. "I'm no pedophile, asshole, and you know it. It's such a shame, you know? What you create with your photographs and films is truly a work of art. It's too bad you have such ugliness inside you."

Hannah couldn't agree more, but now wasn't the time for a philosophical discussion of Richard's shortcomings. Even though he had many. "Joe, can you please check on the florist and caterer's ETAs for me?" She put a hand up when it looked as if Richard wanted to add another dig at Joe's expense.

Joe took a deep breath and nodded. She knew she could count on him. He'd never let her down in nearly twenty-five years of friendship or as work partners. "Of course, hon. There's no reason to waste any more time on *Dick*, is there?" After one final glare in Richard's direction, Joe exited Fellowship Hall, presumably to check on the florist and caterer.

"Have you taken the pictures and shot the footage you need before everyone gets here?" she asked Richard as she placed her bag down on the table closest to them.

"I'm so sorry, Hannah," Jennifer began. "If I had known you and Richard were involved in any way I never would—"

"We're on a break," Richard blurted out. The liar.

Hannah laughed. Hard. And it felt wonderful. Cleansing. "What are we? Ross and Rachel now? A break. That's hilarious."

Poor Jennifer seemed confused, glancing between them. "So, you're together then?"

"Yes."

"No. We're not. Not anymore, just like Joe said. And to be honest, we were never really together. Richard was never truly committed. I tried, but it just didn't work out. So, like Joe said, you two will have to carry on somewhere else because the flowers and food will be here soon."

Hannah picked up her clipboard and flipped to the page with the room's table diagram. Surveying the current room's layout, she was pleased. It was close. Some minor table placement changes and they'd be all set.

Jennifer glared at Richard with a disgusted look on her face. "I'm not going *anywhere* with him."

Richard rolled his eyes. Hannah didn't care. They'd have to work out whatever happened next between them on their own time. They were now on Jake, Cassie, and Darren's time.

"No offense, Jennifer, but it makes no difference to me. I don't care one way or the other. I need to adjust a couple of tables, so don't mind me." Hannah pulled out the chairs from the table where she'd placed her bag and moved it to where it needed to be.

She was relieved Richard's glare no longer had an effect on her. She would be all right. She'd put their awful time together behind her and move forward. To something and someone better. Just because Richard wasn't interested in her didn't mean no one else would ever be. As long as they passed the Patty test of appropriateness as far as her mother was concerned. Considering the disaster Richard had been, and he was Patty-approved, the only test of appropriateness that mattered anymore was hers and hers alone. Hannah needed to have a long overdue chat with her mother. No more stalling. *After the wedding.*

Jennifer followed Hannah to the next table she wanted to adjust and began pulling the chairs out. "Richard, either help us or go find something else to do."

He grunted and scowled at her. "Fine, I'll get lost. But we're going to talk about this later." Without waiting for Hannah's reply, he stormed out of the room.

Good riddance. Hannah wasn't surprised. If it wasn't photo- or film-related, Richard wanted nothing to do with it. In all the events their companies had worked together, never once had he lent a helping hand. How could her mother think she'd want to spend one second with him was beyond her. She shook her head. It didn't matter. *He* didn't matter. Not in a personal way, at least.

In silence, Hannah arranged the table the way she preferred and she and Jennifer put the chairs back in place. She noticed Jennifer's hands shook and she sighed. God, she hated Richard sometimes. If he ruined the ceremony because of his man-whore tendencies, the gloves were coming off.

She placed her hands on Jennifer's shoulders in a comforting gesture and smiled. "It's all right, honestly. Please don't be upset. Don't let Richard's behavior upset you. I know I'm being selfish, but I really need your A-game today."

Jennifer's eyes widened. "Of course! You'll have it. You've done enough weddings here to know I take my musical responsibilities seriously. I won't let you down. You have my word. I just feel awful about the Richard situation. I feel so stupid."

Hannah could relate. Richard was a piece of work. "Don't. He can be persuasive and he comes in a pretty package." That much was true. The man was handsome—blue eyes, thick wavy blond hair, and well over six feet tall with a toned physique. When he wanted to, he could turn on the charm.

"But that ugliness inside. I can understand why you don't want a personal relationship anymore. And I don't want one with him either. Thank you for not holding what happened against me. I've enjoyed working with you." Jennifer hugged her quickly as the caterers and florist entered Fellowship Hall.

"Same here. Enough about Richard. Let's get to work." Hannah picked up her clipboard and smiled encouragingly at Jennifer.

She smiled back, seemingly in better spirits. "You're right. I'll double-check everything one last time while you take care of everything in here."

Hannah nodded and Jennifer left with a smile still on her face. With the Richard drama finally behind her, she directed the caterers and florist for the room setup. Long rectangular tables had been placed near the center of the room where refreshments would be available for guests after the ceremony and before it was time for the reception at Cucina Antonetti's where everyone would enjoy a scrumptious Italian family-style dinner. Circular tables of eight were arranged around the rest of the room's space so ceremony guests could relax and socialize whether or not they had refreshments.

After the bright white tablecloths were in place, she and florist made quick work of placing the cornflower-blue and white rose low-profile vases of flower arrangements on each table. Just as she was reviewing her work one last time, her mother, followed by Richard, entered the room.

Hannah knew the space was arranged perfectly and hoped her mother wouldn't find fault with something. She regarded the woman who gave birth to her. Taller than her daughter by several inches, Patty was impeccably dressed in a powder-blue pencil skirt power suit with her dark-blonde locks in a tidy bun. Her shrewd baby blues did a quick but thorough scan of the room. Hannah held her breath, waiting for the verdict.

Before her mother could comment, Richard chimed in. "I think the room looks nice. A kind of sneak preview of the reception setup. Don't you agree, Patty?"

Hannah nearly rolled her eyes. What a kiss-ass. The sooner she had a chat with her mother about Richard, the better. The sweet smile Patty rewarded him turned her stomach.

"Yes, you're right. It looks like everything is well in hand here. Are you ready to meet up with the bride and bridesmaids at the Fairchild Hotel?" Patty asked Richard.

"Of course. I just need a minute with Hannah and I'll be on my way," he assured Patty with a pacifying smile.

Of course, her mother fell for that smile. Most women did. She had herself until she'd gotten to know the man better. When Richard turned on the charm, he was nearly impossible to resist, a fact he took full advantage of. Hannah felt pride she no longer let him affect her on a personal level. She wanted more than a pretty package with ugliness inside.

Patty turned to her with a neutral expression on her flawlessly made-up face. "I'll see you a little later after the ladies arrive before the ceremony." Her heels clicked on the tile floor as she left Fellowship Hall for the hotel.

Hannah let out a deep sigh. No criticism or Patty-requested adjustments were small victories she'd happily accept. If Richard would stop looking at her expectantly and leave, she'd be able to joyfully continue on with the day.

He frowned and shook his head. "You're not even going to thank me?" He stepped closer and she instinctively stepped back.

What was he up to now? "Thank you for what?"

He grasped her hands and she felt nothing. Not exactly nothing, something similar to disgust. *That* was what she felt. Maybe if she let him have his say, he'd leave.

"For saving you from Patty's critical opinions of your work, that's what." Richard stroked her palms in what would have been a sensual gesture if she cared about him. His touch just turned her stomach.

She yanked her hands away. "The room is set up exactly the way we planned it. No opinions needed." She knew her mother though. And so did Richard.

He raised a blond brow, gazing at her skeptically. "That wouldn't have stopped her from making some unnecessary adjustment or criticism if I hadn't have been here complimenting your work, don't you agree?"

What a sad testament to her relationship with her mother. He was absolutely right and they both knew it. Hannah believed without a doubt she did an exemplary job for Hailey's Events. Her mother's never-ending quest for perfection, prestige, and elegance had little to do with her daughter and everything to do with Patty's need to erase the trailer-park days of her youth.

From Hannah's perspective, Patty's mission had been accomplished. She'd fled the St. Louis trailer park, her lush of a mother at the time, came to Chicago, and never looked back.

Richard had ulterior motives for running interference between her and Patty, but she was grateful to be spared Patty's never-ending judgment for once. "You're right, thank you." She made to step around him so she could check in with Joe but Richard blocked her escape.

"Not so fast, Hannah. Tell me we can put what happened earlier behind us so we can get back to us." He tucked a strand of hair behind her ear. She cringed and stepped back slightly.

Determined to make him understand there was no *us*, and never would be, she tried a different tact. Gently brushing off non-existent lint from his narrow pin-striped navy-blue Brooks Brothers suit, she took a deep breath. "You and I both know there never was an *us*. *Us* was some ill-conceived notion our mothers pushed on us and nothing more. If they don't trust each other enough to form a joint venture between our companies without trying to force us together, that's on them. I'm out. I'm done playing this stupid game with you *and* them." There. She didn't think she could make herself any clearer.

He flashed her that pacifying smile which no longer worked on her. "That's not true," he lied. "And just think of the publicity and clients both companies will get when we announce a professional *and* personal merger."

And there it was. To him, she was just a means to an end and nothing more. She'd known it all along, but it stung to hear nonetheless. Most importantly, a personal merger, as Richard put it, wasn't necessary if Hailey's Events and Hayes Studios wanted to join forces. Let their attorneys, her father Denton and her brother Eric on their side, hash out all the legal details.

Hannah squared her shoulders, her resolve firmly in place. "Grow some balls and tell your mother you're not interested in me and leave me the hell alone."

He had the nerve to scoff. "You grow some and tell yours you don't want *me*," he countered.

She smiled brightly and nodded. "I was already planning to after Jake and Cassie's wedding. So, we're good then, right?"

Hannah made to sidestep Richard again and leave, but he grabbed the middle of her forearm and squeezed. She winced, trying to pull away.

His eyes narrowed to thin slits. "Listen to me, you little trailer-trash bitch. You're going to do as you're told. I've got plans. This merger will help me transition to cinematography and filmmaking completely, and hopefully lead me to Hollywood. Where I belong. You're going to smile pretty, play along, and do your part. Got it?"

Hell no, she didn't *get it*. How dare he threaten her? With strength she didn't know she possessed, she shoved Richard hard, sending him backward and nearly causing him to fall on his ass. She rubbed her arm, trying to ease the pain from his grip.

"No. You listen to *me*, asshole. Figure out a Plan B, because I refuse to let you *or* Patty use me like that. Because our mothers are friends, I won't mention this little incident. Touch me or threaten me again and I'll take out a press release telling everyone what a lying, cheating, self-serving piece of shit you *really* are. I'm sure Dad and Eric would be more than happy to sue the shit out of you for assault while we're at it, too. *Got it*?"

She took a moment, reveling in the look of utter shock on Richard's face before leaving Fellowship Hall to find Joe. "Get your ass to the Fairchild Hotel. Patty's waiting for you," she called out as she walked away.

Chapter Two

Rocco Moretti stood just inside the vestibule doors of Grace of God Lutheran Church and *had not* gone up in flames, as star pitcher for the Chicago Cobras and good friend Luke Stryker had teased him a few minutes ago. Dixon-Shaw Security had assigned him to manage and oversee Luke's security detail for the weekend. Good thing he considered Luke a good friend so his Italian and Catholic jokes didn't bother him. They were all in good fun.

Through his close friendship with Heath Jackson, fellow Marine he'd met in Sangin, Afghanistan, back in late 2010, he'd met Luke and was now close friends with the bride, groom, and their families, along with Heath's and Luke's. Somehow, he'd fit in with their clan and he thought of them as his non-Italian family. His *American* family.

Looking up at the masterfully painted domed ceiling, he smiled. The religious scenes above him were reminiscent of the many churches and cathedrals in Catania and Palermo, Sicily, where his family was from. How long had it been since he'd visited his extended family? *Too long. Not since Nonna and Nonno passed away four years ago.* His heart still ached. He missed his grandparents so much.

They'd become his parents after his mother left him and his baby brother when they were six years old and three weeks old, respectively. His abusive drunk of a father hadn't wanted to be bothered with his young sons and had disappeared himself shortly after his mother escaped, leaving his grandparents to pick up the pieces. He was grateful every day that they had.

Rocco shook his head, not wanting to delve too deeply into the dark corners of his early childhood. Today was a day for celebration, new beginnings, and with Luke in town for the wedding, joyful reunions. He needed to stay focused on *that*. That and standing in the way of the paparazzi, press, or anyone else who wanted a piece of the celebrity pitcher. Luke had repeatedly stressed the focus of the day and weekend needed to be on Cassie and Jake, the bride and groom.

Rocco sensed someone behind him before they spoke and turned around. It was Cole Palmer, his second for the weekend and an off-duty Chicago firefighter.

"*Dimmi.*" He'd been teaching the man a little Italian.

Cole smiled. "I'll *tell you*. We're all clear at this point. We have someone at every exit," he began.

Rocco shook his head. "Not at the parking lot entrance I just watched Luke enter through, even though he wasn't aware I was watching him."

Cole nodded and chuckled. "Actually, we had someone from the team get there just as Luke started chasing after Hannah Hailey, the event planner. She grabbed a cooler he had and he was going on about needing it for a groom mission. We weren't briefed on a groom's mission, though. What else do we need to know?"

Rocco grunted, shaking his head. He retrieved a copy of Luke's mission note from his suit pants pocket and handed it to Cole. It was a clever idea. He watched Cole read the note, knowing he'd get a kick out of it.

"What a unique idea, for *civili*, right? Like a cross between *Taken* and *Mission Impossible*. The cooler has the beer for before, during, and after the ceremony. No wonder Luke was upset. As the best man, it was his responsibility to bring the beer." Cole handed him back the mission note.

"Exactly. *Cos'altro hai da dirmi*?" He wasn't sure if Cole understood but gave it shot.

Cole's brow furrowed as he tried to discern what Rocco had just asked him. "Um … the other things I have to tell you are the Elmhurst PD already have extra patrols in the area and will have them at Cucina Antonetti's before we head over there. Then later tonight, the Oak Brook PD near and around the Fairchild Hotel. Dixon arranged for an Illinois State Police presence too, just in case."

He wasn't surprised. Eli Dixon and Eason Shaw were both former CIA, taught at the US Army Military Police School at Ft. Leonard Wood in Missouri, and had countless military and law enforcement connections far beyond his Marine paygrade. Those connections and expertise were what made Dixon-Shaw Security sought after in the Chicago metropolitan area and beyond.

"I'll look around before I meet up with the groom and his groomsmen. Thanks, Cole."

"Sounds good. I'll go to my post. *Ciao*," he said, smiling, and left through the vestibule doors.

Rocco chuckled after the firefighter. "You did good. I'll throw something harder at you next time," he called out after Cole.

"Give it your best shot, *compagno*," Cole teased, his voice growing fainter the further away he got from the doors.

Buddy. Yes, they were buddies. Like he was with many of the associates at Dixon-Shaw. Their collective military, law enforcement, and service backgrounds helped to form a bond between them all. Similar to being in the Marines, but much less dangerous.

He took a seat in the last row of pews on the left side of the aisle and rubbed his tired eyes. He hadn't slept well the night before, woken up by a combat nightmare coupled with dreams of his late father's abuse. He'd been close to calling Heath, but the man had called him first, needing support after waking up from a combat nightmare of his own. Though he hadn't mentioned his own nightmares to Heath, speaking to him had helped anyway.

He closed his eyes and performed the sign of the cross. He prayed for the souls of his grandparents, fallen soldiers, and their families. Next, he prayed for the health and happiness of the rest of his family and friends. Finally, he prayed the day and the rest of the weekend were trouble-free. "Amen."

Rocco took a deep breath, stood, and admired the beautiful white and cornflower-blue flower arrangements placed around the sanctuary and tied around the end of the pews. For a minute, he wondered what color scheme he'd choose for *his* wedding.

He shook his head and snorted. He was thirty-six, wasn't dating anyone, and had no current prospects. According to his long-lost mother, he and his brother were useless and were no good, just like their late father.

Disliking the direction his thoughts were heading, he stood, felt for his SIG P226 sidearm, and proceeded through the sanctuary out a side door on the right of the altar. After a quick walk through the building, admiring the beautiful stained-glass windows along the way, he acknowledged his security detail were in place and alert, and made his way to the office where Jake, Heath, and Luke were getting ready for the ceremony.

He knocked on the door. "Hey, it's Rocco. Can I come in?" He waited for one of the guys to answer.

Instead of one of the guys, he was greeted by a dark-haired angel with her hair up in a messy bun. A few shiny dark-brown wisps had escaped the bun and his hand itched to tuck them behind her delicate ears. Even the one with the Bluetooth in it. Beautiful, big brown eyes, slightly dilated, gazed back at him in surprise and a pretty blush stained her cheeks. The conservative navy-blue pantsuit she wore did little to hide her luscious curves. His heart skipped a beat and his dick twitched. *Who* are *you?*

Movement from behind the tempting vixen broke the unwelcome trance he found himself ensnared in. He stepped around the mystery temptress and greeted Jake and Heath with quick man hugs before he embarrassed himself. *What the fuck is wrong with you, idiot?*

She joined them further inside the room. "Guys, you've got to get dressed. Time to get serious, all right?"

He nearly groaned. She had the voice of an angel, too. He needed to get a grip and fast.

She touched her earpiece and nodded. "Thank you. I'll be right there. I'm going to take a look at the flower arrangements while you all get dressed."

She had to be the event planner, Hannah Hailey, Cole had mentioned earlier, if she had to check flower arrangements. Mystery solved.

"I think I need help getting my t-shirt off," Luke said, seeming unsure.

What the hell was going on and how did everything suddenly seem out of his control? "What's going on?" Why did Luke need help with his t-shirt? He hadn't mentioned anything was wrong when they rode together to church.

Rocco did his best to ignore his racing heart as Hannah explained Luke had been in a motorcycle accident and hurt his shoulder. On his pitching arm, no less. Shit. Luke's shoulder was severely bruised. Rather than wear a sling like they all thought he should, he wanted to wear a discreet shoulder support under his clothes. No one was supposed to say a word about his injury. It wasn't public knowledge.

Hannah scooped up some cream onto her fingertips from a jar she'd retrieved from her travel bag and touched Luke's shoulder with it. When Luke hissed as if in pain, on instinct, Rocco grabbed her wrist lightly, just to stop her. And maybe because he'd wanted to get his hands on her and he'd been given the perfect opportunity without it appearing obvious. Or so he hoped.

"You're hurting him." He growled at her. There. He *thought* he sounded menacing. That was what he was going for.

He heard Luke tell him to stand down because he wasn't hurting, but he just stood there, mesmerized as he looked into Hannah's eyes that shot daggers and lust back at him. The feel of her warm, soft, supple skin against his own sent his heart hammering in his chest. His cock joined in the festivities and he was grateful his suit jacket was buttoned to hide his growing hard-on.

He was getting an erection inside a church. It made no difference it was a Lutheran church. It was official. He was going to Hell. His grandparents and the Pope would be so disappointed in him. What was she doing to him?

Hannah yanked her arm away and although he knew she was angry at him, he immediately missed her touch. Ignoring him, she proceeded to gently rub the cream on Luke's bruised shoulder. And like an idiot, he became jealous she was touching Luke instead of him.

"It's natural, don't worry," she explained to Luke. Good, he needed to get the focus back on his ward for the weekend and off the much-too-tempting event planner. *Get your head back in the game, Marine.* "It has healing botanicals and emu oil in it. It'll help with the soreness and the bruising. If you need relief later in the day, I'll apply more."

He knew a little something about botanical skin care. Many of his female cousins preferred them to most store brands that contained harsh chemicals.

"Thanks, Hannah. It's helping," Luke assured her. "We'll get ourselves ready. You go do whatever you need to do. We're good here."

Hannah put the lid back on the jar and shoved it at Rocco's chest. Clearly, she was angry, but a faint blush stained her pretty cheeks. He didn't know why, but he was pleased he an effect on her. "Think you can hold on to this for Luke?"

Utterly dumbstruck and tongue-tied, he nodded and took the jar from her.

"Good." And with that, Hannah left, closing the door quietly behind her.

Jake smiled at Heath and Luke, then turned to him. Shit. "That sure was interesting. I think maybe Rocco's got a thing for little event planner Hannah," Jake teased.

Rocco's mouth fell open and he quickly closed it. So much for being subtle. "Bullshit, no, I don't. She's bossy. I'm not used to that." That was a lie. The women in his family were opinionated and assertive. Hannah would fit right in. *Don't go there.*

Luke took his own little dig. "Uh huh. When you grabbed her, I didn't know if you wanted to hurt her or fuck her, man."

Fuck her, definitely. In some other empty room in the building. Damn it. He needed to go to Confession before his trip to Hell.

"And the way you watched that ass as she walked out the door. Yup, I agree with Jake and Luke. You want her. She's got some nice curves under that little pantsuit of hers. Can't say I blame you," Heath added and chuckled.

The thought of Heath laying one hand on Hannah made his blood boil. They were friends. Marine brothers. The man had most likely saved his life on the battlefield in Sangin after the Taliban had shot him, but he'd better not touch Hannah. Ever.

A short while later, after bullshitting around with the guys, a few sips of beer which he rarely drank, and making a spectacle of himself *again* in front of everyone, including Hannah over breath mints, no less, he got back to the job he was hired to do. Ensure the day and weekend were trouble-free.

Rocco did a sweep of the building, confirming his security team was still in place and alert. He did his best not to let the fact that Jake had announced Cassie was expecting their first child bother him. He was happy for the man but envious. He had no children of his own, just a niece and nephew he adored, Adrianna and Massimo, Junior. As close as he was to his brother and his family, at the end of the day, Adrianna and little Massimo, or MJ, weren't his.

The conversation about babies had his mind immediately picturing Hannah swollen with his child. He'd started getting hard again while they had all discussed the happy news in sign language. He would have to make several visits to Confession before his trip to Hell.

They had all learned to sign after Heath was injured in Afghanistan and had lost about seventy percent of his hearing. He managed well with hearing aids, but learning sign had been a necessary precaution.

Ceremony guests were arriving en masse, so he needed to be on his toes. So far, no press, paparazzi, or would-be troublemakers had made an appearance. He prayed it stayed that way for the duration of the day and weekend.

On his final walk-through of the premises, Rocco stopped just outside the entrance of Fellowship Hall where he heard voices.

"Dick said *what* to you?" the unfamiliar-sounding man asked.

"He called me a trailer-trash bitch and said I needed to toe the line. Look, it doesn't matter what he said—"

Rage like he hadn't felt since his days in Afghanistan roared through him. How *dare* this *Dick* refer to Hannah in that manner. Rocco's protective instincts soared into overdrive. Did *Dick* have a death wish? He'd be more than happy to help the fucker out.

He stormed inside Fellowship Hall to find Hannah. A few feet inside the room, she stood speaking with a dark-haired man in a gray, slim-fit suit. Not an Italian-made suit, but it fit the man's frame well.

But now was not the time to discuss suit makers. "What the hell is going on? What did this Dick say to you? Did he disrespect you? Hurt you?"

"And who are *you*?" The gray-suited man studied Rocco suspiciously.

He took a deep breath, willing himself to calm down. "Rocco Moretti. I'm with Dixon-Shaw Security and in charge of Luke Stryker's security detail this weekend."

That got the man's attention and he noticeably relaxed. "Ah. Former military?"

"Marine."

"Really?" Hannah seemed surprised, though he wasn't sure why. Did she have something against the military? The possibility hurt him more than he cared to admit.

"Just like Heath Jackson, one of the groomsmen. I'm Joe Burke, Hannah's right-hand man and her closest friend since we were kids." He extended a hand and Rocco shook it. The man had a firm grip. He and Hannah were only friends. Good to know.

"Yes. Our units served together in Sangin, Afghanistan. I consider Heath a brother."

"Thank you for your service," Joe and Hannah said in unison with smiles on their faces. He was relieved at Hannah's response to his military service, even though it shouldn't matter.

"Enough about me. What's going on? Someone named Dick hurt Hannah?" He wanted to deal with Dick before the wedding ceremony began, if possible.

Hannah seemed hesitant, but Joe wasn't. "Dick is Hannah's dick of an ex who didn't get the memo she's through with him. We caught him and the church cantor in a compromising position here in Fellowship Hall earlier. Something else happened later, and Dick said some things or did some things, but Hannah won't tell me." Joe's eyes pleaded with Rocco to help. The man obviously cared about her. He could respect and work with that.

"Please, Hannah," Rocco whispered, hoping to ease her concerns and doubts.

As Hannah hesitantly explained what Richard the Dick said and did while they were alone earlier, he felt his blood pressure rise. Her own mother encouraged this asshole? His anger nearly boiled over.

"Let me see your arm," he barked out, harsher than he'd intended. He was holding on to his temper by a thread.

"It's okay, guys, really. He didn't mean to hurt me. He's got a huge ego, that's all." Hannah was nearly in tears. Joe clenched his hands, his face turning red.

"Please?" he asked again in a calmer, more soothing tone.

Hannah nodded and removed her jacket, revealing the angry, finger-shaped bruise marks on her delicate skin. It was all Rocco needed to see. Richard the Dick was a dead man.

****

Hannah stood frozen in place, mesmerized in a corner of a small empty banquet room at Cucina Antonetti's with Rocco, the much-too-sexy-for-his-own-good former Marine. Jake and Cassie's wedding ceremony had gone off without a hitch—mostly. Everyone in attendance had been stunned, herself included, when it appeared Jake had changed his mind about getting married.

Unfortunately, it wouldn't have been the first time she'd witnessed a bride or groom being left at the altar. Jake had been committed, though. When he'd seen his beautiful bride, he'd wanted to escort her to the altar himself. And it had been fun to watch the groomsmen alternate wearing the black top hat throughout the ceremony. She was thankful Patty hadn't uttered one criticism and was back at their corporate office in Oak Brook working on another event. She had the night all to herself—and because of this ridiculous scheme—with Rocco.

"This ploy you and Joe cooked up is silly. We don't need to do this." She winced when Rocco applied the botanical cream she'd used on Luke to her bruised arm. Damn it was cold when it first made contact with the skin. No wonder he had thought she'd hurt Luke and grabbed her wrist.

Like a fool, she'd pulled away, when what she had really wanted to do was feel his hands all over her. Heat and pleasure pulsed through her veins as he now gently, almost seductively tended to her bruises. Her nipples tingled and beaded painfully. She was grateful for the light padding in her bra cups or he'd clearly see the effect he had on her. The man exhibited such raw sensuality, seemingly without effort, and she was at a loss as to how to react.

She'd gotten a glimpse of the tattoos that peeked out from under his suit jacket sleeves and shirt cuffs. She wondered how far up they went and how much of his warm, Mediterranean-toned skin was covered in ink. The man made Richard look like an idiot. Like a boy pretending to be a man.

"Maybe it is silly. But since you wouldn't let me shoot Richard the Dick, we're doing this. Joe's on board with our plan." He surveyed his handiwork. He nodded, seemingly pleased with himself, put the cap back on the jar, and tossed it in her event travel bag on the table beside them.

"That's not saying much. Joe hates Richard." That much was true. On a personal level, she didn't care for Richard either.

"So do I. Stop making excuses for him, Hannah." Rocco's intense dark-brown gaze made her shiver. She could get lost in those eyes. "A *real* man doesn't hurt women and children. A *real* man takes care of his family. He treats them with respect. He does *everything* in his power to make them happy."

She sighed, knowing Richard hadn't been and would never be any of those things to her. And even if he'd tried to be more the like man Rocco had just described, like the man she believed the Italian standing in front of her was, she felt nothing for Richard. She never had. Not like she did for the man she'd just met that day and who looked at her with such deep emotion and resolve she'd follow him anywhere. Where had *that* thought come from?

"Well, yes, I don't disagree with you. But how does pretending you're my date to this wedding and putting on some PDA display in front of Richard help matters any?" That was the brilliant plan Joe and Rocco had come up with when she'd refused to allow Rocco shoot Richard for being a dick.

"It's payback for his mistreatment of you. Even though it's obvious he doesn't care about you, his ego will get in the way and he'll be jealous of all the attention I give you. You'll see. And you'll feel better exacting a little revenge. Unless you want to get back together with him?"

He looked at her expectantly, as if daring her to admit she still wanted Richard.

"No way. I told you and Joe. After the wedding, I'm telling my mother I'm not interested in Richard and she and his mother need to figure out another way to work out their joint venture ideas that *doesn't* include me and Richard together." She and Richard were over. Her mother had no right to put her daughter in such a precarious position and she'd have to get over her disappointment once Hannah put her foot down. Enough was enough.

She was rewarded with a seductive smile and thought she felt wild need pass between them. It couldn't be. This was all supposed to be an act.

"Good," he whispered. Her heart raced when he removed the pins holding up her hair. "Your hair has been trying to escape this bun all day. Time to set it free, as it should be." She heard herself moan when he massaged her scalp and ran his fingers through her loose dark, wavy locks.

She preferred her hair down, but Patty insisted that the female planners at the firm put it up at events as she believed it portrayed a more professional image. Just another thing, among many, mother and daughter disagreed on.

When he leaned in close and she felt his body heat, a delicious shudder shot through her. Her body lit up with a burning need like she'd never felt before with any other man. She thought her heart would beat right out of her chest.

"You feel it too, don't you, *bellissima*?"

Too tongue-tied to speak, she nodded. Yes, she felt it. It was unexpected, but she would go with it. Richard had made her feel so unattractive and unworthy. Rocco made her feel beautiful and desirable. When he flicked open the top two buttons of her white silk blouse, she instinctively reached for his belt buckle.

"What the hell?" Richard barked.

Startled, Hannah nearly jumped out of her skin. God, she hated Richard sometimes. Rocco looked down at her with a smirky, mischievous grin and her heart fluttered. When he winked, her heart sank.

He must've sensed someone had stepped into the room. She felt like a fool. This was just a part of their act to make Richard jealous. Rocco wasn't interested in her. He was just carrying out their plan to get back at Richard. She was so stupid. A man like Rocco would never want a woman like her.

She made to button up her blouse, but his strong, warm hands stopped her. "Don't," he whispered.

Rocco let go of her and turned to face Richard head on. She held her breath and chided herself for wishing he was still touching her. *It's just an act. Don't forget that.*

"What's going on in here? *You*. Aren't you supposed to be watching after Luke Stryker?"

Hannah wouldn't have believed it, but Rocco was

right. Richard wore a scowl on his face, his hands were clenched, and his eyes shot daggers at them both. He was jealous. Huh. And it actually felt good. No. It felt *great* to get back at him for treating her so poorly while they were "together."

"I have a competent team in place that can handle Luke's safety in my absence. Luke and the groom are close personal friends of mine. I'm also a guest at this wedding and you're intruding on private time with my date."

She nearly laughed out loud. Richard appeared ready to detonate. Kudos to Rocco and his performance. He'd nearly convinced her he wanted her and Richard was falling for the act hook, line, and sinker. Although Richard was six-foot-three to Rocco's six feet, Rocco stood his ground. He was imposing and lethal. If Richard were smart, he'd back off. Richard wasn't smart.

"Your *date*? You've got to be shitting me. Hannah's with *me*, pal." Richard didn't even bother glancing at her for confirmation. Unbelievable. Hadn't she made herself clear in Fellowship Hall? Did he truly believe he could *order* her to be with him for the sake of *his* plans? For a moment, Hannah considered asking Rocco to shoot him after all.

"I'm not your *pal*, asshole. Hannah told me she made it clear she doesn't want you. She's attending the reception as my date once her event-planning duties are over, which they nearly are. Isn't that right, *cara*?"

"She didn't mean it, *pal*. We're just having a little disagreement. Hannah, come on, tell Guido over here we're together and to back off."

She scoffed. What nerve. Did he actually believe the lies he was spewing? She took a few steps forward, closer to where Rocco stood.

"We *are* having a disagreement. It's true."

Rocco turned to her, a confused expression on his handsome face. Richard, the arrogant ass, smirked.

"I don't agree to be with someone who treats me like I don't matter. Like I'm a doormat who will put up with anything and just smile pretty through it all. Isn't that what you said I needed to do? And I certainly *do not* agree to be used as a means to an end for our mothers, and I *never* will."

She meant the words which were a long time in coming with all sincerity. And she felt fantastic, empowered to finally have said them. Although they were acting in front of Richard, she believed the look of pride on Rocco's face was genuine. Even though it shouldn't, her heart skipped a beat at his approval of her declaration.

She could do this. Carry out their jealousy-revenge plan and then move on, stronger for it. She'd enjoy Rocco's company and "attention" at Jake and Cassie's reception and decide what to do next afterward. Weddings were a time of celebration and new beginnings. Hannah was more than ready for both.

Rocco extended a hand. "Come, *cara*. Let's go have some fun."

"Hannah, come on. Don't be stupid," Richard pleaded with her. He couldn't even beg properly, the jackass. Not that there was anything he could say that would or could change her mind.

It was all an act, even though Richard hadn't caught on. But Hannah could have some fun. She and Joe had worked hard for Darren Stryker and the happy couple today. They'd been invited to attend as guests long before Joe and Rocco had devised their jealousy plan. Joe had prior plans with his boyfriend, but Hannah was free for the evening.

Yes, it was all an act. Even so, she would enjoy

the next few hours with the sexy Italian Marine. She deserved to have a little fun and the fact that it bothered Richard so much was a bonus.

She clasped Rocco's offered hand and swore sparks practically flew between them. She shook her head and giggled. The sparks were from her, not him. And that was all right. He was a kind man. A decent man who was trying to defend the honor of a practical stranger when he didn't have to. And for that, she'd always be grateful.

With a smile on her face and ignoring Richard completely, she nodded happily. "Yes, let's do that. Richard, you need to get ready to film the bridal party in a few minutes as they're introduced, before dinner is served," she called out behind her as Rocco led her out of the banquet room.

A short while later, Hannah stood with the rest of the guests and applauded enthusiastically as Jake and Cassie were introduced and made their grand entrance into the reception room. Rocco whistled beside her when Cassie did a little twirl, showing off her beautiful gown, and proceeded with the happy groom to their places at the head table.

Cassie had seated her and Rocco at the table with Pastor Jenkins, who'd performed the ceremony, and his lovely wife, along with the DJ and, much to his obvious displeasure, Richard and his crew from Hayes Studios. Against her will, pleasure pulsed in her veins when Rocco held her hand during Pastor Jenkin's prayer over the happy couple and everyone in attendance. Richard's not-so-subtle snort could also be heard at their table.

"So, Rocco," Pastor Jenkins began as Rocco filled her plate with enough food for a week. "Where in Italy is your family from?"

Richard slid the chopped salad bowl toward her.

Another not-so-subtle hint he thought she wasn't thin enough for his liking. Not that she cared. Rocco glared at him with murderous intent for a moment before turning his attention back to the pastor.

"My grandfather was from Catania, Sicily, and my grandmother from Palermo, Sicily's capital," he replied with a wistful expression.

"Really? We spent three weeks in Italy on our honeymoon ten years ago," the pastor's wife said and then gazed lovingly at her husband. "We ended our trip in Catania. Have you taken Hannah to Italy yet?"

Her stomach clenched. She hadn't expected that question. Richard looked on with narrowed eyes and pursed lips. Richard's crew and the DJ enjoyed their delicious meals, seeming oblivious to the tension at the table.

"Not yet, unfortunately. But I'm looking forward to showing Hannah everything Italy has to offer very much."

She was torn between unease and arousal when his warm lips kissed the top of her hand. Richard gasped softly, but Hannah heard him. *In your face, asshole.*

"You're going to love Italy, Hannah," Pastor Jenkins assured her and dug into his dinner.

"You've worked so hard today, *bella*. Eat some chicken marsala. You need the protein." Rocco glared at Richard and then started in on his own dinner.

She nodded. "You're right, I did and I'm starved." She enjoyed her meal as much as she enjoyed pissing Richard off. This was going to be fun. If only her body would stop reacting to Rocco like it was, she'd feel more comfortable.

"Are you going to be able to join us for Sunday brunch tomorrow at the Fairchild Hotel?" Rocco asked. Was it her imagination or did he appear hopeful?

She wasn't sure but was disappointed because she wasn't available. "I have a baby shower for the Oak Brook mayor's daughter at the Drake Hotel tomorrow. I'm sorry, but I can't."

Richard smirked from across the table and Rocco frowned. "Next Sunday afternoon, Jake and Cassie are having their wedding gift reveal party," Rocco tried again.

Yes! She was available next Sunday. Hope bloomed until she remembered they were only acting. "I'm free. I'd love to join you." She hoped she sounded enthusiastic but not desperate. Judging by the angry expression on Richard's face, she'd succeeded.

She enjoyed herself on the dancefloor with Rocco for several songs. The man had some serious moves. She couldn't help but wonder how he moved between the sheets. Then she chastised herself because his attention wasn't real. She'd probably never see him again, even though they had exchanged cell phone numbers at Joe's insistence.

He unexpectedly stopped dancing and grabbed her hand. She followed his gaze toward the banquet room doors where Luke Stryker was dragging Abbey, the bride's younger sister and the pitcher's ex-girlfriend.

"*Cara*, I need to go after them. I'll be right back." Then he surprised the hell out of her and kissed her so sweetly, with such tender care, she nearly swooned.

She stood there on the dancefloor and touched her lips, watching him go after Luke and Abbey. She was in big trouble.

"I've had enough of this shit. This needs to stop. Right now." Richard growled, startling her. She hurried off the dancefloor, distancing herself from him, but he followed close behind.

"I don't give a shit what you think and I warned

you earlier about threatening me. I've tried to make you understand we're through. Maybe you'll understand this. I'm the only thing that's standing between you and a bullet since Rocco saw the bruises you left on my arm. For the last time, stay the hell away from me unless it's about business." Hannah left Richard standing there stunned, with his mouth hanging open, and exited the banquet room in search of Rocco and hopefully another kiss.

Chapter Three

With a smile she knew didn't reach her eyes, Hannah nodded at the bride-to-be and her entourage the following Sunday afternoon as she admired herself in the full-length mirrors at Blumenthal's Discount Bridal in Lombard. She checked her watch for the tenth time. She was going to be late for her date with Rocco. A date she still couldn't believe she was going on, that had nothing to do with making Richard jealous, if the handful of stolen kisses she'd shared with Rocco throughout Jake and Cassie's reception were any indication.

She wanted to hurry things along but knew it wouldn't be fair to the bride. It was all about the dress, after all. And the dress the bride had on, wasn't "the one." It was pretty with the illusion of an off-the-shoulder neckline, but it just wasn't right for her destination wedding in Maui.

Co-owner Cora Blumenthal elbowed her. "You know which one would be perfect for her, don't you?" Cora and her older sister Nora referred to her as the wedding-gown whisperer. Both were nearing eighty years of age, still going strong but were looking to retire in Florida. More importantly, they wanted *her* to buy their bridal salon. She was tempted. So very tempted but had fended them off up to this point.

"Actually, I believe I do. Lynn," Hannah called out to Cora's sales consultant. "Get the Vera Wang. The special." Lynn's face lit up and she nodded as she went to fetch the gown Hannah believed would be perfect, so she could continue on with her afternoon with Rocco and his friends-slash-family.

"Um … Hannah? Since we're getting married in

Hawaii, the budget is kind of tight for the dress." Taylor, the bride, turned to her mother with a concerned expression on her face. Taylor's mother turned to Hannah, frowning.

"Ladies, the dress Lynn's bringing out is on clearance special. Trust me. It's the one *and* it will fit in your budget. Taylor, go back to your dressing room and wait for Lynn. I *promise* you it'll be all right." *Come on, Taylor. I know what I'm doing and I need to leave as soon as I can.*

Taylor nodded, though looking unsure, and left for the dressing room as Hannah had asked. "Dear, this should be *your* salon, offering *your* spectacular designs. You know I'm right." Cora held her hand and squeezed, as she'd done many times before, hoping to convince her.

Hannah sighed, like she always did when pressed by Cora or Nora on the subject. They *were* right. She *could* turn the over thirty thousand square foot, three-story space which was barely being used into something spectacular if only she dared to break away from Hailey's Events and strike out on her own.

Before she could recite her worn-out, lame excuses for not accepting the shop owners' buyout offer, Taylor emerged from her dressing room with "the dress" and tears streaming down her face. The bride's entire entourage squealed and cheered.

The gorgeous gown was soft and elegant with its stunning beaded lace and textured netting. A diagonal seaming defined and flattered Taylor's waist and finished with a chapel-length train. Hannah knew the gown was clipped in the back since the sample was a size too large. With some slight alterations, it would be perfect for her Maui wedding.

Taylor nervously gestured for everyone to calm down and wiped her eyes. "Cora? Hannah? Lynn wouldn't tell me how much the dress costs. I don't think we can afford this."

Taylor's mother shook her head. "This is the dress. We'll figure out a way."

Cora walked over to the nervous bride and placed a comforting arm around her. "Honey, don't worry. This is the last sample we have. It's been discontinued and it's only two hundred dollars. If you want it, it's yours."

****

Rocco turned down 2nd Street in Lombard in his new, fully loaded black Chevy Silverado 1500, courtesy of Luke. The black rosary his *Nonna* Moretti had given him years before was wrapped around the rear-view mirror, keeping him safe. He would've enjoyed driving his grandmother around in this truck. His grandfather *Nonno* Moretti, too.

He parked in his brother Massimo's driveway and cut the engine. He still had some time before he had to pick Hannah up and bring her to Jake and Cassie's for their wedding gift reveal get-together.

He wasn't sure what had possessed him to kiss her on the dancefloor at Jake and Cassie's wedding before chasing after Luke, but once he'd had a taste of her, he knew he'd need more. He smiled, remembering the look of disgust on Richard the Dick's face when he'd stolen a few more kisses throughout the evening. *In your face, motherfucker.*

His brother came out of his front door with a smile on his face, wearing jeans and a gray Northwestern University t-shirt. Rocco couldn't be prouder of the man anxious to take a look at his new ride. His brother had earned a computer science degree, met the love of his life at Northwestern, married her right after graduation, and had been blessed with an adorable daughter who was four and a half and a son who'd just turned six months old. His little brother had everything Rocco wanted for himself. He'd learned to live with just being single *Zio* or Uncle Rocco.

He exited the truck and gave his brother a quick hug. Max, as most people called him, whistled and looked over Rocco's new truck. *One* of his new rides. He shook his head at how the truck-buying excursion with Luke had turned out on Wednesday.

"Look at you, big brother. It's about time you got rid of that piece of shit you were driving. I don't understand why Luke bought it for you, though. Between all the money you saved during your time in the Marines and what you got from *Nonna's* and *Nonno's* life insurance policies, you could've bought something new a long time ago." Max glanced at him and shrugged.

It was true, but his grandparents had taught them to be responsible with their money. To save more than they spent. His old truck was … old, but it ran fine. "The money I sent home during my twelve years in the service was *supposed* to help pay your college tuition."

Instead, his grandmother had saved every penny he'd sent home and had it waiting for him when he'd been honorably discharged. He'd invested it and his inheritance from both grandparents. He'd done well but hadn't touched a dime.

He lived off of his salary from Dixon-Shaw and what he earned from his part-time gig at Chicago's newest BDSM club, Club Envidious. Mostly serving as a bowtie-wearing server for the club's erotic book and social club, the Twisted Tea Society, and occasionally as a Dungeon Monitor. He wasn't sure what he was waiting for to spend some of it. He'd know when the time was right, he supposed.

"You risked your life for twelve years to earn it. The money you sent home was *yours*. I did fine working part-time jobs and with my scholarship. No student loan debt, so it all worked out." He hopped in the front seat and made himself comfortable. "So why did Luke feel the need to get you behind a new set of wheels?"

Rocco sighed. That had come *after* the chaos that had ensued after they'd finished Sunday brunch at the Fairchild Hotel following Jake and Cassie's wedding. It had been divine intervention Hannah hadn't been able to attend. She'd been spared the shitstorm that had played out in front of the paparazzi because of Hollywood starlet Brenna Sinclair, Luke's *friend*, not his girlfriend like everyone had been led to believe for the past three years. Brenna had cleared everything up at the Cobras' HQ press conference on Monday, but so much more had been revealed after the brunch blowup. Not all of it good.

"After the Sunday brunch clusterfuck, we had a family meeting in the honeymoon suite. Jake was pissed. Everyone was keeping secrets because they wanted to spare him and Cassie, but he'd had enough. He was put off by some of the stuff Luke had done to make the day special, the expensive champagne at dinner, the block of hotel rooms, and other things. It was Luke's Uncle Darren who hired Hailey's Events to organize and plan the entire day."

That had also been divine intervention because it had brought Hannah into his life. He smiled when he looked over past Max to the wrapped bouquet of pink roses on the passenger side of the bench seat. Joe had clued him in that pink was her favorite color. That and they preferred Shamrock Garden Florist for their flowers.

He watched as Max felt the plush leather seats and down the side of the driver's side seat. "What's this little button?"

Rocco's new LTZ Z71 had been the showroom's display model, which meant it had every bell and whistle

Chevy had to offer from the crew cab, leather seats, to the tow package, the 6.2 liter V8 engine, a five-year contract with Sirius XM radio and OnStar®, and more. "Heated seats, man."

Max's eye widened and he nodded. "Sweet! Perfect for cold Chicago winters. So, the family meeting."

"Turns out Luke was pissed because everyone gives him a hard time when he wants to spend some money on us. He and Darren got us all to agree to just shut the hell up about it and just say thank you when they offer to get us something. Because it's coming from a place of love, not charity. That's how I ended up with this … *and* the stone-gray Cadillac CT6 sedan Platinum. Luke's buying Jake and Cassie a house in Elmhurst so they can get settled before their baby comes."

Max's mouth fell open. Rocco could relate. It had all been surreal. What he'd managed to save and invest was nothing compared to the billions Luke was now worth since Monday's press conference.

His brother seemed to think for a moment after regaining his composure and nodded. "That's what family does, right? They help each other. If we had that kind of money, we'd do the same thing."

He chuckled. His little brother was a good man. He couldn't be prouder. "Yeah, we would. That was exactly the argument Luke made, so we all shut the fuck up about it and said thank you to his generosity."

Max popped the hood and got out of the truck. They pulled the hood up to take a look at the gleaming new engine. They stood in silence for a minute, each of them lost in thought.

"Me and Sydney lit candles at Sacred Heart Tuesday morning over Darren's surgery. Sydney's mother watched the kids for us," Max admitted quietly.

Rocco's eyes stung and his stomach knotted. He nodded his thanks. The most devastating secret revealed after brunch had been learning the owner of the Chicago Cobras, Luke's Uncle Darren, had stage 1B exocrine pancreatic cancer and the five-year survival rate was about twelve percent. He assumed Max had researched the diagnosis and treatment options online after Darren's condition had been made public during Monday's press conference.

"Everything legally belongs to Luke now, huh? And he's marrying that pretty blonde, Abbey, sometime next year?"

They were getting married in a little over two months on Labor Day, but he wasn't at liberty to share that information, even with his brother. "He asked me to be a groomsman."

Max smiled and clapped him on the back. They closed the truck hood, their mood now more somber. "So I take it the pretty pink roses on the passenger side aren't for me," his brother teased.

Rocco chuckled, appreciating his brother's attempt to lighten the mood. "Fuck no, they're not."

"You like this one, don't you? She's not like the women at that club."

His brother meant Hannah. And yes, he did like her. Very much. He just wasn't sure if he should. "You channeling *Nonna* and *Nonno* again? It's not the 1940s. And there's nothing wrong with the women at *Club Envidious*. I do like her, but she's way out of my league." It was the God's honest truth.

"Bullshit."

He appreciated his brother's high opinion of him, but it didn't make Rocco's assessment any less true. "I invited her to Jake and Cassie's to make her dick of an ex jealous. I thought she would have canceled by now."

Every time they'd spoken or texted throughout the week, he'd expected her to say she'd changed her mind, but to his surprise, she hadn't. Yet.

His cell phone rang. It was Hannah and the dreaded cancelation call. He knew it. He answered, putting the call on speaker so Max could hear.

"Hi, Rocco," Hannah began. "I've got a little problem."

He looked at Max and mouthed, *See?*

"It's not a problem, don't worry. You could've just texted me you were canceling. Richard won't know."

"Oh, ummm … I wasn't canceling. Did *you* want to cancel?"

Max threw his hands up in frustration and mouthed, *Idiot*, back at him.

Rocco shook his head. Maybe Max was right and he *was* an idiot. "No, not at all. What's wrong?" His stomach knotted at the thought she might be hurt or in some kind of trouble.

"Nothing's wrong, I'm just running about a half an hour late. I can meet you at Jake and Cassie's if that's easier for you," she suggested.

Max immediately waved his arms at him. He frantically mouthed, *No! Pick her up! Pick her up!*

Rocco shoved at his brother somewhat playfully to calm him down. "It's fine, Hannah. I'll pick you up."

"Great, thanks for understanding. I'll see you soon." She hung up and he sighed. She still wanted to see him. He was surprised how much that meant to him.

Max shook his head at him and grunted. "You've got to stop thinking that you're not good enough, man. The shit Allegra said to you before she left us was just that—shit. Did you look into any of the non-medical PTSD treatments I emailed you? Think about going back into counseling, at least. There's no shame in asking for help, considering what you went through, even before Afghanistan."

The abuse he'd suffered at his father's hand as a little boy and the berating from his mother Allegra before she'd abandoned them, added to what he'd experienced in combat in Sangin had affected him deeply. He'd been trying to deal with it all himself. Sometimes it worked. Most of the time it didn't. Speaking with Heath, since they'd fought in battle side by side, helped getting over combat nightmares somewhat.

"I'll consider it. Thanks."

Thirty minutes later, he was permitted to enter the Oak Brook Club Condominium gated community. He'd nearly called Max to tell him she lived in a fancy gated community in Oak Brook but thought better of it. Considering she was a single woman living alone, she'd be safer at the Oak Brook Club.

His heart raced as he rode the elevator, roses in hand, to her floor after he'd been buzzed in. He had to adjust himself since he didn't have the cover from a suit jacket. He wore jeans and a navy button-down shirt. The sleeves were rolled up nearly to his elbows, his tattoos on display. He'd been tempted not to roll the sleeves up, but it was a warm July afternoon. Hopefully, Hannah wouldn't be put off by his ink. It was a part of who he was now.

He knocked on the door marked *4*, anxious for another taste of her before they headed to Jake and Cassie's. He had it bad for the tempting event planner and needed to calm the fuck down. This could very well end up being the last time he saw her. She would probably end up back with Richard the Dick. That thought didn't sit well with him, but there wasn't much he could do about it.

Joe's smiling face greeted him when Hannah's

door opened. That was a surprise. "Is Hannah home? She told me to come pick her up now."

Joe stepped aside so he could enter her condo unit. It was just as he'd imagined it. Soft, delicate, feminine, and of course with pink accents. This was his Hannah. *His*? For today, yes.

"She's finishing up getting ready. I got the outfit crisis call so I walked over real quick to help. I live in the building next door, in a smaller one-bedroom unit. Great choice with the pink roses. Shamrock Garden?"

Rocco nodded. He liked Joe. He seemed to truly care about Hannah, which made him good in his book.

Joe turned his head toward the unit's hallway. "I'm heading out since Rocco's here. Have fun. See you at the office tomorrow," he called out.

"Thanks, Joe. I'll be a couple more minutes. Make yourself at home, Rocco. I've got drinks in the fridge. Help yourself." Hannah's sweet voice floated through the air and he couldn't help but smile.

Rocco stepped into the living room after Joe left. He was about to sit down when he noticed what looked like two large drawing pads on her coffee table. Curious, he set the flowers down and picked up one of the pads.

He couldn't believe what he was looking at. Had Hannah drawn this? He flipped through the pages with wonder at page after page of detailed, exquisite bridal gown renderings. He was a closet *Say Yes to the Dress* fan but hadn't seen anything like the amazing sketches before him. He quickly snapped shots of several dresses with his cell phone before he heard Hannah. Everything was back in place just as she entered the living room.

"Sorry to make you wait even longer. I'm ready now."

Lust pulsated through his veins at the vision in front of him. Her lovely flowery, buttoned-down dress with pink rose highlights accented her luscious curves perfectly. His fingers itched to undo the entire row of buttons and get a glimpse of what was underneath. She wore her thick glossy locks down so they fell gently around her shoulders. The kissable lips he'd tasted just over a week ago glistened. Her pink pedicured toenails showed sweetly from her flat, strappy white sandals. His cock responded immediately, so he held the flowers in front of him.

An adorable blush stained her cheeks as she assessed him right back. He stood tall, hoping she liked what she saw. When her gaze stopped at his uncovered, tattooed arms, he held his breath and waited for a look of disapproval. His heart soared when she smiled.

"Wow," she whispered and stepped closer to get a better look. "Your arms are a work of art, just like the Sistine Chapel." He'd had the Bellatoni brothers in Envy, Texas, do all his ink. Much of it religious in nature. He'd spent time in Texas after being discharged from the Marines and tracked Heath down. It had been the early days of their recovery from combat in Sangin.

She glanced at the flowers and her eyes lit up.

Thank you, Joe. "I brought these for you." He held the bouquet out to her and her eyes glistened as if she was going to cry. Hadn't anyone given her flowers before? Not even Richard the Dick who had *supposedly* been her man?

Hannah accepted the bouquet and kissed him on the cheek. He needed more than that. More of *her*. So much more. He stroked her soft, warm cheek with his thumb. Her eyes dilated and he felt her shiver. It did something for his ego to know he affected her with no one watching.

Unable to hold back any longer, he claimed her lips. They were warm and welcoming. He felt her smile and she eagerly opened for him. Their tongues teased and tangled until they were both panting. He pulled away and bit her plump lower lip. "You're so beautiful, baby," he whispered against her lips.

Her eyes widened, seemingly surprised. "You're beautiful, too." She giggled. "I mean, handsome. Let me put these in water. I don't want to make us any later than we already are."

****

Hannah's heart raced when Rocco helped her out of his truck at Jake and Cassie's in Elmhurst. There was something about him. Arousal raced through her whenever he touched her. And the kiss they'd shared at her place had made her head spin. She'd never responded to a man like that before. She chided herself for even entertaining the idea of being with Richard at all. What a waste of time the entire exercise had been. Tomorrow, she would tell her mother they were over.

Rocco took her by the hand and led her to their building. His hand felt warm and powerful around hers. "Are you sure we're not too late?" Hannah felt terrible. She hoped everyone hadn't waited on them to eat.

Hannah entered the elevator when the doors opened. "We're fine, I promise. Don't worry," he replied as the elevator doors closed.

Luke answered Jake and Cassie's door after a quick elevator ride to the third floor. His happy, dimpled smile was infectious. He kissed her on the cheek and gave her a quick hug. "I'm so glad you came."

He gestured for her and Rocco to enter and she was greeted with a lively bunch chatting and laughing. She'd enjoyed getting to know the group while planning the happy couple's wedding. It wasn't always the case with clients. But with this group, she felt right at home.

She was greeted with hugs and kisses from the

women and men. Rocco with hugs and kisses from the women and man hugs and back slaps from the men. She was relieved no one appeared bothered they were a little late.

"Here, give this a try. It's Moët & Chandon Bicentenary Cuvée Dry Imperial 1943 from the wedding with some sparkling cranberry juice. It seems to be the drink of the choice for the ladies right now." Cassie handed her a flute with the light-burgundy-colored liquid.

She took a small sip. Crisp and refreshing. "It's good, thanks." She turned to Rocco and offered her glass to him. "Want to try some?"

He smiled at her and her heart fluttered. When he looked at her with those dreamy, espresso-colored eyes, her insides turned to mush. "I'm fine with water." He kissed her on the cheek and her insides warmed. Cassie shot her a knowing glance and her cheeks heated.

She'd noticed at the wedding he'd only had a sip of champagne during the toasts and had stuck with non-alcoholic beverages all night. She'd attributed that to the fact he was on duty for Luke's security. But now, in a casual setting, he was still shying away from alcohol. He was driving, so there was that. But so were Luke, Heath, and the couple's fathers, and they were drinking beer. She'd have to think about how to ask without offending him.

She and the rest of the women in attendance stood back while Rocco helped set up two six-foot folding tables and cushioned folding chairs in the open-concept kitchen and family room area. Although the younger men in the room were all handsome, to her, Rocco stood out with his European good looks.

"Now that we have the tables and chairs set up, please help yourselves. We kept it casual today. We've got Brown's grilled chicken, their chicken tenders and lots of sides, so don't be shy," Jake announced to the group.

Rocco placed an arm around her waist and she leaned in, enjoying the warm, strong feel of him. "Sit down and let me fix you a plate so you don't end up with a plate full of salad. I bet you haven't eaten at all today, have you?"

Her mouth fell open. How did he know that? "Well, I had a busy morning then the bride was late at Blumenthal's. You can fix me a plate *only* if you promise not to load it up with enough for three meals like you did at Jake and Cassie's reception." She appreciated his consideration and concern more than he could ever know, but she didn't want to push her luck with too many added pounds.

He frowned at her and sighed. "Fine," he conceded and went off to fetch her lunch. She sat down and while she waited to be served, Luke, Abbey, and Abbey's parents joined her with their plates. Everything looked and smelled wonderful. Her stomach growled. Maybe Rocco had a point.

Rocco returned with two plates, one heaping with food she hoped was his and another with less on it, but still too much. He placed that one down in front of her and winked. Her heart did that fluttery thing again. God, she had it bad, or she was so starved for real male attention, she was drawn to it. No, she shook her head slightly and dug in. It was the man giving the attention, not the attention itself.

"Mom, Hannah's here on a date, so you can't hound her about our wedding plans, okay?" Abbey warned her mother. Luke kept his mouth shut and let mother and daughter battle it out. Smart man.

Abbey's mother frowned and nodded, taking a

few bites of her lunch. She wiped her mouth and turned to her. Hannah didn't mind talking about their plans. They had much to do in a little over two months.

"Am I allowed to say how much I appreciate all you did for Cassie and Jake? And how happy I am you're working with us again for Abbey and Luke? Several friends asked for your business card."

Hannah squeezed her hand and nodded. "Of course. And thank you, on both counts. I have cards with me." She giggled when the men at the table sighed, seemingly relieved. She dug in her purse for a few business cards and handed them to her.

She ended up seated next to Abbey's Grandma Ruth and Jake's Grandma Beverly after everyone finished eating. She wasn't allowed to "help" in any way. As the Maid of Honor, Abbey would record the gifts and card contents.

Rocco was commandeered to make cappuccinos. Apparently, it tasted better when an Italian made it.

She'd spoken with the sassy widows at the wedding a bit. They were quite the pair. Lovely women who adored their families.

Grandma Ruth waggled her eyebrows at her. "So, you snagged yourself the Italian?"

Her cheeks heated. She wasn't trying to *snag* anyone. But she couldn't deny the attraction she felt toward him and her instincts told her he was different. Special.

"Don't mind her, honey," Grandma Beverly said. "You're a lovely girl. You can have any man you want. He's one of the good ones, though. Treats us like his own. His *American* family. He spent the entire day with us on Thursday. Took us to our hair appointments, shopping at Target, and then out to lunch in his new truck." Both silver foxes nodded with smiles on their faces.

Just as she'd suspected. He *was* one of the good ones. Her mouth fell open when Grandma Ruth produced a strip with four condoms from her purse and handed them to her.

"Here you go, in case Rocco forgot them for when you have hooking-up sex later," Ruth said happily.

Hannah frantically glanced around the room, hoping no one noticed them, but Luke had and just shrugged with a smirky grin on his face. Her face went up in flames as she quickly tucked them into her purse.

She hadn't expected to sleep with Rocco after they left Jake and Cassie's. Now with condoms in her purse and the idea in her brain, she couldn't think of much else. Her nipples tightened and her core slickened as she waited on him and her cappuccino.

Rocco approached the three of them with a tray holding two white coffee mugs and two smaller cappuccino cups. "*Nonne*, decaf with cream and sugar for you and Hannah the heart cappuccino for you."

She gazed at her cup with three foam hearts, each larger than the one above it. It was too pretty to drink. His had a pretty foam leaf.

"Why didn't me and Abbey get hearts? We just got boring leaves," Luke teased.

Rocco shook his head, rolled his eyes, and took a seat in the folding chair he'd placed next to her at the end of the couch. "Is the big-shot ball club owner feeling unappreciated?" he kidded back.

Abbey elbowed Luke in the ribs playfully and shook her head. "You'll take whatever design he gives you and like it. Be nice." Luke gave his fiancée a quick kiss and drank his leaf-designed coffee in silence. Good man.

Everyone enjoyed a pleasant afternoon chatting,

oohing, and aahing over the lovely gifts Jake and Cassie unwrapped. When they opened Rocco's box, they paused a moment. "Wow, Rocco, thank you, but this is too much," Cassie said sweetly. "This Rules for Marriage wood sign says *listen, say I love you, tell the truth, forgive, speak kindly, fight fair, don't bring up the past, be romantic, be happy, keep your promises, laugh together, complement each other, and enjoy each other.* Plus Memories *and* Baby Wishes Glass Jars." Cassie retrieved a small envelope from the box and opened it. She teared up and gave it to Jake.

Hannah squeezed Rocco's hand and was thrilled when he squeezed hers back. His gifts were so thoughtful. Abbey had told her Cassie was a little over eight weeks along. *He's one of the good ones.*

"Come on, man. You didn't have to give us Nordstrom's gift card, too. Cassie's right, this is too much." Jake gave her back the gift card and wiped her cheeks.

"No, it's not. Plus the gifts weren't on your registry. Use the gift card for something on your list," Rocco shot back.

Hannah watched on as Cassie opened her and Joe's gift. It wasn't on their gift registry either, but she hoped they liked it. They usually gave their wedding clients a small gift but she and Joe had really enjoyed working with Cassie and Jake. Since they were also Darren Stryker's family, they'd chosen something special.

He was an important client and they wanted him to understand he was valued. He was also missed, as he was still in the hospital after having surgery to remove his pancreatic tumor. What a heartbreaking turn of events. From what she knew, the early stages of his recovery were going well.

Everyone marveled at the shimmering oval stainless steel decorative bowl. Fourteen hundred silver-colored and clear Swarovski crystals were embedded around the bowl's edge. It was a unique showpiece and Hannah was relieved Cassie and Jake both seemed to like it.

Cassie looked up at her with watery eyes after turning the bowl over. It was engraved with their names and wedding date. Poor thing. Pregnancy hormones and all. *That's probably how I'd be if I was pregnant with Rocco's baby.* What? The condoms in her purse were making her loopy.

"First, you and Joe didn't have to get us anything. And secondly, this is absolutely stunning. Thank you so much. It'll look gorgeous next to the engraved bottle of Moët & Chandon Dom Perignon White Gold Luke gave us, right, Jake?" She turned and gazed at her new husband lovingly.

Jake nodded at his lovely bride and turned to Hannah with a tender expression on his face. "This is beautiful, Hannah. Thank you."

After finishing up with the gifts and wedding cards with cash and checks, including a "huge" unexpected check from Darren, she and Rocco headed back to her place. Everyone who wanted to had written wishes for the Baby Wish jar and Cassie and Jake had written up several memory notes for their Memories jar. She'd had a wonderful time and had only been unnecessarily texted by her mother three times. She considered that a win.

They sat at a red light, holding hands. "Thank you for inviting me today. I had such a nice time." Her heart fluttered when Rocco kissed her knuckles. No one had ever done that to her before. Who knew it could be so erotic?

He eased into traffic when the light changed. "I'm glad. I did too. A couple of them can be real pains in the ass, but I feel lucky to have them. It's really because of Heath. We first became friends in Afghanistan."

Hannah had been briefed on that story from Jake's sister Leah as they were all getting ready to leave. Apparently, she and Heath were now an item after decades of friendship. She liked them together. They seemed to suit each other.

Rocco escorted her to her door and she hesitated, not putting the keys in the lock. She didn't want their evening to end but wasn't sure how to express what she wanted, which was all of him. She looked into his deep brown eyes, losing herself in his dreamy gaze.

"So beautiful," he whispered before claiming her mouth in a soul-searing kiss that left her needy and wanting. He pressed her up against her door and she felt his thick, hard length against her belly. She ached to feel him inside of her, elated that she affected him as much as he affected her.

"I want you," she whispered, hoping she didn't sound whiny.

"Oh, *bella*, I want you too, but I'm trying to be a gentleman."

When he spoke Italian, it turned her on even more. "Why?" She appreciated it, but they were consenting adults. If they both wanted to, they should.

He growled and nipped at her lower lip. Her breasts felt heavy and her core was slick. "Open the door," he whispered with urgency.

With shaky hands, she unlocked her door and led them inside. He slammed the door shut and took possession of her mouth again, backing her up to the living room couch. She giggled and fell onto the seat cushions. She unbuttoned her dress as she watched him unbutton his shirt.

She'd left a light on in the living room but took a quick glimpse at the masculine beauty before her, and then he was on her. When they had more time, she wanted to get a good look at his ink. At all of him. He was a work of art and she couldn't believe he wanted *her*.

"Pink is now my favorite color, baby." He unhooked her front-clasp bra and slowly peeled back the cups. His eyes dilated and nostrils flared. "Jesus, you should always go topless."

Her already hard nipples tightened further when he covered one nipple with his mouth and suckled while his fingers worked the other. She felt a jolt straight to her clit and moaned, arching her back. She gasped and sucked in air.

She grabbed his head and pulled him up. They could go slow next time. "I have four condoms in my purse that Grandma Ruth gave me for hooking-up sex," she said.

Rocco sat up so quickly her head spun. He frowned and ran a hand through his mussed-up hair. Now feeling self-conscious, she tried to cover herself with both ends of her dress. Tears stung her eyes.

"I'm sorry. I didn't put her up to that. You must've been so embarrassed. There was a mix-up at a family meeting after brunch last Sunday and Ruth and Beverly got confused about dates versus hooking up and then hooking-up sex—"

She giggled. Then full-out laughed. Ruth and Beverly were something special. Rocco looked panicked for a minute, then joined her.

"Baby, I'm not fucking you using Grandma condoms. I just can't. Unless *you* have some?" The hopeful expression on his handsome face made her heart hurt.

She shook her head. "This is so unfair. You told Pastor Jenkins you were going to show me everything Italy has to offer," she teased him.

"I made you a cappuccino with hearts on it."

She snorted. "I can get that *anywhere*."

He gasped, as if insulted. He pulled her hands away from her dress and drew the ends apart. "I know something you can't get *anywhere*."

When he tore her pink panties off, a thrill pulsed through her and her clit throbbed. Had he changed his mind about the grandmother condoms? Hannah didn't care where the condoms they used came from, as long as he was inside her and they were protected.

He scooted down between her legs. Was he going to? She nearly detonated when his tongue found her sensitive nub and worked it over. It had been so long. Richard hadn't liked going down on her but was rather demanding about getting his dick sucked. None of that mattered. They were over and the man between her legs *now* was eager to please her.

Rocco's talented tongue set off a searing heat inside her. He continued to tease and flick her swollen clit until she was writhing against his face, panting. She squeezed her eyes shut and lost herself in the moment until she crashed over, shouting his name as she did. She felt him smile against her moist folds as he gently lapped at her juices and eased her back down to earth slowly. *Oh God.*

Hannah opened her eyes when she heard him chuckle softly. He licked his glistening lips with a smug look on his face.

"Not God, just me." He pulled her up and kissed her. She tasted herself on his lips and tongue. She'd never done that before either. She hardly knew the man and already she'd experienced so much. "Come to my place for dinner on Friday and I'll show you more of what Italy has to offer," he whispered after ending their kiss.

"By more, do you mean this?" She slid her hand along the hard bulge in his jeans and was rewarded with a groan. He placed his warm hand on hers and stopped her.

"Yes. That and more," he said sexily.

"I accept." She hated having to wait five days to get her hands on all of him, but she knew he'd make the wait worth her while.

A few minutes later, after she let him hear her lock her door before he left and had just washed her face, she heard her cell phone ring. She dashed out of her en suite bathroom to her bed to answer it. Without looking at who was calling, she answered the phone.

"Changed your mind? You don't want to wait until Friday after all, do you?" She smiled, heading toward the front door.

"Friday? What about Friday?" Richard's voice on the other end of the line immediately decimated her post-orgasmic bliss.

Anger simmered at his arrogance and insistence on pushing himself on her when he really didn't want her. Let alone *she* couldn't stand the man very much anymore. "Listen to me carefully, Richard. Unless it's during working hours or at an event, don't call me."

She hung up as he started to speak. She couldn't wait to tell her mother she was through with him. "See you later, *Dick*."

Chapter Four

"I just don't know what's gotten into you. Richard is beside himself," Hannah's mother complained into her Bluetooth. It was Friday night and she was anxious to get to Rocco's. She turned at the light on Camden Court and 22nd Street in Oak Brook as he'd instructed. His apartment building had been vacant a few short months ago. It was strange. There were no signs that she'd noticed as she turned into the crowded parking lot and pulled into one of the few available spots.

She shut off the ignition and sighed. She'd gone over this with her mother on Monday and didn't feel the need to repeat herself. "Nothing's gotten into me. Like I already told you, there's nothing between Richard and me. There never was. You and Maggie were wrong trying to push it. If you want some kind of joint venture together, let the lawyers work out the details. You know, like your husband and son?"

Her mother sighed. Hannah rolled her eyes. "Richard's a catch and you know it. You're going to throw everything away over some Marine? This Rigo Mancini is a bad influence on you. It's affecting your work and it's going reflect badly on the firm."

Richard was such an asshole. Crying to her mother when he knew damn well he didn't want to be with her and had cheated on her when they were together. She'd bet he hadn't mentioned *that* little tidbit of information to her mother.

Hannah exited her car and grabbed the bag in the backseat with the pound cake and fruit topping she'd made for dessert. She noticed several people carrying duffel bags and small travel bags make their way toward the building's entrance. Were they Rocco's neighbors? Were they all traveling?

"First, his name is Rocco Moretti and Richard knows that. He's not just *some* Marine, either. Don't talk about him that way. He's served this country. Honorably. He's a hero. And I'm not twelve years old, Mother. He's not a bad influence. I don't need to put in sixteen-hour days to serve my clients. No one should have to do that." *If I buy Blumenthal's from Nora and Cora, I can call the shots and finally be free.* She made the short trek from her car to the lobby doors, ready to get off the phone and start her evening.

"His service and sacrifice are appreciated, of course. It doesn't mean you have to date the man when you should be making plans for the future with Richard," her mother insisted.

Hannah stepped inside the luxuriously appointed lobby. It had been beautifully renovated. She was impressed. "This conversation's over, Mother. Have a nice evening." She disconnected the call and waited in line behind the people she'd seen in the parking lot. *What is this place?*

A pretty blonde appeared to be checking the people in front of her in at some sort of granite-covered counter and collected some of their cell phones. This couldn't be Rocco's building. When the people in front of her entered through a door on their right using a key-card scanner, she knew she was in the wrong place.

She was about to ask the blonde for directions when a tall mountain of a man, with thick blond hair and bright blue eyes, wearing a white-sleeved shirt rolled up to the elbows and black suit pants, walked into the lobby through a door on the left. What she saw of his forearms were covered in ink like Rocco's, but the man's tattoos were of exotic animals like lions, tigers, and various other jungle animals.

The mystery man smiled, showing off his dimples, and took a seat behind the check-in counter. "You must be Hannah," he stated in a southern drawl.

Still unsure of what to make of everything going on around her, she nodded. "How do you know that? I was told this is where Rocco Moretti lives. But all those people just went through those doors over there. What is this place?" What had she gotten herself into? Had she been wrong about Rocco? Her stomach knotted and she trembled.

Before the mystery man could answer, the pretty blonde did. "I'm Grace Asher. This is my brother Kyle," she explained, gesturing to Kyle, who appeared to be her older brother. "This complex houses a members-only club on the first two floors with the entrance on the right. The executive apartments are on the third floor, and the entrance is over there on the left. You're in the right place. Rocco let us know you were coming."

"Thank you, baby girl. Hannah, we need to check your ID before we let you through. Its policy," Kyle informed her with a serious expression on his face.

"Oh, of course. I understand." She dug through her purse and handed Kyle her driver's license. He jotted down her information and handed it back with some paperwork. "What's this?"

Grace rolled her eyes at her brother. "That's an application for the Twisted Tea Society. He shouldn't have given you that." Hannah quickly tucked the application into her dessert bag. Why shouldn't she apply for whatever the society was?

"Why not? Hannah, do you read steamy romance novels? Like tea and snacks? Need a little time away from your busy life to just relax?"

She smiled at Kyle. She liked the southerner's

style. "Yes."

Kyle turned to Grace with a smirk on his face. "Good. Rocco can tell you all about the Twisted Tea Society. He's quite familiar with how it all works."

"Kyle," Grace warned.

Kyle ignored his sister's warning and smiled brightly, showing off his dimples and straight white teeth. "Go on up, Hannah. Rocco's waiting for you. I'll disengage the door lock. Take the elevator at the end of the hall to the third floor. He's on the left in Unit Four."

Hannah wasn't sure what to make of the southerners but wanted to get to Rocco. Several more of who she assumed must be club members entered through the lobby doors and she took that as her cue to leave.

She strolled down the empty, nondescript hallway toward the elevator doors. Restrooms were on her right. She noticed two offices with high-end office furniture on her left and just before the elevator, a large carpeted room with what looked like a small kitchenette with a sink and granite countertops as well as luxurious leather chairs and couches. Some chairs were arranged in a semi-circle in the center of the room. The Twisted Tea Society might be a steamy or erotic book club, she pondered. Why was Grace upset Kyle had given her an application? The idea sounded fun. She'd ask Rocco about it, but she wondered why he would know so much about it.

As she rode the elevator up to the third floor, she felt giddy. Butterflies took flight in her stomach and her heart rate sped up. She'd looked forward to tonight all week and had several non-grandmother-purchased condoms tucked away in her purse—just in case. She was wearing her favorite black jeans that made her ass look good and a lace neck, off-the-shoulder dusty rose t-shirt. Rocco had promised her all Italy had to offer and she was more than ready to receive it.

She laughed when the elevator doors opened and she saw Rocco waiting for her, wearing snug jeans and a tight black t-shirt that read *Italians Do It Better* in white letters. Three-quarters of his skillfully inked arms were on display and his sexy grin made her body heat up and tingle all over. The man was lethal in the best of ways.

"Do they now?" she teased when he reached for her and pulled her against him. She loved the feel of him. Strong and hot, and there was no mistaking his obvious erection grinding into her. She had plans for that hard cock tonight. Powerful hands glided from her torso to her hips and then her ass and squeezed. She reveled in the masculine energy that dominated her.

Seemingly not bothered they were in his hallway, he claimed her mouth. His masterful tongue teased and tempted her until they drew apart, both panting. "You tell *me, bella*. Have I done it better so far?" He held her tight and nibbled on her earlobe, then peppered kisses along her neck, inhaling deeply. "You smell *fantastico,* baby. I love your scent."

She swayed in his arms, thankful he was there to hold her up. "It's called *Falling in Love,*" she whispered. She knew it was crazy and much too soon, but she couldn't help but feel it was exactly what she was doing.

She felt his lips smile against her neck. "*Perfetto.* It suits you." He pulled away from their embrace and she immediately missed the contact. Their connection. Crazy as that also sounded, she believed they shared one.

He held her hand and led her to his apartment door. She was greeted with the delicious aroma of what she knew had to be Italian food as soon as they stepped inside. Her stomach growled and she giggled.

"What's this?" he asked, glancing at the bag in her hand.

"I made dessert. It's nothing fancy, but I didn't want to come empty-handed."

Rocco kissed her nose and shook his head. "You wouldn't have come empty-handed without dessert because you brought *you*. That's all I need."

Her heart fluttered. *Falling in love*. That was what was happening, for certain.

"Dinner's ready. I'm guessing by your growling stomach it means you didn't eat like you should have today. I'm sorry I was too busy to text you a reminder. Please take care of yourself, *bella*. If you don't eat right, it can make you sick."

She followed him deeper inside his space to a generously large common area boasting hardwood floors, a full-sized kitchen equipped with cherry cabinets, sparkling black granite countertops, a large eating area, and a spacious family room with comfy-looking leather couches and a big screen television. His place exemplified the man—dark and masculine.

"Please, sit. I'll bring everything to the table for us," Rocco said.

He took her dessert bag and placed it on the counter while she sat down at the table. Pink roses with baby's breath graced the center of the set table and gave off a subtle scent. She watched as he deftly plated lasagna and meatballs. He placed a bowl with tossed salad and a plate with focaccia bread on the table and sat down. Her stomach growled again and he frowned.

"You're right. I skipped breakfast and didn't have much for lunch. Your reminders have been sweet. Are you trying to fatten me up even more with all this?" she kidded. It all looked and smelled wonderful, but as usual, when he prepared a plate for her, he gave her too much.

"Don't do that. You're not fat. You're perfect just the way you are. Let's eat while everything is hot," he said and dug into his dinner.

That was Richard's opinion of her figure, which he hadn't been shy about expressing. She supposed after hearing him berate her so many times, she'd accepted his opinion as fact. It did something to her heart knowing Rocco didn't share Richard's opinion. *Richard's history. What he thinks doesn't matter and never will again.* Regardless of what the future held, *that* was a fact.

"Okay. You're right. I'm starved." She took a few bites of the best Italian food she'd ever eaten. Antonetti's must have updated their recipes or brought on a new chef. "Cucina Antonetti's really stepped up their game. This is delicious."

Rocco raised a brow and shook his head slightly. "I wouldn't invite you to dinner and pick something up. I made everything on the table, including the balsamic vinaigrette on the salad. I didn't have time to bake so I *did* pick up the focaccia bread from Antonetti's. My recipe is better though," he stated proudly.

The man had a gift when it came to cooking. "This is amazing, Rocco. Better than anything I've ever had, truly. You should have your own restaurant. I mean it." She continued eating with gusto.

He scoffed but smiled. "I don't know about all *that*, but I'm glad *you* like everything."

She received a text from Richard and cringed.

Richard: **this is stupid, we need 2 talk about things**

Hannah: **I told u there's nothing personal left 2 say, we can talk biz tomorrow at the wedding, bother me again and I'll block your number**

"Dick?" Rocco asked with a smirk on his face.

She waved a hand dismissively. Richard didn't matter. Where he was concerned, she truly felt free and it was wonderful. "He's not important. I had a nice little

chat with Kyle and his sister Grace in the lobby. Tell me more about the building. This members-only club and the Twisted Tea Society. Kyle said you knew all about it."
****

Falling In Love was her scent. As Rocco sat across from the dark-haired beauty eating dinner with him, he could admit it was indeed the case for him. He was smitten. Enchanted. Falling hard.

When the elevator door had opened, revealing his dinner companion in her perfectly fitting black jeans and off-the-shoulder, deep-pink top, he'd nearly taken her against the wall. He wasn't an exhibitionist, per se, but was comfortable with his body and sexuality. He was a trained Dominant at Club Envidious, was a Dungeon Monitor from time to time, and had scened at the club in Envy, Texas, as well as their new club in Oak Brook.

He also enjoyed serving the women who were members of the Twisted Tea Society. He felt like he made a difference. Helping the ladies take a break from their hectic lives. Aside from the fact the servers only wore a bowtie, to him, his enjoyment wasn't sexual in nature. It came from helping others. From service.

He was more than pleased Hannah enjoyed his cooking. She was the first woman or date he'd ever cooked for. All his cooking gifts, or talents, as she referred to them, were shared with his family and a few of the men he worked with at Dixon-Shaw, until now.

Kyle and his big fucking mouth. Heath had warned him. It was at Kyle's suggestion Heath ended up taking Leah to Club Envidious after their first official dinner date at Kyle's restaurant Golden Horns. Kyle's expansion of Envy Entertainment to Chicago was in full swing. Fortunately, Heath's association with the club hadn't scared Leah away, but she'd been in love with the man for years.

He and Hannah were new. Just getting to know each other. Now he faced the real possibility she could decide he wasn't what she wanted after all and went running back to Richard the Dick like their mothers wanted.

He wasn't a dick like Richard and she deserved the truth. She'd been lied to and treated badly for far too long. He had no intention of being yet another person in her life who didn't do right by her.

She looked at him expectantly with her soulful, deep-brown eyes and he was helpless to do anything but tell her truth. He took a deep breath and nodded. *Might as well get it over with.*

"This building, or complex, houses executive apartments on the third floor. Right now, only I, Grace, and Kyle occupy a unit. The first and second floors are a part of a BDSM club called Club Envidious, which Kyle and his older sister Lauren own. They also own the Golden Horns restaurant. The original locations are in Envy, Texas, and these new Chicago locations are the first leg of Envy Entertainment's expansion." He continued with his dinner, nervous about her response.

She seemed to think for a moment. "Okay. That explains why the people I saw were carrying duffel bags and travel-type luggage. They were bringing club wear and uh … other things, right?"

So far so good. She didn't appear upset and was still enjoying her dinner. He doubted she was in the lifestyle, but she seemed curious rather than put off. He could work with that. "Yes. Members are required to wear street clothes if they're in the parking lot or the lobby. And many bring their own toys or implements."

She nodded slightly. "Makes sense. Are you a member?"

His stomach knotted. His honest answer could

very well be the beginning of the end between them. "I was trained as a Dominant at the Envy location so I could perform my duties as a Dungeon Monitor. I receive full-member benefits because of that. Do you know what a Dungeon Monitor is, *bella*? What they do?" He was stunned but relieved she hadn't run out the door.

She laughed and nodded. The sound was music to his ears. "I'm not in the lifestyle, as you'd say, but I've done some reading. Researched online. The DMs keep everyone safe, generally speaking. I'm not freaked out or anything. Chicago is a large metropolitan area. Kyle was smart to expand here. For the club and Golden Horns. I've heard great things about the restaurant. And how does this Twisted Tea Society fit into all of this? Kyle made it sound like an erotic book club. No big deal. He gave me an application. It's in the bag with dessert."

Considering what she had to put with on a daily basis, he couldn't believe how accepting and nonjudgmental she was. She was perfect for him, though he'd already suspected that. Now he was certain.

Kyle had no business butting his nose in his business like that. It should've been up to *him*, not Kyle, to reveal his association with Envy Entertainment, when *he* was fucking ready to do it.

He took a deep breath. This was the last of the explanations. If she didn't leave after this, he was hopeful there could be something between them. As long as Richard the Dick and Hannah's mother didn't make things more difficult.

"It is an erotic book club, yes. But it's more than that. It's a ladies' social club, really. With a touch of kink." He waited, his stomach doing flips over her next move.

"Kinky how?"

Hannah didn't seem upset, just curious. He was

relieved. "The male servers provide refreshments, give footbaths, foot, hand, and shoulder rubs wearing only a bowtie. There's no sex or play of any kind, and the ladies are dressed."

Her eyes grew wide for a moment before a sly grin graced her lovely face.

"I'm a server."

Her mouth fell open and he knew she was moments from leaving. He was going to fucking kill Kyle.

"Really? Then I'm definitely going to fill out the application. Oh! Can I ask for you to be my server? Is that allowed? When do they meet? Kyle didn't give many details." She was nearly bouncing in her chair while nibbling on her dinner. What a relief. He might not have to kill Kyle after all.

He chuckled, feeling as if a weight had been lifted. "Slow down, *bella*. Yes, you can ask the Server Supervisor if I can serve you. They meet on the second and fourth Wednesday of the month from seven to ten PM. Go to their website for policy and etiquette information. You'll also have to sign an NDA and a Hold-Harmless Agreement or HHA."

Hannah's smile lit up her face and she clapped happily until something seemed to concern her and she frowned. Damn it. She was second-guessing herself. "The second Wednesday is next week. What book are they reading? I have to get it so I can prepare."

He laughed. He needed to calm down. She was fine. He pulled up their website on his phone for the current read. "They're reading *Dawn* by Erin M. Leaf."

He finished his dinner as he watched her purchase and download the book on her phone, all the while with the sweetest grin on her face. He was done for, but he didn't care.

"So, now let me ask *you* something. What about those beautiful bridal gown drawings I saw at your place? Why are you not designing rather than planning events?" He believed he knew the answer but wanted to understand from Hannah's perspective.

Some of her light dimmed and he felt like an asshole for asking. She shrugged. "I went to design school at the School of the Art Institute of Chicago. My mother thought it was a waste of time since she'd expected me at Hailey's Events. But my father and brother Eric were supportive and encouraged me to attend. I dream up ideas for gowns to relax and unwind sometimes. It brings me peace. I guess you could say it's my bliss." Again, another shrug. "It doesn't really mean anything."

He heard her words but felt her regret from unrealized dreams. "Hannah, those designs matter. They're stunning. They mean something. I've never seen trains like what you've drawn."

Some of her light returned, making him feel ten feet tall. "They're royal trains or luxury royal trains. They can be drawn in a variety of lengths, or even be detachable. And how do *you* know so much about wedding gowns, Marine?" The smile he'd come to adore was now back.

"Ah … well, I may or may not like to watch *Say Yes to the Dress*." It was his turn to shrug this time. "I sort of got into the show when my younger brother Massimo was getting married. Don't tell anyone, though. I have a reputation to maintain." He'd helped out with the wedding preparations in ways his brother didn't know.

His brother had gotten married soon after he and his girl Sydney graduated from college. They'd had a tight wedding budget, so Rocco had offered Sydney's parents money to upgrade to a full open bar and a plated dinner rather than a less expensive buffet at their reception.

She laughed and he felt his cock twitch. He was ready for more of her. "I won't say a word, I promise. I told you mine, now you tell me yours. What's *your* bliss?"

That was easy. "Cooking. Spending time with my grandparents learning to cook during those early days of living with them full-time after my parents abandoned us. It saved me, emotionally. After a while, though, I found I had a knack in the kitchen. I'm not sure it's a gift, but I enjoy cooking very much. Not only Italian food, though my grandfather's recipe for sauce is amazing."

Hannah shook her head. "You're wrong. You have a gift. What you made for us tonight. It's as good— better than much of the Italian food I've eaten anywhere, and I've been to many restaurants and venues over the years."

It meant a lot to him that she believed that. It made him almost believe himself. "Kyle won't let me near the kitchens at the club *or* Golden Horns."

"He's wrong about that. Trust me," she assured him.

"And *you* should trust *me* when I tell you that you should be designing couture bridal gowns rather than running after caterers and florists. You're an artist and don't let anyone tell you otherwise." He knew what he needed to do. He knew who would be inspired by her designs. The question was when to share her gift with them. It was all about timing.

She gazed at him with a pained expression on her face. "The sisters who own Blumenthal's Discount Bridal want to retire and sell me their salon."

What an amazing opportunity. A *perfect*

opportunity for her. It hurt him to know that because of her mother, she most likely had doubts. "Please tell me you're considering it. Seriously considering it. Hailey's Events is your *mother's* dream, not yours. She's come a long way from that trailer park and has nothing more to prove. Neither do you."

He held her delicate hands in his, hoping to instill some confidence. She'd likely regret it if she let the opportunity slip through her fingers and end up resenting her mother. They'd shared some of the painful details of their pasts over the phone. Somehow, it had seemed easier.

She sighed and his heart ached for what should be a simple decision. The *right* decision for her and her future. "You're right. I know you are. I don't have to decide right now, though. There's still a little time. They're looking to move to Florida by next spring, so I have a few months. Thank you." She smiled at him with that angelic smile and he leaned in for a quick kiss. The feel of her soft, warm lips made his blood pulse through his veins. He couldn't wait much longer before he had her beneath him.

"Do you have a little dinner left that I can take with me? To make sure I eat like I should?" She offered him a shy smile and he knew he could never refuse her. He'd made plenty, in order to send her home with enough for several meals anyway.

He kissed her knuckles and noticed her eyes dilate. Good. "Of course. Let me wrap it up for you and then more of what Italy has to offer and dessert a little later? I hope, so far, I'm doing it better."

She giggled and his heart did that little flip thing again. "Yes. So far, *much* better."

Chapter Five

Hannah rinsed their dinner dishes and placed them in the dishwasher while Rocco packed up enough leftovers for her host her own dinner party. It was just as well. Kyle Asher might be a successful businessman and club owner, but he was a fool not to have Rocco in one of his kitchens. She had an idea she believed would pay off and give Kyle a moment of regret. A few of what she thought were protein bars were also added to her leftover bag. She couldn't help but feel special when Rocco doted on her the way he did. No other man aside from family had ever cared if she ate properly or at all.

He pointed a remote control toward the family room and the elegant, seductive sounds of Roxy Music began to play softly. She liked Bryan Ferry, the singer, very much.

"Take a seat in the family room and I'll make you a quick cappuccino." He kissed her lips softly and her body warmed.

"With a pretty foam picture?"

"Of course."

Hannah grabbed her purse and set out for the family room. She took a seat in the center of the couch, relaxing into the comfy leather, the sultry sounds from the stereo speakers relaxing her. She smiled when she heard the whirring and hissing from the kitchen and wondered what design he'd surprise her with. She'd regretted not snapping a shot of the pretty hearts design he'd created for her at Jake and Cassie's, so she pulled her phone out. She would post it on her blog on Hailey's Events website.

Her heart rate picked up speed when Rocco

joined her on the couch with a white cup and saucer in his hands. He'd created another culinary work of art—for *her*. A foam version of a single long-stemmed rose complete with leaves and thorns on the stem.

"What do you think?" he asked in a low sexy timbre that matched the music drifting through the room. He looked at her expectantly as though he thought she wouldn't like it.

"I think it's too pretty to drink, although I think we should share it. Let me take a couple of pictures for my blog on the company website. Maybe some other time you can recreate the design you made at Jake and Cassie's so I can get a shot of that too?"

Hannah hoped she wasn't sounding presumptuous that there would actually *be* another time. She wanted there to be, but in the back of her mind, she worried that after tonight, after they slept together, he wouldn't want to see her again socially. Richard hadn't been interested in her very much sexually. She hated him for making her doubt Rocco's interest and her own desirability. She didn't want to believe Rocco's interest in her was insincere.

Hannah snapped a couple of photos of his foam art and bit her lower lip, waiting on his reply. He offered her a smirky grin that made insides tingle and anticipation pulse through her.

"I can recreate the hearts design for you anytime. I have many other designs I can do for you. You really want to put them on your company blog?"

She could kill Kyle for making Rocco doubt his culinary skills. If her plan worked like she believed it would, he'd be eating crow soon.

"Absolutely. I'll do a write up on the chef who created the masterpieces too." She giggled when the man blushed. He was humble in addition to all the other wonderful things he was. The total opposite of Richard the Dick. She vowed right then and there to put Richard out of her mind. He had no place in her head anymore on a personal level and especially not when she was with Rocco. "Let's drink it while it's still hot, okay?"

His lip twitched and he nodded. He held the cup and saucer away from them. "Sit on my lap, facing me, and we'll share."

Taken by surprise at his request, she hesitated for a moment and then carefully positioned herself on his strong thighs, his body heat warming her. When he used his free arm to pull her up closer, she felt his hard cock press against her. Her nipples hardened and her pussy slickened. She was close to suggesting they forget about the coffee, but he'd gone to the trouble of making and decorating it for her, she didn't have the heart.

He brought the cup up to her lips and she took a small sip of the rich blend he'd prepared. Sweet and not bitter. He'd prepared it perfectly. She licked the foam from her lips and felt a sense of feminine pride as he watched her do it. His nostrils flared and his eyes dilated. He was just as affected as she was. "Delicious," she whispered.

Hannah placed her hands on his, warming further, and guided the small cup to his lips. She watched in fascination as he took a sip. Rocco sat for a moment with foam on his lip and raised a brow as if in a challenge. She leaned in while grinding against his erection and swiped at the foam with her tongue until it was gone.

He moaned softly and closed his eyes briefly. "I agree, *delizioso*. Here, baby, take another sip so we can finish this and then *ti voglio scopare*. You've been driving me crazy with need since the moment the elevator door opened."

Her eyes widened. She had? She assumed he'd

said he wanted to have sex with her. "Really?" She took a larger sip and ground against him again, eliciting another moan.

He shook his head slightly and her stomach flipped. So, he didn't want her after all? "Actually, I've wanted to fuck you since the day we met at Grace of God when I grabbed you by the wrist in the guy's changing room." He took his sip and guided the cup back to her.

Her breasts ached and felt heavy, and her pussy was hot and slick. She quickly took her sip, needing for them to finish, her lust making her mindless with desire.

Rocco took one last large sip, placed the empty cup and saucer on the floor away from them beside the couch, captured her mouth, and kissed her rough and deep. She ran her fingers through his thick, dark hair and kissed him back, pouring everything she had into the kiss.

They broke apart, gasping for air. Itching to feel his skin, she yanked at his t-shirt to loosen it out of his jeans. He leaned forward, helping to make her task easier. A giggle escaped and she pulled his t-shirt up and off. She tossed it aside and kissed him again while he tugged at her blouse. With little patience left for fumbling around, she pulled away slightly and removed her blouse and tossed it to where his t-shirt now lay.

Old insecurities returned and she covered herself with her hands. Rocco held her face in his strong, warm hands. Disappointment showed in his dreamy brown eyes. "You don't need to hide from me, *bella*. Whoever has you believing you're anything but beautiful, perfect, should be ashamed of themselves. *Capisci*? Understand? I'll keep telling you that until you believe it. I told you last Sunday that you should always go topless. Now, take your bra off and let me see your luscious tits."

The desire and lust on Rocco's handsome face

left little doubt *he* considered her beautiful. That was good enough for her. After all, beauty was in the eye of the beholder. She channeled some of his confidence, reached behind her back, and unhooked her lacy pink bra. His eyes never left hers and he wore the slightest of grins. She slowly peeled it away from her breasts and tossed it to where their other clothes were on the floor. Her nipples pebbled under his watchful gaze and when he licked his lips, she nearly groaned.

He captured a tight bud with his teeth and gently tugged, causing a moan to escape. She didn't need gentle. Her pulse raced and her clit throbbed as he laved and suckled her breast. When he turned his attention to the other peak, she shivered she was so aroused. He moaned against her flesh and she grew more desperate to feel him inside her. After he pulled away with one last nip at her aching nipple, she groaned in disappointment. She was panting, she was close. Just from this.

Rocco gazed at her with such hunger, his pupils so dilated, they were nearly black. "You're delectable, *cara*. I'm going to carry you to my bed because I can't wait to fuck you anymore. You're not going to make any comments about being too heavy, right?"

She leaned in and ran her tongue lightly along his lower lip. She smiled, feeling feminine power for the first time in her life when he groaned and closed his eyes. "Not a word. I need you. I can't wait either," she murmured against his lips.

Suddenly, he was standing, barely exerting any effort, and she quickly wrapped her legs around his waist as he took quick strides through the apartment to his bedroom. "Good, because I need you too. Now."

That knowledge thrilled her even more. The lustful sensations she was experiencing were also new to her but she welcomed them almost giddily. Hannah wanted whatever Rocco was willing to give her.

He set her down in his room that was decorated like the man himself. Dark, masculine, elegant, and with a king-size bed. A nightstand lamp cast a soft, intimate glow, setting the mood perfectly while Roxy Music continued to play, albeit a little softer, from the family room.

She quickly toed off her shoes and shed her jeans while he did the same. Her mouth went dry when she saw Rocco in only his black boxer briefs, his hard cock straining against the front of them. He was a work of art. Literally. Even with the scars on his torso she was able to make out in the dim light. And he thought *she* was beautiful? Wanted *her*?

In a flash, he stood before her, glancing down at her with a hunger she'd never seen from a man directed toward her—ever. His lips twitched as he made slow work of looking her over. He seared her skin when he placed his hands on the waistband of her lacy pink boyshorts.

"You forgot something, *bella*."

She gasped when he ripped them off and brought them to his nose and inhaled. He offered her a crooked grin and opened the nightstand drawer, tossing her torn panties inside. "These are mine now. I told you pink has become my favorite color. Get in the bed, *cara*."

She vibrated with need, imagining what it would feel like to finally have him inside her but remembered her purse. "I brought four condoms, non-grandmother condoms. They're in the family room in my purse."

He chuckled and shook his head. "Those *nonne*. I bought four *boxes* earlier today. In bed. Now," he sexily commanded her. If this was his Dom persona, she had to admit she rather liked it.

She eagerly climbed into his big bed, feeling the

cool burgundy sheets against her warm skin. The faint scent of fabric softener lingered and she smiled, knowing he'd gone through the trouble of changing the bedding for her. She made herself comfortable in the center and was about to mention he had too much on when he discarded his boxer briefs, revealing his magnificent rock-hard cock nestled in dark curls. Pre-cum glistened from the tip and she licked her lips, desperate for a taste.

He tore open one of the condom boxes, removed a packet from the strip, and tossed it on the bed next to her. "If you keep looking at me like that, it'll be over before we get started. I'm barely hanging on as it is." He climbed onto the bed and on top of her, resting on his elbows.

Her heart thudded in her chest, feeling his warm, muscled skin pressed against hers. "I don't care. We can go slow next time." Didn't he realize how much she wanted him? Ached for him?

His brow furrowed, as he seemed torn between wanting to take his time, which she appreciated, and wanting to fuck her right now, hard and fast, like she needed him to. He sighed, sat back on his knees, and quickly sheathed himself.

He positioned himself at her entrance but held still. "Just this one time you get to top from the bottom, *bella*. You understand what that means, right?"

She knew from her reading, though not from personal experience. "I do. I'm so—"

Rocco pushed into her slick, waiting pussy to the hilt with one thrust, the tendons in his neck straining. She gasped as he was bigger than she was used to. He filled her completely, stretching her almost painfully. She wrapped her arms and legs around him, holding him tight.

"So tight, so perfect, Hannah. Just like I knew

you'd be," he whispered and pulled out slowly before plunging back in. His body felt hard, hot, and primal against hers.

"I've thought about us like this since the day we met." She moved under him, moaning as he began fucking her.

"So have I, *cara*. I've thought of us together in so many ways."

She lifted her hips to meet his rough, hard strokes. It was exactly what she needed. What she craved. He pressed into her body harder, rocking into her. She was close already.

He groaned when she tightened her internal muscles around his thick cock, pulled out, and drove back in. He pistoned in and out of her again and again with hard, sure, possessive strokes. They were both panting, their bodies damp. When he reached between their joined bodies and expertly stroked her clit, she detonated and crashed over, shouting her release. After a few more strokes, his movements became jerky and he growled out his own release. She felt him pulse his cum into the condom, filling it.

Until Rocco, sex had always been so boring and unfulfilling. He'd just set the bar for other men a hell of a lot higher, although she didn't like the thought of being with anyone else now that they'd slept together. It was too soon to think long-term. She'd enjoy the moment and see where things led. *One step at a time.*

When they'd both calmed a bit, Rocco pulled out carefully and smiled down at her. She couldn't help but smile back since it appeared he'd enjoyed their time together as much as she had. He kissed her tenderly and her body warmed again. How did he do that?

"I'll be right back." Another quick kiss and he got out of bed and padded to the en suite bathroom. She heard water running and stretched. A giggle escaped. She felt fantastic even if a little sore.

Suddenly "That's Amore" by Dean Martin began playing in the room. Rocco emerged from the bathroom with a concerned expression on his face. He found his jeans from their pile of clothes on the floor and retrieved his phone. She sat up, worried because of his concern.

"It's my brother Massimo. Something could be wrong with him or the kids."

She nodded her understanding.

He swiped and pressed. "What's wrong?" he barked at the phone, his body tense. She made room for him when he sat down on the edge of the bed.

"Hey, big brother. So, how did the big date go?" Massimo asked with a smile in his voice. Rocco visibly relaxed and made himself comfortable in the bed beside her, both of them leaning up against the headboard with pillows behind their backs.

Hannah pulled the sheet up to cover herself and Rocco promptly pulled it away, exposing her from the waist up. A giggle escaped and she quickly placed her hands over her mouth.

"Shit. Hannah's still there, huh? Sorry, dude, didn't mean to cock block you." He didn't sound sorry at all to her. She found him funny, but from the irritated look on Rocco's face, he didn't.

"You didn't block anything, *stronzo*. I only picked up because I thought something might have been wrong with the kids."

"Everything's fine. I told him he shouldn't bother you. Hi, Hannah, it's Sydney, Rocco's sister-in-law. I'm so sorry for intruding on your date."

Sydney sounded sweet. She liked her already. "It's okay. You didn't actually intrude on anything."

"Thanks, Hannah," Massimo replied. "Hey, how

about I cook dinner for you and Rocco sometime soon, as an apology. I'm a *much* better cook than he is."

Rocco shook his head. Although it stung, she wasn't surprised he didn't want her to meet his family yet. "Bullshit, you are not. *I'm* the better cook and everyone knows it. And Hannah will know it too." Hope bloomed. It was a sibling rivalry thing that had nothing to do with her. She could work with that.

"How about we let Hannah decide? Let us know when you're free for dinner and then you're going down. I'm also the better-looking Moretti brother, but I'm already spoken for."

Massimo hung up and Rocco rolled his eyes. He tossed his phone on the nightstand and pulled her to him so she was straddling his lap. His skin was still warm and she felt his length harden under her ass. More. She definitely wanted more.

"The *nonne* thought we could fuck four times in one night. Shall we prove them right, sweet Hannah?"

Her pussy pulsed and slickened at the idea of having Rocco three more times. "I say yes, we should. I'm enjoying what Italy has to offer very much and I'm ready for more."

****

Rocco heard Hannah moving around in his bedroom as he prepared their omelets, wearing only a full-length apron that read *The only thing better than being Italian is being Sicilian*, a gag gift from Heath, whom he was on the phone with.

"It was an amazing night until I fucked it up by having a combo nightmare. At least it wasn't a bad one where I woke up begging him to stop hitting me, thinking IEDs were going off around me. Hannah took it pretty well. Thank God, and we both got a little more sleep."

Heath grunted. "I wish that piece-of-shit old man

of yours was still alive so I could put a bullet in his head for what he did to you and your mother."

Rocco snorted. *Get in line.* "He got his in the end." They'd all received word about five years ago Matteo, his father, had smashed his car into a tree in Wisconsin and had died on impact. His blood alcohol level had been so high, the authorities couldn't believe he could actually drive at all. "Thanks, brother."

"No need to thank me, man. We're not keeping score on the nightmare phone calls. Tell Hannah I said hello. Talk to you later."

He hung up as Hannah entered the kitchen. She took his breath away every time he looked at her. She glanced at him and blushed. She was a shy one, but she needn't be. He'd had to give her one of his t-shirts to sleep in before she agreed to spend the night. He should put a bullet in Richard the Dick just on principle for making her feel anything less than gorgeous.

"Come sit. Breakfast is just about ready. I have your Twisted Tea Society application on the table. I'll give it to Kyle for you after you fill it out." He extended a hand and she took it. After a much-too-brief kiss, she sat down and completed the application.

He placed their breakfast plates on the table and removed his apron, hanging it on one of the kitchen chair backs, and took a seat beside her. Her eyes widened and her cheeks stained pink.

"You're going to eat naked?" She busied herself with her breakfast, but he noticed her sneaking glances his way. His ego enjoyed a boost, knowing she liked what she saw, even if she felt embarrassed.

"Why not? This is a private space. You should eat naked too." He dug into his omelet, wondering how she'd respond.

He watched her as she enjoyed her breakfast but

appeared deep in thought. Perhaps she was considering his suggestion. He hoped so.

She sat back in her chair slightly and pulled her pretty deep-pink blouse out of her jeans, lifted it off, and placed it on her lap. He enjoyed the view of her full tits in her lacy pink strapless bra but preferred the bare view much better. She took a deep breath, unhooked her bra, and also placed it on her lap.

"You said I should always go topless, right?" she asked, doing her best to seem unaffected, but her pebbled dusky nipples gave her away. He knew this was a big step for her and didn't want to scare her any more than she probably already was.

He nodded and took a sip of orange juice. "I did. And I meant it." They continued eating in compatible silence for a moment. "I propose from now on, when we're alone together here at my place or yours, we remain undressed."

She looked up, eyes wide but not seeming alarmed. "Like a contract?"

With all the directions she was pulled in on daily basis, especially from her mother, and the situation with Richard the Dick, he didn't want to add to her burdens, even though a contract between the two of them would be different than the contracts she was used to.

"Let's call it a verbal agreement—for now."

She furrowed her brow, obviously contemplating his proposal. It was a start. He wanted her to feel comfortable and confident in her own skin. It was a crime she didn't already. Richard the Dick's bullet count had just increased to two.

"Yes. I agree." She smiled and gazed at him so sweetly his heart skipped a beat. He was in trouble but had no desire to do anything about it.

"We have a wedding in North Barrington today

with a fun retro disco and karaoke theme after dinner. Would you like to be my date?" She bit her lush lower lip and looked at him expectantly. She thought he'd turn her down?

"Under one condition. After all the arrangements are set, you change into something pretty like the dress you wore to Jake and Cassie's. Not a pantsuit. And wear your hair down." He knew he was pushing her, but there was a passionate, remarkable woman underneath all the crap she dealt with every damn day. It was time to let her out. Let her shine.

"Yes. I'll bring something pretty, and wear my hair down."

He nodded, feeling relieved he hadn't scared her. "Text me the details. I can come by early and help out if you want. Will Richard and his people be there?" He assumed they would be. It seemed Hailey's Events and Hayes Studios worked many events together. He didn't particularly give a fuck if Richard the Dick was there but wanted to be prepared ahead of time.

She frowned and nodded. After a beat, she said, "But who cares, right? We'll still have a great time anyway, won't we?" Her angelic, hopeful smile lit up her face.

His heart flipped and he nodded. "Hell yeah, we will."
****

About two hours later, Rocco pulled his truck into the North Barrington Country Club parking lot. Dixon-Shaw had been contracted to provide security details for high-profile clients at the venue before, so he was familiar with the layout of the property.

Dressed casually in jeans and a gray Marine t-shirt for work detail, he grabbed his garment bag with a dark-gray Armani suit, coordinating tie, and white dress shirt and shoes from the backseat. He rubbed his whisker-covered jaw and grinned. Hannah had asked him not to shave, liking his "scruff," as she called it.

He made his way through the club's grand entrance and to the ballroom. He spotted Joe right away, dressed in jeans as well, holding two clipboards, reviewing his notes. Round tables were arranged with bright white tablecloths and place settings were set. They were missing chairs, centerpieces, and Hannah.

Joe noticed him and smiled. Rocco nodded. "Where's Hannah? Shouldn't she be here by now?" His stomach knotted at the thought something could be wrong. He chastised himself for not suggesting they drive in together. *Next time I will.*

Joe placed a hand on his shoulder, most likely hoping to calm him down. "I just heard from her. She said she had an important errand to run. She's on her way. Just a few minutes away."

"Good. Where do you need me?"

"They're just about finished with the platform outside. Ah, here are the chairs. The florists are due any minute. Let's get this room set up."

After a few minutes of setting up chairs, assisted by staff employees, Hannah arrived with a bright smile on her face. Though she was wearing simple black capri pants and a white top, his cock twitched, taking notice.

"Thanks for getting started without me," she said as she made her way to him.

Falling in love. He held her face in his hands and took quick possession of her lips. He reluctantly pulled away when someone cleared their throat.

Patty Hailey, Hannah's mother, stood a few feet away, dressed to perfection in a burgundy pencil skirt suit and crisp white blouse. Her blonde hair was pinned up neatly and her makeup was flawless. She was taller than Hannah and too slim in his opinion. He much preferred Hannah's more natural, dark-haired looks and curves.

Although she appeared calm and collected, he sensed her tension and disapproval as she gave him a quick once-over. She lingered a moment, gazing at his arms before she managed a tight smile as she advanced closer.

"Richard and his team are here," Patty stated happily. Yes, Patty was on Team Richard all the way and wasn't shy about letting him know.

"I should hope so. Kristen and Ben want shots and footage before, during, and after the wedding." He was relieved Hannah's reply was all business. No indication of caring on a personal level about Richard's presence.

Patty's expression faltered slightly and she turned her attention directly to him. Shit. He hoped for Hannah's sake her mother wouldn't cause a scene.

"I trust Hannah explained the proper attire for after the event setup is over, seeing as you're her … date for the reception?" She regarded him coolly. He felt sorry for Hannah, for what it must be like to deal with Patty like this every day. He wondered if she wouldn't have been better off without her. Happier. Fulfilled. More confident.

He spoke before Hannah could. "Yes, ma'am. We had a specific conversation about attire for this evening. I hope a custom-tailored Armani suit is acceptable. And I'm sure Hannah brought something equally appropriate to wear, didn't you, *bella*?"

Rewarding him with a knowing grin, she nodded. "Yes, Mother. We spoke about what we should wear to the reception over a delicious breakfast Rocco prepared for us this morning after our date last night. What I brought to wear to the reception is *exactly* what he and I discussed."

He heard Joe snicker from across the room but kept his own expression neutral. Now was not to time for a mother-daughter showdown. Kristen and Ben, the bride and groom, were expecting their best and he wouldn't be the one to ruin their day.

"Patty, everything will be fine," Joe said from beside him. "Rocco's been a big help. You have nothing to worry about."

Surprisingly, Patty's expression softened a bit as she regarded Joe. She nodded, seemingly conceding. "Thank you, Rocco. And for your service as well. I'll leave you all to it then. I'll go to Hoffman Estates and check on the preparations for the Clark/Sanders wedding."

After Patty left the ballroom, Hannah let out a breath and Rocco picked her up and twirled her around. Her giggles soothed his soul.

"All right, all right, we still have a bit to finish before guests start arriving. We'll have plenty of time for fun a little later." He put her down and kissed her forehead.

For the next hour, he shadowed Joe or Hannah around the property, double- and triple-checking all the arrangements, conferring with the facility's staff, and confirming everything was in place as the bride and groom wanted it. After dinner, the ballroom would be transformed into a retro-style disco with flashing lights, a karaoke machine, and a DJ. He had an entirely new appreciation for event planners and all the work that went on behind the scenes. Joe and Hannah were amazing. They worked well together and he was confident Kristen and Ben would be pleased. Richard the Dick had been within his peripheral vision the entire time with a disgusted look on his face. *Too fucking bad, asshole.*

He and Joe had just finished getting dressed in the men's locker room for the day's festivities when Richard the Dick stormed in with a scowl on his face.

"What the fuck, *Semper Fi*? You're Hannah's *date*?" Richard the Dick's voice was shrill and he had beads of sweat on his upper lip and forehead. He was angry but afraid. *Good, he should be.*

Joe got up in the asshole's face before Rocco could say anything. "What's it to you, *Dick*? You don't care about Hannah anyway."

"Fuck off, *fag*, the *real* men are talking." So Richard the Dick was a homophobe in addition to all of his other less-than-desirable character traits. He'd just earned his third bullet.

Joe advanced on Richard, but Rocco held him back. They didn't have time for this shit. "Let me handle this, Joe. Can you check on Hannah for me? Please?" Hannah's name appeared to calm Joe down slightly but he didn't move. "*You*, shut the hell up for a second," he said to Richard. "It's all right, Joe. I've got this."

With a curt nod, Joe left the locker room. He blew out a sigh of relief. Hannah's mother was pushing this asshole on her? What the fuck for? Regardless of his so-called artistic talents, he was a piece of shit as a person.

"I know what you're doing, *Guido*. No way in fuck you're interested in Hannah. This jealousy game you're playing won't work. I know she's pissed about what happened at Grace of God. We've got plans, and you're in the way. You don't fit, so move on. I'm warning you."

He was a real piece of work. Warning *him*. He knew he didn't fit, but he couldn't walk away either. "That's where you're wrong. I'm *very* interested. As long as Hannah wants me around, that's exactly where I'll be. Count on it, *Dick*."

Richard clenched his fists but stood back slightly, like the pussy he was. Rocco wouldn't need a gun to put the fucker down. "Yeah, right. Her pantsuits do it for you, do they? And all your *bella* and *cara* crap. Give me a fucking break."

He shrugged. "Her pantsuits don't bother me. I prefer her naked, like she was last night and early this morning. I happen to think she's beautiful and I can tell her that in Italian, Spanish, German, or Hindi."

Richard's eyes narrowed and were cold, hard and flinty. "None of that matters. In the end, Hannah will do what Patty wants, she always does."

And that had been Rocco's concern all along. That he was just some sort of temporary rebellion against Hannah's mother. "Maybe, maybe not. But know this, asshole. Whether I'm with her or not, if I find out you hurt her again, you're a dead man. I'm with Dixon-Shaw and their reach goes nationwide to DC and across the globe. You hurt her, I'll crush you and nothing will happen to me afterward. That's the only warning you're going to get, *Dick*. Be a man and make your *own* way to Hollywood instead of riding there on Hannah's and your mother's backs."

He left Richard standing there with a dumbstruck expression on his face and went to find his Hannah. And she *was* his, as long as she wanted to be. He exited the locker room to find his woman across the hallway near the ladies' locker room door, waiting on him. Joe stood next to her with a huge grin on his face.

He heard Richard gasp behind him. *That's right, asshole, she's gorgeous and all mine—for now.*

Appearing unsure, she waited on him, wearing a beautiful white summer maxi dress decorated with pink florals, a sexy low-cut collar showcasing her luscious tits, and a thigh slit on the dress skirt, and finished off with pretty high-heeled strappy sandals. She was perfection and his for the night. He was one lucky fucker. His cock responded immediately but he wasn't concerned. They weren't in a church and he had cover from his jacket.

He smiled what he hoped was an encouraging smile and extended his hand. "Stunning, Hannah. Are you ready to have some fun?"

The smile she rewarded him with lit up her face and warmed his heart. She clasped his hand and squeezed. "Hell yeah, I am."

After intermittent event-planning duties and a decent roasted beef tenderloin dinner Hannah assured him he could have better prepared, they were on the dancefloor in a makeshift retro disco karaoke club. He had to admit, he was having a great time at the unusually themed wedding reception. Mostly, he felt like the luckiest man in the world with Hannah by his side. The few glances at Richard filming the event with a nearly constant scowl on his face added to his enjoyment of the evening immensely.

After several guests karaoked their renditions of popular disco hits, the bride and groom were before them. Both appeared happy and in love. "Hannah, what about *your* song? When are you going to sing?" The bride looked at Hannah expectantly and Hannah blushed. No one seemed to care whether or not guests had good singing voices. Everyone was just enjoying themselves.

"Kristen's right, baby. Go on and sing your song," he encouraged her.

"Come on, Hannah. You worked so hard today giving us the perfect day. Now it's time for you to have some fun," the groom said.

"But I picked this song before we met," she said, glancing at him, unsure.

There was no reason for her to be worried about some disco song. The karaoke was all in good fun. "I promise it'll be okay," he assured her.

He acknowledged the moment she conceded and decided to sing her song. The bride dragged Hannah to the karaoke machine and introduced her to applause from the guests on the dancefloor.

When the music from "Ring my Bell" by Anita Ward began to play, everyone cheered. He grinned at her from the crowd and waited for her to begin. Tentative at first, she began and everyone including him murmured in excitement. She had an outstanding singing voice. He watched and listened in awe as she belted out the disco tune, swaying sensually to the music in her sexy party dress.

"She's amazing, isn't she?" Joe stood beside him, beaming with pride. Rocco was grateful she had such a good friend in Joe. He didn't give a shit if the man was gay or not.

Rocco nodded. "She truly is." He looked forward to ringing her bell later, over and over until she understood what she meant to him. He prayed Richard was wrong and she wouldn't end up just going along with her mother's plan for her future. Rocco wanted to be a part of her future.

Chapter Six

Hannah parked in the Club Envidious parking lot fifteen minutes before the Twisted Tea Society was set to meet the following Wednesday evening after Kristen and Ben's wedding. She felt conflicted. On the one hand, she was excited. She'd done nothing like this before. Attend a ladies' social gathering where servers only wore a bowtie. On the other, she felt overwhelmed. Rocco overwhelmed her. His attention overwhelmed her. She was in way over her head and didn't know what she should do. He was so far out of her league it wasn't funny. She feared one of these days he'd realize it too and where would that leave her?

"You're overthinking this, Hannah," Joe stated plainly.

"I'm with Joe," her older brother Eric added on their three-way call. "And don't start with that golden child shit, either. Mom's so-called outrage over whatever the fuck Richard told her about you at Kristen and Ben's wedding last Saturday disappeared pretty quick after she read all the raving reviews on Yelp, Twitter, and Facebook."

"And the new clients we got as a result of the amazing job we did with their wedding," Joe said.

She sighed. They didn't understand. Neither of them had the strained relationship she had with her mother. Not that she resented Joe or her brother because of it, but it didn't make her current predicament any easier. And neither of them felt as insecure as she did with the opposite sex. In Joe's case, with either sex.

"What's really bothering you, hon? Be honest."

She knew she could tell Joe anything but with her

brother on the line, she didn't feel as comfortable.

"But I don't need details about you hooking up with Rocco, okay?" he brother asked.

She chuckled. That wasn't going to happen.

"You haven't said much, but what's happened since the wedding?" Joe inquired.

Her face heated as she thought back. She'd spent the rest of the weekend at Rocco's place. Naked. In his bed, mostly, but not only having sex. They'd talked, laughed, and had made plans to visit his brother Massimo and his family so she could tell him Rocco was the better cook and the better looking of the two brothers. They'd even enjoyed gelato as they watched episodes of *Say Yes to the Dress*. Her time with him had been perfect. And it scared the hell out of her. The other shoe was going to drop, she just knew it, and she would be wrecked when it did.

"We spent the rest of the weekend together. It was wonderful." There, that was enough. Joe and her brother could infer whatever they liked.

"Nothing at all like your time with Richard, right?" Eric wasn't fond of Richard either, for which she was grateful. It was only her mother who was insistent on the two of them getting together.

She snorted. "Complete opposite. He makes me feel beautiful. Talented. Intelligent. He thinks I should take Cora and Nora's offer and buy their salon. He thinks my designs are amazing."

"He's right," both men said in unison.

She wanted to believe them, she truly did. She knew she couldn't continue on her current path with her mother and Hailey's Events forever, but she was conflicted about taking a chance on herself with her own salon. And there was Rocco, who had the power to really hurt her emotionally like Richard never could because she'd never cared about him the way she did Rocco. She'd noticed all the flirty glances, winks, and napkins with phone numbers he'd been given at Kristen and Ben's wedding. So had Joe.

"Everything's new right now. Just relax and take things one step at a time. What did he do with the numbers he got at the wedding?"

She smiled when she recalled what he did as they left the reception to head back to his place. "He tossed them all in one of the trash bins in the lobby without a second thought."

"You see? He's a good guy. There's a lot more to him than his good looks. He cares about people, his family, his friends. Even this thing with the book club. It's kinky, but it's about helping people." Joe was right. She just needed to believe it herself.

"I'm with Joe on this, Hannah. It's time you took a good look at what you really want out of life and I don't just mean Rocco. Everything. Mom's got issues none of us can fix so you've got to take care of yourself. Take a chance on yourself. You're capable. You can do anything you set your mind to. What's the alternative? You wither away at Hailey's for the rest of your life?" Eric was also right.

Everything they'd both said was true. Things couldn't continue on like they were indefinitely, she knew that, too. She just needed a little more time to work up the courage to take that terrifying leap of faith.

"You're both right, thanks. I better get going. I've got a book to discuss and a naked server waiting for me."

"I didn't need to hear that," her brother said with a smile in his voice.

"I'm so jealous of you right now," Joe quipped.

She chuckled and disconnected the call. After presenting her Twisted Tea Society membership card and driver's license, she was cleared to go through the left door toward their meeting room. She hustled to their room and took a calming breath before stepping inside. Her stomach growled and she frowned. Rocco had texted her a reminder to eat earlier in the day but she'd been in back-to-back client meetings and had several venue visits so she ended up skipping lunch.

Her feet sank into the plush taupe carpeting and she inhaled the relaxing scent of lavender. The lighting had been dimmed and soft spa-like music drifted throughout the room. She immediately felt the stresses of the day begin to ease. *Heaven already.*

Two very pregnant brunettes sat on one of the plush leather couches. One had a pretty blue maternity blouse on and the other a pink one. Both appeared exhausted but also had that pregnancy glow about them. Both were barefoot. Not wanting to make the ladies get up, she approached them and extended her hand.

"Hi, I'm Hannah Hailey," she said and shook both of their hands.

"I'm Penny," the blue-bloused woman said.

"I'm Carmen," the pink-bloused woman replied. "From Hailey's Events, right? Your firm planned my cousin's destination wedding in Cancun last year. It was amazing." Carmen rubbed her protruded belly and offered her a sweet smile.

Hannah beamed with pride. Although she didn't travel to the firm's destination venues any longer, she assisted with the planning and organizing from their corporate office. "I'm so glad to hear that."

"And you've been showcasing Rocco's cappuccino art on your blog," Penny said happily.

Hannah clenched her teeth and her stomach burned. "I requested him as my server tonight," she blurted out before she could stop herself. Christ, was she jealous of two pregnant women's interest in Rocco? She was in big trouble if that was the case.

Penny and Carmen turned to each other and smiled, and then teared up. Damn it, she was making pregnant women cry.

Carmen wiped her eyes and smiled so sweetly Hannah felt like a total bitch. "We're not upset. You don't have to be jealous or anything."

Penny nodded and rubbed her belly. "We're both happily married, Hannah. It's the hormones that have us emotional, you know?"

She nodded, although she didn't know from personal experience what pregnancy hormones felt like. At least she hadn't upset them. She'd have to examine her jealousy issues another time.

"If you're with Rocco, that's great. This group is fairly new, but from what we've seen so far, he's never been inappropriate with any of the members."

Hannah sighed in relief but knew she was getting ahead of herself. They hadn't said they were exclusive, but she had no interest in seeing anyone else. Logically, she understood he'd had past relationships, her heart was a different story. It was already fully invested. Yup, she was in big trouble.

Before she could respond, she heard Leah Tyler, Jake's sister, call her name. She was a member? Was Heath a server as well? She wasn't sure how she'd feel if that were the case. Joining the group was so far out of her comfort zone and she'd only done it because Rocco was a server. If she knew any of the other servers, she'd be embarrassed even more than she already was.

After a quick hug, Grace Asher entered the room with two other women she didn't know. After introductions were made, the other members removed their shoes, so she followed suit. She admired her pedicuring handiwork and her deep-rose-painted toenails. There was still no sign of the men.

"Let's all take a seat. The servers are getting everything ready for us," Grace announced and took a seat in the semi-circle of comfy leather chairs in the center of the room.

Hannah sat next to Leah, feeling comforted as she was at least a casual acquaintance. If she and Rocco continued seeing each other, they'd most likely become closer. She found she liked that idea quite a bit. She was getting to know the Stryker clan a little better already since she was planning Luke Stryker's wedding and had already planned Leah's brother Jake's. They were a good group of people she'd be happy to call friends.

She retrieved her Kindle with *Dawn* by Erin M. Leaf queued up. She'd enjoyed the story so much she'd also purchased the first two books in the series, *Dark* and *Dusk*.

Suddenly, a door behind the granite countertop near a full-size sink opened and several men she knew were naked except for their bowties walked in, carrying trays of assorted refreshments. The cabinetry hid their bodies from the waist down. When Rocco walked in carrying a tray with what looked like assorted cheeses, her body heated.

She watched him look for her and he smiled when they made eye contact. Her heart thudded and her core slickened. How was she expected to get through the next three hours and seem unaffected? Even when he was dressed, she was overwhelmed.

And to experience him and the entire premise of this ladies' social club was entirely new and uncharted territory for her. The most daring and out-of-the-norm thing she'd ever done. And if she were being honest with herself, she loved it. In a way, she felt free, more like herself in some ways. It was a heady feeling. One she didn't think she could give up.

When the servers had everything in place, they made their way to the club members. It was proper etiquette to refer to Rocco as *boy* or by his first name.

He stood before her in all his glory, a wicked grin on his face. When had bowties become so sexy? Her heart raced and her nipples pebbled. She felt her face heat.

"The Server Supervisor informed me you requested I serve you today." His soft, sexy voice made her shiver in delight.

"Ye … yes, I did … *boy*." Her stomach chose that moment to growl. She sighed and Rocco shook his head. Damn it.

"Would I be correct in assuming you may not have eaten as you should have today, even though you might have received a text reminder to so?" He kept his voice low, calm, and sultry, although she suspected he was disappointed in her.

Embarrassed she'd been busted, all she could do was nod.

"May I prepare a plate for you? With the sustenance you need? And a soothing footbath as I suspect you've had a long hard day?"

Aside from where she was, in a room full of naked men there to serve women, his offer sounded wonderful. "Thank you, *boy*. I'd like that very much," she replied softly. *This is surreal.*

The women chatted casually as the servers prepared footbaths in white plastic rectangular tubs. Hannah handed out some business cards with promises of being contacted about upcoming events members wanted her to plan. She hadn't expected to acquire clients from this group and was relieved Grace Asher, the apparent leader of the group, wasn't upset and asked for a card herself.

She smiled when she considered what her mother would think about planning some sort of BDSM-related event. It would be a first, but she imagined her mother would refuse the business. So *not* Patty-appropriate.

Rocco kneeled in front of her and gently placed her feet in the warm, lavender-scented footbath. She nearly groaned it felt so wonderful. The other ladies in the room had similar reactions. Aside from the kinky aspect of the evening, she really needed this. "*Boy*, would you like to give me a foot massage after my soak?"

His nostrils flared and his soulful, dark eyes dilated. She wasn't supposed to blatantly gawk at the men, but from her seated position, she could see he was semi-erect. It gave her ego a little boost.

"It would be my pleasure, Miss Hannah. Let me wash up and prepare your plate first," he replied in a sensual, low tone.

She held in a giggle when he discreetly covered his groin and retreated back to the kitchen area. All the men took great care to keep their hands washed and sanitized. She was impressed.

"Let's get started with an excerpt from *Dawn* while the servers prepare our plates," Grace suggested.

The attendees all nodded in agreement. Grace swiped at her Kindle for a moment until she found what she apparently wanted to read aloud.

No, she isn't a stupid woman, he corrected himself. The female looking up at him had too much life experience and determination to be anything other than a fully grown adult. "Saige," he said, voice going low. "What are you doing?" His cock hardened as her warmth seeped through his clothes, and he shifted slightly so she wouldn't feel it. God help him, he wanted her with a desperation bordering on insanity. Her emotions skittered over his senses, and he almost stopped breathing when he sensed her arousal suddenly spike.

"Shut up, Isaac." She slid her arms around his neck and pulled his head down. "I'm going to regret this," she muttered, and then she put her lips against his.

She smelled like mint. Isaac shuddered, and then he pulled her tight against his body, seizing control of the kiss. He coaxed her lips open, dipping inside when she gasped.

"Holy moly," Saige said, voice breathy.

"You have no idea what you do to me," Isaac said, hands splayed across her shoulder blades. "You're playing with fire." She felt so tiny against him, but her energy put the lie to her physical appearance. Her small frame held enough spirit for someone three times her size. He kissed her again, cock throbbing against her hip.

"God, you drive me nuts," she said when he came up for air. She pushed his jacket off his shoulders. "Look at you. You have muscles on top of your muscles. And you hide them and pretend like you're some nerdy academic."

Isaac shrugged the jacket to the floor, wanting to feel her soft curves closer to his skin. "What are you talking about? I like this jacket. It's comfortable, not nerdy."

"It totally is nerdy," she retorted, and then she kissed him again, clearly determined to steal every last shred of control that he had left.

Hannah leaned back in her comfy chair and wiggled her toes in the soothing, warm, lavender-scented footbath Rocco had prepared for her. She was looking forward to his rubdown even if it was only her feet and possibly her shoulders. She was tense and long overdue for some spa time. Her stomach growled again and she rubbed her tummy discreetly.

Chancing a quick glance in Rocco's direction, she sighed when he frowned at her just as he'd finished preparing her plate. She couldn't help but frown herself. He'd been thoughtful by texting her earlier in the day about eating and she'd just ignored him, not intentionally, but she now felt disappointed in herself. She didn't want him to think she didn't appreciate his concern. Just the opposite. She'd never felt so cared for and appreciated with a man—ever.

Grace looked up from her Kindle with a smile on her pretty face. "So, ladies, what did you think of *Dawn*?"

"I think Saige and Isaac are good together. I love how she gives as good as she gets," Leah offered enthusiastically.

Hannah agreed completely. She'd really enjoyed the story. "I like the supporting characters, too. I got the first two books so I can get up to speed on the series." Everyone nodded in agreement.

"I'm with you, Hannah. There is some snazzy world-building in *Dawn*. I definitely need to read the first two books because I could tell I was missing some stuff by starting with the third one," Penny commented from behind her.

Grace nodded. "The sci-fi aspects and bad aliens, not just including the spiders, made for some great action scenes. If you love sci-fi romance and some hot action between the sheets, *Dawn*'s a must read."

Hannah felt a lightness in her chest and her pulse picked up speed as Rocco returned to her with a plate of scrumptious-looking refreshments and a mischievous grin on his face. She couldn't wait for the rest of the evening to unfold at her first meeting of the Twisted Tea Society.

****

Rocco washed his hands for the last time after he'd prepared a treat bag for Hannah and helped the other servers clean up the kitchen area. He'd been battling a hard-on all evening and couldn't wait to get Hannah alone upstairs in his apartment. Why he thought being her server would be a good idea, he didn't know. It had been sweet torture, but he believed he'd made his woman's day a little less stressful. He intended on making her evening even better.

Brody Dobbs, a mountain of a man from Envy, Texas, and a bartender at Kyle's Golden Horns restaurant, looked at him with an amused expression. Women were drawn to the man's tall, burly frame, long, thick blond hair, neatly trimmed beard, and southern accent. Little did they know they didn't stand a chance. Leo, as some of his pals called him, was looking for someone special, someone *unique* he hadn't found yet. Anyone else held little interest for the man.

Brody chuckled and shook his head. "Next time I should serve your girl if you can't keep your dick in check, brother."

Rocco knew Brody could easily put him down if he wanted to, but that didn't stop him getting in the man's face. His chest burned and he saw spots before his eyes. "Don't you fucking touch Hannah. She's *mine*," he snapped. Brody had better *not* lay a finger on Hannah or there would be trouble. As much as he could inflict before Brody took him out.

Brody stepped back and put his hands up, a smug smile on his face. The Server Supervisor stood nearby at attention. "I never thought I'd see the day. I was just fucking with you, brother. No need to be jealous."

Rocco sighed and shook his head. He'd never been jealous over a woman before. This was completely new territory for him. Like so many other things were where Hannah was concerned.

"We'll finish up, Rocco. Don't keep Hannah waiting," Jack, the Server Supervisor, said.

He was in way over his head with Hannah. Apparently, the men of the Twisted Tea Society seemed to realize it too as he glanced at each of them. They all wore the same knowing expression on their faces. *I'm so screwed.*

It didn't matter. Like he'd told Richard the Dick at Kristen and Ben's wedding, as long as Hannah wanted him around, that was where he'd be. He'd figure the rest out as he went along.

He grabbed her treat bag and nodded to the group of men around him. "Thanks." He watched as Grace left the room after she and Hannah said their goodbyes. She turned to him, her smile warm and dreamy.

His heart swelled with affection he'd never felt for a woman before. His cock reacted once again at the sight of her. He hurried to her with his hand extended, needing to get her upstairs as soon as possible. When she didn't hesitate and took it, after glancing at his erection, he nearly dragged her to the couches. He heard the men chuckle as he tore out of the room toward the elevator with Hannah in tow.

Hannah giggled after they reached the elevator door and he jabbed at the button. "Something funny, *bella*?" He was hanging on by a thread, not the least bit amused. God, she drove him crazy.

She shook her head as the elevator door opened. He quickly pulled her inside the cabin, immediately jabbing at the third-floor button. Before the door closed, he had her pressed up against the wall and claimed her lips. He was desperate for a taste of his woman and he was through waiting.

Hannah eagerly opened for him and he sighed at finally getting a taste of her sweetness. And what a tempting treat she was. She clung to him as they rode the elevator up to the third floor where his bed was ready and waiting for her. Their tongues teased and danced. Their kisses hard, then soft, then hard again as the elevator door finally opened on his floor.

Hand in hand, they raced to his front door. Not fearing security since only he, Grace, and Kyle currently occupied units, he opened his unlocked door and ushered Hannah inside. He placed her treat bag on his kitchen counter and led them to his bedroom. "We have a verbal agreement, baby. We're alone in my apartment now. Take your clothes off." His voice sounded strained, but he needed her desperately and was out of patience. He couldn't wait any longer. His cock ached for her.

He went to unhook his bowtie but Hannah stopped him, placing her warm, delicate hands on his. "Can you leave the bowtie on?" She shrugged and graced him with a shy smile. How could he refuse her?

"You like the bowtie, do you?" He grinned back at her, gently removed her hands from his neck, and tenderly kissed the knuckles on each hand. She moaned softly and her eyes dilated.

She nodded and then surprised the shit out him. "If you don't mind wearing it, I'd appreciate it, *Sir*."

He gripped her hands tightly and took a deep, calming breath. She would be the death of him. He'd imagined her wearing his collar more times than he cared to admit. They weren't there yet and if he were being honest, he wasn't sure if they ever would be. There were too many potential obstacles in their way at the moment.

He needed to take things one day at a time. Enjoy their time together, one day at a time.

Claiming her lips again, even though she was still dressed, he kissed away any doubts she might possibly have. When she moaned and ground against his aching dick, he pulled away, leaving them both panting.

"Since you asked nicely, I'll leave the bowtie on, *cara*. As long as you get undressed immediately and get in my bed."

He snickered when Hannah's eyes widened and she made quick work of shedding her jeans, pretty blue top, and matching bra and panty set. He preferred her in pink but found her sexy as hell regardless of what color she wore. Shit, but he had it bad.

When she climbed into his bed, that was his cue and he fumbled in his nightstand for condoms, relieved when he retrieved a couple from an open box. He tossed them on the bed and joined his woman, ready and waiting for him.

His eyes feasted on her beauty. Hannah's skin was flushed and her dusky pink nipples were tight peaks waiting to be sucked and nibbled on. How had he gotten so lucky?

With his bowtie still in place, at his woman's request, he positioned himself on top of her, soothed by the feel of her warm, silky skin. He ran his tongue along the fluttering pulse on her neck and she shivered. He smiled as he kissed her shoulder, inhaling her intoxicating scent, a mixture of her personal essence and her favorite fragrance *Falling in Love*. Rocco knew with certainty he was falling, and falling hard.

"You drove me crazy downstairs, baby. I kept trying to hide my hard-on." He kissed his way down her torso, captured a taut a nipple in his teeth, and tugged gently until Hannah groaned.

She arched her back and he laved at her nipple. She ran her fingers through his hair and tugged. "I wasn't trying to. You drove me crazy, too. I didn't realize how tense I was until you massaged my feet and shoulders." He focused his attention on the other tight bud, earning himself another groan. "And you were so distracting without your clothes on."

He let go of her nipple and felt ten feet tall when she moaned in frustration. "You were *dressed* and distracting as hell, *bella*. I'll give you a massage anytime you want, baby. Full body. Would you like that?"

Hannah giggled, music to his ears as he settled between her legs.

Her delicious, musky flavor burst onto his tongue as he swiped it along her drenched slit. He felt an overwhelming sense of pride that she was ready for him. Unable to wait much longer to sink into her tight, wet pussy, he focused and devoured her, flicking her swollen little clit with vigor until she was tugging on his hair and grinding against his mouth. He added two fingers, her cunt clenching around them, and fingered her as he continued his assault on her bud until his sweet Hannah detonated and shouted his name.

Rocco lapped up her juices and slowly eased her back down. With shaking hands, he sheathed his aching dick and sat up against the headboard, ready for his woman. More than ready.

"Hannah, I need you, *cara*." He sounded desperate, even to his own ears. He felt a lurch of excitement when she obediently positioned herself on his lap and rubbed her still-slickened pussy against his rock-hard length. "Don't tease me, baby. Ride me."

She smiled down at him, skin flushed, eyes dilated with a dreamy expression on her angelic face. He could so easily lose himself in her. *Could?* Hell, he already had.

Tentatively, she kissed him, no doubt tasting herself on his lips and tongue. To him, she tasted divine. She slowly lowered herself on his aching dick after quickly adjusting his bowtie. He'd find some fun tie designs to keep his woman entertained.

She slowly began to ride him, her tight slick heat enveloping him. It was as if she'd been made just for him. *Only* him. "I couldn't wait until we got back up here," she whispered and picked up the pace, like she'd read his mind. Rocco didn't want or need slow and gentle. Not right now.

He held on to her hips and guided her, faster and harder up and down his needy dick. Her snug cunt driving him crazy with need. As he took a beaded nipple between his teeth and tugged, she groaned and continued to bounce frantically up and down his length, exactly the way he needed her to.

"Just like that, baby. I've been waiting for you too." He turned his attention to her other tight bud and tugged, eliciting another moan from his Hannah.

Feeling his spine tingle and his balls draw up tight, he ran little circles around her engorged clit with his fingers as she rode him for all she was worth. God, how he needed her. In bed and out. He despised feeling unsure about their future, but he couldn't let her go. Wouldn't let her go.

She threw her head back and closed her eyes as she crested again. Satisfied he'd pleased her, he allowed himself to follow her, emptying his balls into the condom. He shuddered and held her close, never wanting to let go, his heart racing, and gasping for air.

He gathered her gently, both of them hot and slick with sweat as they slowly eased back down. "I think I like the Twisted Tea Society if this is how the meetings end every time." He closed his eyes as she lovingly ran her fingers through his hair and kissed him so gently he felt but a whisper's touch of her lips against his.

"If you request *me* as your server they will." He couldn't help himself. The jealousy he'd suffered at Brody's comments unsettled him. He opened his eyes, searching Hannah's for an indication she may want someone else the next time she attended a meeting. He didn't know what he'd do if she did. He'd be crushed, but he didn't want to let on. It had to be her decision, not his.

Her eyes grew wide and she frowned. "Of course, I'd want you. I wouldn't request anyone else, unless you'd prefer I did." Her eyes glistened like she might cry and he felt like shit for doubting her. Relief flooded through him that she didn't want anyone else serving her, *touching* her. He'd obviously become a caveman where Hannah was concerned and he didn't care. While they were together, she was his and *only* his.

"No. I do *not* prefer. In fact, what I'd like is for us to be exclusive." He held his breath. He may have been pushing his luck but he wanted to be up-front with her. Always. She had enough people with demands and personal agendas aimed at her in her life. He wanted to be someone different, someone better for her.

The smile she rewarded him with lit up the room. *Thank God.*

"I'd like that too." She held him tighter, making him feel like the luckiest man in the world. It was a start. An amazing start. *One day at a time, Marine.*

He felt himself soften and regrettably eased her off his lap. He kissed her forehead and got up. "Let me take care of the condom and I'll bring in your treat bag. How about that?"

She nodded enthusiastically. "I like that idea a

lot. Thanks." She perched herself up against the headboard, bunching the sheets up to her waist, leaving her luscious tits exposed just the way he liked them.

He poured Hannah a large glass of milk after he'd quickly gotten them both cleaned up. When he returned to his room with her milk, treats, and napkins, he found her busy on her cell phone. "Bored with me already?" he teased as he slid back into bed.

She mocked looking offended and shook her head. "Of course not. I just wanted to download the next book we're going to discuss. It's *Third Wheel*, by Lynn Burke. It's the first book of her Elite Escorts series. Other than hearing the excerpts Grace reads at meetings, have you ever actually read a romance novel? Erotic or otherwise?"

She placed her cell phone on her lap and took a sip of milk after opening her treat bag. He'd filled it with cookies and other sweet treats Club Envidious's chef had prepared. He tried not to let it bother him that she believed his culinary skills were good enough for a commercial kitchen even though Kyle didn't think so.

"Actually, no, baby. I've only listened to excerpts." He wondered why she'd asked. He assumed mostly women read them, but he had no way of knowing.

"Why don't I read a little bit of *Third Wheel* before you have your way with me again?" She giggled and his heart did that fluttery thing it did so many times when it came to her.

He settled in beside her. "Is that what I did earlier? Have my way with you? Let's start the book, sure." He kissed her shoulder and she shivered. So responsive—to *him*.

She grinned and shrugged. "Maybe you did *a little*. Let me pull it up." She pulled up the book on her cell and scrolled to what he assumed was the beginning of the story. "Okay. Here we go. Chapter One, Reid."

Chapter Seven

Rocco pulled up to his brother's house on a warm Saturday July afternoon, a week and a half after Hannah's first Twisted Tea Society meeting. He'd been able to convince her to stay over and sleep without one of his t-shirts on. It took some convincing, but after she'd read the first chapter of *Third Wheel* aloud and they'd fucked again—twice, by the time he'd explained the benefits of sleeping naked, she'd fallen asleep.

Sleeping with Hannah beside him, her soft, silky skin against his all night had been just what he needed. Thankfully, he'd slept a sound, nightmare-free sleep. He was grateful for small miracles.

It was a beautiful summer afternoon, but his woman seemed upset. She hadn't said much on the ride from her condo to Massimo and Sydney's place in nearby Lombard. Had she changed her mind about lunch? About meeting his family?

They were now exclusive, so he was confused. Maybe it was too soon. He'd never been exclusive with a woman before. Massimo had been so insistent on showing off his cooking skills, Rocco should have consulted with Sydney before agreeing to bring Hannah over.

Holding the dessert she'd prepared on her lap, she turned to him and took a deep breath. She bit her lip and seemed ready to bolt.

He turned to her and clasped of one of her hands. She was trembling. "Baby, what's wrong?" He kissed her knuckles gently, hoping to calm her down.

"I'm nervous, what do you think?" she replied in a whisper and squeezed his hand.

He nearly chuckled because she had no reason to be nervous. He didn't so as not to upset her or dismiss her worry. "I promise you, you don't need to be. They're going to love you."

She glanced at him nervously, seeming unsure. "I know you have a big family, and next to your grandparents, who are no longer with us"—she pointed at his brother's house—"the people in that house are the most important people in the world to you. Can you tell me a little about them? Please?"

Poor thing. Rocco hugged Hannah the best he could in his truck, rubbing her arms, hoping to comfort her. Of course, he could tell her.

"You already know Massimo or Max is my baby brother. He's six years younger than me. He's a computer whiz, a DBA. They let him telework full-time from home now."

"Oh, that's nice, especially while the kids are little." She took a deep breath and relaxed a bit.

He thought so too. Being at home, Max wouldn't miss those precious "firsts" with his babies. He ignored the tiny pang of jealousy in his gut and continued. "He met his wife Sydney their sophomore year at Northwestern. She was a finance major and a cheerleader. She was really good, competed even. She and her squad were more like gymnasts. I was told that's a part of it."

"Really? Wow. So she didn't graduate?" Hannah frowned up at him. She must have thought Max hadn't wanted her to get her degree.

Rocco shook his head. "She did. Graduated with honors like Max did. They got married soon after graduation. Her family owns a mid-sized accounting firm. She's a CPA, works part-time right now. I think she's planning on going full-time after little Massimo or

MJ is in school full days."

She nodded, seemingly satisfied his brother wasn't trying to hold his wife down. It was quite the opposite. His brother supported his wife's ambitions and dreams completely. Considered her his equal, as Rocco believed it should be. It was the same way he felt about Hannah, except he hoped she would break away from her mother's company and purchase Blumenthal's Discount Bridal and design her own gowns. He believed it was what she was meant to do. Her true bliss. He wanted to help her realize her dreams.

Hannah took a deep breath and nodded again. "Sounds like they've got everything planned out. And your niece and nephew? I know they're still little, but they've got personalities too."

He chuckled at that. His niece Adrianna had quite the personality at only four and a half. "Little Massimo or MJ—sometimes I call him Maxie, depends on how I'm feeling, he just turned six months old. So far, he's been a pretty good sleeper, has quite a little appetite on him, too. He seems to be a happy little boy. I think he recognizes me when I visit. He smiles at me all the time."

Hannah giggled and kissed him all too briefly. "Of course, he does. I'm sure he's crazy about his Uncle Rocco."

He hoped so. He had a close relationship with Adrianna and trusted he'd have one with MJ when he got older. "Adrianna is four and a half, going on thirty."

Hannah full-out laughed and his heart did that little fluttery thing it always did when he was with her. "She's full of energy. Inherited her mother's athletic skills is already quite good in tumbling and gymnastics. Sydney helps coach, she's still rather good herself. Adrianna is bright and curious and speaks Italian fluently. I taught her Spanish. And it's a secret, but I've taught her German too."

Hannah's brow furrowed. "I won't say anything, but why the secrecy?"

He opened his truck door and motioned for Hannah to do the same. He'd noticed Adrianna peeking through the curtains in the living room at them. He rounded the truck and helped Hannah out as she held on to her dessert carefully.

Taking her free hand, he led her to his brother's front door. "Because Adrianna had started not speaking English at home and half the time they couldn't understand her when she spoke Spanish. She's since promised to stick with English or Italian, but she and I decided to keep the German only between us. I want to teach her Hindi at some point too."

He watched her take another deep breath. He felt for her, but she didn't need to worry. When she gave him a quick nod, he rang the doorbell.

His brother Max answered the door with a stupid grin on his face. Maybe bringing Hannah over had been a mistake. Max could be an ass when he wanted to. He hoped like hell his baby brother didn't embarrass him. Rocco stilled a moment as he realized this was the first time he'd ever brought a woman over to meet any member of his family. He squeezed Hannah's hand, acknowledging to himself there hadn't been anyone worth bringing—until now.

Hannah gasped, glancing between both Moretti brothers, her eyes wide. Max gestured for them to come inside, into the living room. "I know what you're thinking, Hannah. I'm *so* much better looking than the Moretti brother you're stuck with."

Rocco rolled his eyes and made to leave, dragging Hannah with him. "Come on now, be nice," Hannah teased.

"Right, listen to your girl. Be nice to your little brother."

He grunted and placed a possessive arm around his girl's waist, as Max had put it. "Maybe my *baby* brother should be nice to *me*."

Before his idiot brother could answer, Adrianna came bounding into the room, wearing the latest animated movie princess leggings and matching t-shirt. "*Zio! Ciao bello!*"

He picked up his giggling niece and his heart swelled when she hugged him tight and showered him with little girl kisses. She may think she was a "big girl," but she smelled like baby powder and baby shampoo.

He'd always remember her that way, even after she grew up. She'd inherited Sydney's bright blue eyes and blonde hair and his brother's Mediterranean skin tone. She would be a knockout when she grew up, just like her mother—and his Hannah. Sydney was close behind, wearing a matching outfit. For a quick second, he wondered if Hannah would wear matching outfits if they ever had a daughter. *Don't get ahead of yourself.*

"Who's this?" she asked, placing her arm around his shoulders.

Rocco replied the way he'd never done before in his life. "This is Hannah. She's my girlfriend." There, that wasn't so bad. It felt amazing to refer to her that way, even if he wasn't sure how long she'd hold the title.

Hannah beamed and he was relieved. "Hi Adrianna, it's so nice to meet you."

"Hi, Anna. I'm four going on five." Adrianna held up four fingers and nodded. He was about to correct his niece but Hannah shook her head. Rocco was grateful she hadn't taken offense to his niece's mistake with her name. He'd correct her another time.

"Wow! What a big girl you are." She winked at

Sydney and they shared a smile. So far so good.

His niece gasped and her eyes widened. "I know! I like her, *Zio*," she whispered loudly in his ear. "Let me down so I can show Anna my gymnastics."

"Not in the house, you know that. Go on outside, we'll be right there." Sydney shook Hannah's hand, chuckling as Adrianna rushed through the house and out the kitchen patio door leading to the deck and back yard.

With a genuine smile on her face, Hannah offered Sydney the dessert she'd brought. "I brought a little something for dessert. It needs to stay refrigerated until we're ready to serve it."

"Max, why don't you take Hannah outside and I'll help Syd in the kitchen?" His brother eyed him suspiciously before leading Hannah to the deck out back.

"Oh my God, Rocco, Hannah's lovely. I'll make sure Adrianna knows how to pronounce her name correctly. I'm so glad she wasn't upset being called Anna." After she'd stored the bowl of dessert dip in the refrigerator and placed the graham crackers, Nilla wafers, and a bag of toffee chips on the kitchen counter, Rocco handed her a wad of bills.

She frowned and reluctantly took the offered cash. "Rocco, what's this? Again?"

"It's just a little…"

"I knew it. What the hell, man?" Max asked with a scowl on his face.

Where the fuck had he come from? He was supposed to be outside with Hannah and Adrianna. "Don't give me that look. Hannah's fine. I gave her a Peroni and Adrianna's showing her the swing set waiting for Syd so they can show off their gymnastic skills."

Poor Sydney stayed silent, nervously glancing between them both. "It's just a thousand dollars. For the kids. For college." Rocco didn't understand what the big deal was. The kids were his niece and nephew, the only ones he'd ever have since his brother and sister-in-law decided they wouldn't have any other children after little Max was born.

Max sighed and shook his head. "Last time is was seven-fifty. The time before that twelve hundred. You need to stop throwing money at us."

That wasn't going to happen. There was nothing his brother could say. "*Due bambini*." Rocco growled at his brother, trying desperately not to lose his temper in front of Sydney.

Max narrowed his eyes and clenched his hands. "Babe, can you take the money and put it away? Please?"

Obviously happy for the reprieve, Sydney quickly kissed Rocco's cheek and left the kitchen, shaking her head.

"I know how many fucking babies I have. You've got to stop this, man. How do you think it makes me feel? Like I can't take care of my own family, that's how."

Rocco threw his hands up. Max was being ridiculous. "I never once said you couldn't take care of your family. I'm just trying to help, that's all. You've got the mortgage and Sydney's only part-time right now. College is expensive *now*, who knows how much it will cost when the kids actually go."

Max sighed and shoved his hands in his jeans pockets. "We've got it covered, *fratellone*. We're paying down on the fifteen-year mortgage and I've got good money coming in from my freelance gigs too. We're good, I promise."

Placing a comforting hand on his brother's shoulder, he willed him to understand. "They're my God-children, *fratellino*. What I've been giving you for them hasn't been a hardship for me. My military pay investments are still intact. What Kyle's charging me for rent is a joke. I'm good, too, all right? Why not take a page from Luke's book and when I offer, just say thank you?" Hell, that was what had him riding in a new Silverado and Cadillac.

His brother shrugged and nodded. "Fine. Just don't go overboard, okay? We're putting money away for them too. As their *parents*."

"Fine," Rocco conceded, knowing he had every intention of being as generous as he could with MJ and Adrianna. But hopefully not so much that it would upset his brother and Sydney. "So, what are you going make poor Hannah eat trying to convince her you're a better cook than me?" All kidding aside, his brother had also inherited their grandparents' skills in the kitchen. It was more of a sibling-rivalry issue in regard to who was better. Though Rocco believed *he* was the better cook.

"Grilled chicken and flat-iron steak in my secret marinade with mixed vegetable packets. She's going to love it." He and Max stood on the deck near the warming grill and watched as Adrianna and Sydney stretched in the back yard, preparing to show off their gymnastic skills. Hannah stood off to the side with an easy smile on her face.

Rocco noticed his brother grinning like an idiot in his peripheral vision. "What?"

Max shook his head and chuckled. The grill sizzled as he placed marinated meat on the hot grill grates. "It looks good on you."

"What does?" Rocco was lost. What was Max talking about?

"Being in love. What did you think I meant?"

Rocco's mouth fell open. In love? He turned to Hannah in the yard and she enthusiastically waved at him. He waved back, feeling more at peace than he had in a long time.

"Look me in the eye and tell me you're not. You'd be lying if you did." Max waited for him to answer. Rocco knew it was true, and there was no point in lying, especially to his brother.

"*Zio*! Daddy! Watch me and Mommy!" Adrianna was jumping up and down, vying for their attention.

"Okay, baby, we're watching," his brother called out.

"It's a little complicated. Richard the Dick is still trying to weasel his way back into Hannah's personal life. Her mother isn't exactly thrilled she's spending time with *some Marine*, as she puts it."

His stomach clenched as it always did when mother and daughter performed a little synchronized routine. He wasn't sure who he was more afraid for, little Adrianna or Sydney. He didn't know how Max stayed so calm through it all.

Rocco sighed in relief when they completed their mini-routine without incident. Then he tensed up again with Hannah executed a decent cartwheel. He and Max applauded and whistled.

"Great job, ladies," he called out. They all bowed and took seats at the swing set.

Max turned the meat and closed the grill lid. "Tough shit. She obviously wants *you*. What about her brother? How did dinner go with him the other night?"

It had gone rather well. They'd met up for dinner at Golden Horns. Hannah's brother Eric seemed like a decent guy. In appearance, he took after their mother with blond hair and blue eyes, but he was easygoing and seemed to have a good relationship with Hannah. He'd even encouraged her to purchase Blumenthal's Discount Bridal when Rocco had brought it up during dessert, which Kyle had offered on the house.

"We had a nice time. I liked Eric. I think you would too."

They both heard little Max cry through the baby monitor's speaker. "You mind getting him while I finish up here?"

"No problem." Rocco made quick work of changing MJ's wet diaper, placing him in his portable carrier, and warming up breast milk Sydney had stored in the freezer. When he brought the baby and bottle to the deck, everyone was gathered around the table, protected from the hot summer sun by a retractable awning.

"Would you like to feed him, Hannah?" Sydney asked.

Hannah's eyes widened and she smiled so brightly Rocco's heart swelled. "Sure, if you don't mind."

"I help Mommy feed little Max all the time, Anna. It's easy," Adrianna assured his woman.

His heart fluttered as he handed over a fussy, hungry baby boy to the woman he loved. He imagined this was what it would feel like if MJ were theirs and they shared in his care.

He watched in awe as everyone around him stayed busy chatting or cooking while Hannah deftly fed MJ. She was a natural and he couldn't help but notice how beautiful she looked feeding the baby. A baby that could be theirs one day. He chastised himself for letting his thoughts take him there. They were a long way away from *that* scenario.

"All right, everyone, the food's ready. Get ready to be wowed, Hannah." His brother placed everything he'd prepared on the center of the table and Sydney took care of burping and settling the baby back in his carrier.

When Rocco went to sit next to Hannah, Adrianna piped up. "But I always sit next to you, *Zio*."

"Honey, *Zio* Rocco wants to sit next to his girlfriend." Sydney smiled apologetically at him and Hannah. Adrianna frowned and appeared ready to cry.

"There's plenty of room. How about you sit between us so I get to sit next to *you*?" Hannah arranged three chairs and his niece happily took her seat between them.

"Thanks, Anna. Good idea."

Rocco looked over Adrianna's head and mouthed a quick, *Thank you*, to Hannah as they dug in.

"This is really good, Daddy," Adrianna commented after taking a bite of chicken Hannah had cut up for her. He agreed with the little girl, but he still believed he was a better cook than his baby brother. He had six years more experience.

"So, Hannah, what do you think? I'm the younger and more talented Moretti brother, right? Oh … and better-looking, of course."

He grunted when Sydney rolled her eyes and shook her head at Hannah.

"Oh, well, this is all delicious, honestly. Thank you for going to so much trouble. As far as being more talented and better-looking? I think I'll plead the fifth on that." She glanced at him and shrugged.

"Give it up, Max. If you really want to settle this once and for all, let's cook for the aunts and let *them* decide whose best. Like a Bobby Flay throw-down. Think you can handle that?" That should shut his brother up. His aunts, all five of them, were amazing in the kitchen and would *honestly* evaluate their cooking.

"Anna, there's *Zia* Pina, Santina, Claudia, Gisella, and Alba. Five. Like how old I'm going to be," Adrianna reminded her.

"Guys, you really don't have to do that, do you? I think we can all agree you both are very talented in the kitchen, can't we?"

Hannah didn't know his brother. His ego wouldn't allow for a tie. Rocco didn't want one either. It was time to put this debate to rest and have a little fun with his baby brother in the process.

Sydney laughed. "Oh, Hannah, you'll see."

"Fine by me, *fratellone*. Bring it." Max shrugged and continued eating, although it seemed to Rocco his brother seemed a little nervous. He should be, because he knew which dish his brother struggled with, and which *he* was decidedly better at preparing.

"Fine, *fratellino*. Let's throw-down with coq au vin. I'll even do you a solid and give you a couple of weeks to practice."

Max cursed under his breath and Sydney shook her head, frowning. He felt bad for his brother and considered choosing a different dish. Their throw-down was *supposed* to be in good fun.

"Anna, coq au vin is *really* good. You'll like it. Right, Daddy?"

Max squared his shoulders, a look of determination on his face. "It sure is, sweetie. You'll regret *doing me a solid*. Text *Zia* Alba since she's the oldest and she'll round up the other four. You're going down this time, Rocco. Count on it."

For a split second, Rocco worried. Coq au vin wasn't a difficult dish in his opinion, per se, but his brother tried to get fancy and consequently altered its intended taste. Rocco kept his recipe more traditional and used two Antonetti red wines he believed were the key to making his version of the dish exceptional.

He texted his Aunt Alba and they all relaxed, letting the aunts decide when their throw-down would go down. He felt more at home that afternoon with Hannah as his companion than he ever had before visiting his brother. Rather than panic, he enjoyed himself.

Hannah kept up well with his young, spirited niece, helping her with the tempting dessert dip she'd prepared for them. When Adrianna needed more toffee chips, Hannah didn't hesitate helping the little girl get her serving just right. "Anna, this is so yummy! I like it with the Nilla wafers best."

A few times, Max and Sydney flashed him knowing glances. The adults around the table all got on well, he acknowledged. He understood what his brother and sister-in-law were trying to tell him without words. If he gave it a chance, it could always be like this, assuming Hannah wanted him in her life and he wasn't a temporary distraction for her. He hoped like hell Richard the Dick was wrong and she wanted him around and wouldn't just go along with her mother's wishes in the end, especially if they were contrary to her own.

****

Later that evening, after demonstrating how he felt about Hannah, twice, Rocco lay wrapped around his woman at his place, more content than he ever remembered being in his life. Certainly with a woman. Unable to resist the lure of her warm, silky skin, he kissed her shoulder and felt her shiver against his lips. Her responsiveness humbled him.

"Do you think three weeks is enough time for Max to perfect his coq au vin recipe?" Hannah snuggled in a little closer and his pulse ticked up.

He sighed. He hoped their little throw-down didn't cause any lasting friction between him and his only sibling. Rocco saw their competition as a fun way to introduce Hannah to more of his family in a casual setting, like the afternoon had been.

"If he doesn't get in his own way, I think so." If Max stayed true to the basic recipe, he stood a better chance of beating him, though Rocco still believed he'd win anyway.

"I had such a great time at Max and Sydney's today. They're such a beautiful family."

In the stillness of the night, he smiled. He couldn't agree more. "I'm so proud of him, baby. He's a good man. He takes great care of his family. Has the perfect partner in Sydney."

"Little MJ is so cute. Both he and Adrianna have Sydney's stunning blue eyes."

He chuckled. "I know I'm the better-looking brother, but the kids inherited the best of their parents in their appearance. I'm sorry Adrianna kept pronouncing your name wrong. We'll work on that with her. And her insistence on sitting next to me. Thank you for being such a good sport about everything."

He felt her laugh and it warmed his heart. "I think she's wonderful. You don't have to apologize. She just loves her *Zio* Rocco," she whispered. "And Anna loves him too."

Tears welled up and he held Hannah to him, careful not to hurt her. "I love you, too, Anna. Hannah." No woman had ever told him they loved him. He felt it in his soul that it was always meant to be Hannah. He wished he wasn't scared as shit he'd lose her in the end.

"I've never been in love before, Rocco. I'm scared."

His heart raced. He knew all too well. He was terrified himself. "Me too, baby. Me too. We'll take things one step at a time. That won't be so scary, right?" He tried his best to calm his racing heart and settle in for what he hoped would be nightmare-free sleep.

He felt and heard Hannah sigh and settle in herself. "Yes, I think you're right about that. Like brunch tomorrow with your *American* family. Not scary at all."

She yawned and he knew she was close to falling asleep.

Heath had texted him at Max's just as they were getting ready to leave. The entire clan, except for Luke's Uncle Darren, was meeting at Drury Lane for brunch the following morning and they'd been invited.

He kissed her shoulder again and felt her breathing even out. It had been a long, emotional day. He was feeling it himself. "Brunch with my American family is not scary at all, baby. We're going to be fine." He drifted off, feeling at that moment everything would indeed be fine for them.

Chapter Eight

Rocco rubbed his eyes again, trying to stay alert until the end of his workday at five. It was noon as he sat in the cafeteria at Dixon-Shaw's HQ in Oak Brook. He'd been nightmare-free Saturday and Sunday, he presumed because he'd been with Hannah. But last night, he'd experienced one of the "bad ones."

The ones that started off with his father drunk and angry, taking out his frustrations for who knew what on him until he sobbed, begging him to stop. The dream would then transition to the battlefield in Sangin, Afghanistan. The moment where he thought he'd lose his life to Taliban enemy fire.

Heath, God bless his soul, having just been injured himself, dug the bullets out of his side using a small folding tactical knife, similar to the one he always carried now. Rocco had never felt pain like that before and hoped he never did again. He touched the healed, puckered wounds through his t-shirt and sighed. He owed Heath his life. It was a debt he knew he'd never be able to repay. He'd have to settle for being as good of a friend to Heath as he could be.

"God damn, Rocco but this meat sauce of yours is fucking amazing." Eli Dixon, co-owner of Dixon-Shaw Security shoveled more of his homemade gnocchi in his mouth, smiling happily as he ate his lunch. Lunch Rocco had brought in for the firm's owners.

"I'm with Eli. Your marinara sauce is fantastic, too." Eason Shaw, the firm's other owner spread some on the homemade focaccia bread he'd also brought for them. He'd made extra and had set some of it aside for Hannah. "You should really bottle it and sell it. You'd make a shitload, bud."

"I'm with Eason. Put the guns down and apron on." Eli munched on crisp mixed greens tossed in his special vinaigrette, nodding his head.

Rocco grunted. He wished. He appreciated their sentiment, along with Hannah's. The truth was, if a successful restaurateur like Kyle Asher didn't think his cooking was good enough to serve the masses, it probably wasn't. Not that he'd ever tried it. Whenever Rocco had suggested Kyle give him a shot, even in the smaller Club Envidious kitchen, Kyle had shut him down immediately, stating he had all the kitchen staff he needed.

"Thanks for jarring some of it for *us* at least," Eason said.

Rocco yawned. He needed to do something about his nightmares but wasn't sure what. Heath had some relief with sleeping meds but most of the time he was too out of it in the morning to function well enough for the workday. "Any time. I'm glad you both like it."

He pulled up the email his brother had sent him with non-medical PTSD treatments on his cell phone. Maybe it was time to take a serious look since Massimo had gone through the trouble of researching them for him. It couldn't hurt.

"What's going on? You feeling all right?" Eli asked him.

Rocco shrugged. He didn't want to talk about it, not that Eli and Eason wouldn't understand. Both were former CIA and instructors at the US Army Military Police School at Ft. Leonard Wood in Missouri, and in addition to serving themselves, they'd seen their fair share.

"Just a combat nightmare last night. Didn't get much sleep." He scanned Massimo's email and found the section about sound therapy worth exploring. It seemed simple enough and the Naturespace 3D holographic sound app website had some promising testimonials. He had to do something and he couldn't continue on the way he had been, especially with Hannah in his life now.

Sensing Eli and Eason watching him, he looked up. When Eli held his hand out, Rocco passed him his phone. He studied his bosses as they reviewed Massimo's email and Naturespace's website.

Eason nodded, seemingly approving of what he and his partner were looking at. "Your brother did his homework. I use a sound app similar to Naturespace. It helps a lot. And not only at night. Sometimes I play the app in my office, keeps me more even-keeled."

Rocco hadn't expected that. He'd download the app right away.

Eli nodded. "Meditation and yoga can help too. Don't dismiss the mind-body therapies. And don't get pissed off, but I'll forward a couple therapists who work with veterans suffering from PTSD. You need it, brother, and there's no shame in that. Especially now that you're with Hannah. Eason and I have used both these therapists regularly, so we can vouch they'll be able to help you."

His mouth fell open. He'd always considered Eli and Eason infallible, superhuman in a way. Experienced, capable, and connected far above his own paygrade.

"Don't look so surprised. Nearly everyone at this firm has experienced trauma in some form or another." Eason handed him his phone back just as it rang.

Rocco frowned, glancing at the unfamiliar number a moment before answering. "Moretti."

"Hello, Mr. Moretti, I'm calling for Carlo Antonetti. Mr. Antonetti was hoping you'd be able to meet with him today at the Elmhurst location? And please bring your knife set."

He must be sleepier than he thought. Did the

woman on the phone tell him to bring his knife set to Cucina Antonetti's?

"Miss, this is Rocco Moretti, Marine and associate with Dixon-Shaw Security. I think you're looking for someone else." Eli and Eason were listening intently to his crazy conversation. He rubbed his eyes again and blew out a frustrated breath.

"No, sir. I have the right person. Are you able to come to the Elmhurst location today? With your knives?"

He glanced at his bosses. They both shrugged and mouthed, *Go ahead*.

He had no idea why Carlo Antonetti wanted to see him. As tired as he was, his curiosity got the better of him. "Sure, I can be there within an hour. I have to go home to get my knives."

"Wonderful! Mr. Antonetti will be so pleased. Just tell the seating hostess you're there to see him when you get here. See you soon." The call disconnected and he stared at his phone. *What the fuck?*

"Your knives?" Eason asked.

Rocco stood and rolled his shoulders and neck, hoping to ease the stiffness he felt from not sleeping. "You know my grandparents taught me and my brother how to cook. My first gift to them was a set of Victorinox rosewood-handle executive knives. I still have them and use them every time I cook. I don't know why Carlo Antonetti wants to see me. It's got to be some kind of mistake. I'll go over there and clear up what's obviously a misunderstanding. Then maybe I'll try and get some sleep."

"Bullshit. Your sauces, both kinds, are better than Antonetti's. Call us when you find out what the hell's going on." Eli took a bite of marinara-covered focaccia bread and nodded with determination.

He chuckled and shook his head. "You got it,

boss."

Less than an hour later, he stepped inside Antonetti's Elmhurst restaurant, still unsure of what was going on. He was so certain this meeting was a mistake he hadn't bothered changing into dress clothes and was still wearing a short-sleeved t-shirt and faded jeans.

Rocco waited near the hostess station for Carlo, his knife bag in hand. He yawned and rolled his shoulders. The sooner he straightened out this misunderstanding, the sooner he could go back home and get some sleep. The restaurant seemed busy for a weekday after what should have been the lunch rush.

His stomach clenched with jealousy when Carlo and his son approached. CJ, as everyone referred to the younger Antonetti, was the spitting image of his father. He couldn't help but wish he had a son who took after him. The image of Hannah pregnant with their child flashed through his mind and warmed his heart. He shook his head. Now wasn't the time for thoughts of a pregnant Hannah.

Carlo extended his hand and Rocco shook it. "Good to see you again, Rocco. Thank you for meeting with me on short notice." While Carlo was dressed in a well-fitting gray suit, his son was wearing black jeans and a Cucina Antonetti's logo t-shirt. He shook hands with CJ and waited to be briefed on the reason for their meeting.

"I'll cut to the chase. We think your cooking is outstanding and want to know if you'd be interested in cooking for us, or rather cooking *with* us, a couple of days a week to start."

What? "I've got to be missing something. How do you know about my cooking?"

Carlo and his son turned to each other and grinned. "Hannah Hailey brought some of your lasagna and sauce over to my place before she had to oversee a wedding."

Now it made sense. She must have stopped at Carlo's before heading over to the North Barrington Country Club for Kristen and Ben's wedding. That was why she'd been a little late.

"But you use your mother's sauce recipe." He had no intention of causing friction in the Antonetti family. It was surreal to believe they thought his cooking was good enough to be served at their restaurant. And Hannah. She'd meant it when she'd told him his cooking was good enough to be served to the masses. She believed in him, truly believed in him. He supposed that was what love was. He believed in her as well. It was all so new to him, he wasn't sure how to respond or feel.

"Dude, she *loved* your sauce. Admitted it was better than hers," CJ informed him.

"You're shitting me? Oh, I'm sorry."

Carlo and CJ laughed, causing Rocco to join them. It was crazy. But his heart raced in anticipation of cooking in a commercial kitchen for the first time.

"No reason to be sorry, Rocco. I know this all seems out of left field. But we're looking to expand. We don't have all the particulars sorted out just yet. Our expansion includes recipes *and* staff. I'm guessing you have some special recipes? Maybe some of Antonetti's you think you could improve?"

Rocco's face heated. He did have ideas of how the small restaurant chain could improve and expand their menu. Or maybe it was his ego when it came to his cooking. "Actually, yes."

Father and son shared a knowing glance and smiled. Carlo clapped him on the shoulder and nodded. "That settles it. Let's give this a try today and see how it goes?"

He thought he would pass out either from exhaustion or excitement. He gripped his knife bag like it was a lifeline, feeling his grandparents' presence as he often did, and smiled. "Yes, sir."

"We're not that formal, man. We're a family, remember?" CJ's youthful enthusiasm calmed him down somewhat but he couldn't wait to step inside their kitchen.

"*Parli italiano?*" Carlo asked him.

Rocco chuckled. "*Sì, certo*. Spanish, German, and Hindi, too."

"Excellent. CJ, introduce Rocco to everyone in the kitchen and get him started. Then back to your homework. Don't give me that look. *You* chose summer school, college man. You've got to do the work, *giusto?*"

They walked past the main dining room and his heart galloped. He took a couple of deep breaths and clutched his knife bag. This was it. A commercial kitchen. He wished his grandparents were alive to witness this. And regardless of how things turned out, he'd find a way to thank Hannah for giving him this opportunity.

CJ provided a quick but thorough tour of Antonetti's Elmhurst kitchen. From the gleaming stainless steel prep areas to the salad station, dough room where he would share his focaccia bread recipe, main ten-burner cooking area, and to their huge refrigerator and gleaming cauldrons where they wanted him to prepare his *amazing* sauce as they all referred to it. He was literally on cloud nine. *This is where I belong.*

Carlo's *Zio* Rudolfo, or Uncle Rudy as the non-Italians called him, handed him a black, mesh-top chef skull cap and matching button-down, short-sleeved cook's shirt. He quickly put everything on and rubbed his tattooed arms. No one had said anything about his ink, most likely because he'd be hidden away in the kitchen.

Rudy looked him over and nodded. "You'll look wonderful when you bring out some dishes to our customers," Rudy commented.

Rocco's mouth fell open. "You want me to serve diners?"

He must have commented too loudly as some of the other cooks and wait staff laughed along with Rudy. What the hell?

"Of course. I do it. The patrons love it. And now we have a tattooed Marine cooking with us. They'll love being served by you, too. Sometimes they take pictures. Your tattoos are amazing. They'll want pictures of you, you'll see. It's fun, don't worry."

Stunned, he nodded and began preparing both his marinara and meat sauces. Once he had them simmering, he'd prepare the dough for his focaccia bread. He fired off a quick text to Eli and Eason in response to their *many* texts to him wondering what the fuck was going on. He wasn't sure if he should feel relieved or worried they both intended to visit for dinner.

A few hours later, after preparing several pots of sauce and enough focaccia bread dough to feed several Marine units, Rocco was documenting his recipe for stuffed Chicken Parmesan. Apparently, it had been so well received, Antonetti's wanted to add it to their menu. He couldn't fucking believe it. His hand shook as he finished and heard someone calling for Chef over and over again. Where was Rudy? He'd just seen him a minute ago.

"Chef Rocco!"

Rocco glanced up, dazed to find Chef Rudy and Carlo beside him. Both with amused expressions on their faces.

"You didn't hear us calling you, Chef?"

He felt his face heat. "I didn't know you were calling me. I thought you were calling for Rudy, sorry."

"Chef Rocco has a nice ring to it, don't you think?" Rudy asked with a grin.

Although he never thought he'd hear himself called that, he liked it. "Yes, I think it does." He chuckled and waited for what they wanted to throw at him next.

"So, here's the deal. Both of your sauces are hit with the customers. They're asking for large to-go containers, instead of the small ones we usually give at no cost. So we're going to charge them two dollars for the four-ounce container and three dollars for the eight-ounce," Carlo informed him.

His eyes grew wide. Antonetti's customers liked his sauce enough to pay extra for it? He was at a loss for words. Never had he imagined his cooking receiving this kind of attention. For a minute, he thought about how Kyle had dismissed him. Considering how comfortable he felt in Antonetti's kitchen and with the staff, Kyle had done him a favor.

Carlo clapped him on the back and snickered. "I know you won't be back until Thursday, but could you write up the recipes for the sauces, too? *Zio* Rudy will do right by *Nonno* Moretti."

"Sure, no problem." Rudy had already helped him and had replicated the family recipe to Rocco's satisfaction.

Rudy nodded, seemingly relieved. "First, though, you've been requested in the dining room by Eli and Eason." Rudy's knowing grin made Rocco smile himself. "And a couple of other diners, too."

Carlo shrugged and grinned. "*E così comincia.* And so it begins."

****

With a smile on her face, Hannah reviewed the many positive comments about *Chef Rocco's* culinary expertise on Cucina Antonetti's Facebook and Twitter feeds. He looked amazing in the pictures diners had posted of him in his black uniform with his beautifully tattooed forearms on display. His smile seemed genuine, so she hoped he wasn't upset she'd taken it upon herself to share his leftovers with Carlo Antonetti. Kyle Asher could suck it. His loss was Antonetti's gain.

It was nearly eleven in the evening as she waited patiently for Rocco in the luxurious Club Envidious lobby. She hadn't heard from him, which didn't surprise her. But she wanted to see him personally, even if only for a few minutes, before she assumed he'd want to get some much-needed and well-deserved rest. She'd brought a bag with some goodies in case he wasn't dog-tired. She'd have to wait and see.

Hannah glanced up as a group of club members entered the lobby door, followed by an exhausted-looking Rocco carrying his knife bag. Poor thing. She'd just stay a minute, her goodies could wait for another time.

When his weary but surprised eyes met hers, her pulse sped up as it always did. His warm, welcoming smile made her heart sing. He seemed happy, not upset to see her. Unexpected tears of relief welled up behind her eyelids. She tossed her cell phone into her goodie bag and stood as his purposeful strides quickly shortened the distance between them.

She held her breath, not sure what to expect next. The man appeared drained but happy. He placed his knife bag next to hers on the lobby couch and before she knew it, she was in his arms, being spun around, much to the amusement of incoming club members. She giggled and held on for dear life. Up close, he smelled like sweat and whatever delicious delights he'd prepared before coming home. She loved it, and him, so much.

Hannah had been nervous throughout the day after Carlo had texted her that Rocco was in his uniform and busy in the kitchen. It appeared her worries had been unfounded.

"Save that for the club," someone called out and chuckled.

Rocco placed her back on her feet and turned toward whoever had commented. "No way, she's all mine. *Only* mine. Always."

Her heart fluttered. *Always.* She sure as hell hoped there would be an always for them.

He clasped her hands and squeezed gently. After a much-too-quick peck on the lips, he smiled down at her dreamily. "Baby, what did you do?"

Her face heated and she shrugged. "I might've shared some of your cooking with a preferred vendor who happens to own a three-Italian-restaurant chain. You're not angry, are you?" She hoped he wasn't putting on a show in front of the club members and personnel working behind the building's reception desk.

Rocco's hearty laugh put her mind at ease. "Are you kidding? Today was fucking amazing." He picked up their bags and led her to the non-dungeon side key-carded door.

"No, Rocco. You're exhausted. I just wanted to see you in person for a minute. I'll let you get some sleep."

The hurt expression on his handsome face made her feel like shit. "I want you to stay. Please, *bella.* I just need to take a shower and I'll be fine and ready for *us.*"

She liked the sound of that and couldn't resist his hopeful tone. "If you're sure, I'd love to stay and hear all about your day."

Although he yawned on their way up to his place in the elevator, his smile never dimmed. He unlocked his door and ushered her inside, locking it securely for the night.

After placing their bags on his kitchen counter, he led her to his room. "We're alone at my place. Our verbal agreement is still in place, so get undressed and in bed while I take a shower. I won't be long." He kissed her forehead and disappeared into the en suite master bathroom.

As soon as the door closed, she dashed out to the kitchen and retrieved her bag. She was giddy, never having done what she was proposing for Rocco. He seemed so tired, regardless of what he'd said. He should be agreeable to her plan.

While the shower was running, she pulled back the bed blanket and sheets and covered the bed and pillows in towels. She quickly lit several lavender-scented candles, arranging them around the room, and placed lavender-scented massage oil on his nightstand.

She heard a blow dryer turn on as she undressed, excitement flowing through her veins. On a whim, she put on one of Rocco's bowties, a white one. She adjusted it the best she could but it remained a little loose. Giggling, she supposed it didn't matter. She was going after the effect. She sat on the end of the bed, calmed by the subtle scent of lavender, the candles flickering providing a soft glow in the room.

Hannah couldn't remember the last time she'd felt so blissfully happy, so alive. It was as if the warm glow from the candles was actually flowing through her. *This is what love feels like.* She supposed it was and she was terrified because now that she'd found it, she didn't want to ever give it up.

Her heart jolted and her pulse pounded when she

heard the blow dryer shut off. She hoped her little plan didn't backfire on her.

Rocco emerged from the bathroom in all his sexy glory. Although he looked amazing in whatever he wore, from jeans and a Marines t-shirt to his finest Armani suits, Hannah liked him best like this—naked.

He quickly scanned the room before focusing on her. His eyes trained on hers before they slowly roamed her naked form, stopping momentarily at her neck. His lips twitched before turning into a grin. He glanced over to the nightstand where she'd placed the massage oil.

He came to her and held out his hand. She happily took it, his strength and warmth spreading through her. "What's all this? Do you want a massage?"

She stood and cupped his cheek, feeling feminine pride when he leaned into her touch and briefly closed his weary eyes. "No. This is for you. I'm going to give *you* a massage. I think you need it after the long day you've had."

Instead of laughing or dismissing her like she thought he might, Rocco's eyes widened in surprise. He looked at the bed and back at her. "No one's ever done that for me before. You don't have to," he whispered.

Her heart ached knowing something as simple as a massage was something no one had ever thought to give him. Rocco was such a giving soul, always doing for others. It was about damn time someone did for *him*.

She squeezed his hand assuredly. "I know. I *want* to. I can't guarantee my skills are as good as yours, but I think I can help with what's got to be sore feet, back, and shoulders."

He nodded but stayed silent. She watched patiently as he tried to decide if he'd allow himself the luxury of being taken care of for a change. If he agreed to this, she vowed to be mindful of doing what she could to make him feel valued and cared for.

He nodded with determination, seemingly reconciled to being taken care of. "Thank you, baby. I appreciate it more than I can say. But hopefully, afterward, I can *show* you."

She liked the sound of that, but the exhaustion etched on his face told her he probably wouldn't be showing her until tomorrow. And that was fine with her. Tonight was about *him*.

Gesturing to the bed, he thankfully complied and lay on his stomach in the center. Even the scars on his back, some she knew to be from his father's hand and others from his time in the Marines, didn't detract from his male beauty. Taut muscle under deep-olive skin made for a feast to behold. Her fingers itched to touch and explore.

After grabbing the massage oil bottle from the nightstand and pouring a small amount onto her hands, she began with his feet, like he had done for her at her first Twisted Tea Society meeting. The groan her work elicited made her smile. Rocco's yawn convinced her that her plan for the night was spot-on.

"So, tell me everything. What happened? Did Carlo call you?" She only knew what little Carlo had told her after Rocco was already working in Antonetti's kitchen and what she'd seen on social media. She was curious to hear Rocco's perspective of the day's events.

As she slowly worked Rocco's tight, tired muscles, he recounted the events of the day, starting with his conversation at Dixon-Shaw with the owners and his nightmare from the night before. Damn. As exhausted as he must have been, he'd still worked his ass off at Antonetti's.

She was relieved to learn he'd decided, with their encouragement, to utilize non-medical treatments for

PTSD, including counseling. His trauma began years before his time in the service. He deserved to be as healthy as he could be emotionally, considering everything he'd been through.

"Wow, they're actually charging for containers of *your* sauce, huh? That's amazing." She worked his tight calves until they gave way and relaxed a bit.

"Yeah, I couldn't believe it. Most of the customers were ordering the large container." Another yawn had Hannah wanting to move further up so she could finish and he could rest.

"I'm not surprised. I *told* you your cooking was good enough. *Better* than good enough."

He sighed and groaned as she worked his upper thighs. "Yes, you did. And they added my stuffed chicken parmesan to the menu. And they're using my focaccia bread dough recipe, too."

That all sounded delicious. She was so proud of him. "I saw all the posts on social media. You looked pretty hot in your chef's uniform."

He chuckled as she glided her hands along his perfect, tight ass. "Yeah, well, a couple of women grabbed that ass you're rubbing right now."

Hannah stilled, jealousy burning hot in her gut. Shit. She should've known how women would react to Rocco. The man was gorgeous, had the most stunning ink covering his arms and could cook. For a moment, she wondered again what the hell she was doing. He'd realize she wasn't enough for him and then move on. Tears stung her eyes.

"Baby. I told them my ass is spoken for. Politely, but firmly. I love you, remember? You can trust me. I promise. Like I know I can trust *you*." His voice was getting fainter by the minute. She suspected he'd fall asleep soon.

She worked her way up to his lower back, kneading firmly, hoping to ease the stiffness and soreness away. "I know. I'm sorry." And she did. So far, he hadn't given her any reason not to. He was a straight shooter. "Oh, and aren't Eli Dixon and Eason Shaw handsome? That picture of the three of you was great." She smiled when Rocco stiffened up for a second. So, *he* was a little jealous too. She couldn't help but feel relieved about that. They obviously both felt a little insecure. Maybe that was a good thing.

As she worked his upper back and then his shoulders with him not saying a word, she assumed he'd fallen asleep. "They're too old for you and you're with *me*. *Mine*," he said on a soft whisper and then began snoring softly.

Smiling to herself that she'd relaxed him enough to put him to sleep, she carefully got off the bed. She admired his sleeping form for a moment before pulling the sheets up, covering him. What a shame, she contemplated, shaking her head. He believed she should always go topless, and she thought he should never be dressed.

She blew out the candles and grabbed a sheet and pillow she'd set aside and made herself comfortable on Rocco's couch. Feeling satisfied she'd done good both with Antonetti's and tonight, she drifted off to sleep with a smile on her face.

Hannah startled awake sometime later, being lifted off the couch by a woken and alert Rocco. She wrapped her legs around his waist and held him tight.

"I'm so sorry I fell asleep, baby," he whispered as he effortlessly carried her to bed. One candle was lit on his nightstand, casting a slight glow. Soft nature sounds were playing from his cell phone next to the candle. It was soothing, and she rather liked it. "Thanks for not leaving."

She nuzzled his neck, inhaling his unique scent as he gently placed her in the center of the bed. "Of course I stayed, even though I knew you were exhausted. I'm glad I was able to relax you enough so you fell asleep."

Feeling his warm, solid weight on her made every inch of her light up with burning, urgent need. He was all she wanted, all she ever thought about. She hadn't known what she'd been missing until they'd met.

He feathered kisses along her neck and her pulse fluttered in response. She felt a ripple of excitement as he slowly and teasingly kissed his way to her breasts and caught one pebbled nipple between his teeth. He tugged gently and her core slickened. A delicious shudder shot through her when he slowly kissed, licked, and nibbled his way to her lower stomach. She thrilled at the thought of having him inside her.

"I can't believe you gave my leftovers to Carlo." The first swipe of his tongue along her slickened slit nearly set her off.

She was about to tell Rocco she didn't need him to go down on her because she wanted him so badly but when his tongue grazed her clit, all bets were off. Hannah buried her hands in his thick locks and pulled him closer, grinding her pussy against his talented tongue.

"I … had to." She gasped as he worked her over, his tongue unleashing its magic until she couldn't hold on any longer. Her entire body vibrated as she tumbled over and squeezed her eyes shut. Her toes curled as he left her shattered on the sheets. "Kyle was wrong … not to give you a shot … in his kitchens," she panted out.

She opened her eyes to find him staring up at her with a smug look on his face, the glow from the candle making him appear ethereal. That was how she saw him, as otherworldly. And because of his past, he didn't see the beauty in himself that she did. That everyone else did. She hoped the experience at Antonetti's would bolster his confidence and self-esteem. Help him to realize what an amazing man he was. She'd do her part, too.

When he chuckled and nodded, she believed he might actually agree. "Thank you, baby." He gently kissed her thighs before moving and sitting up against the headboard. He patted his thighs. "No matter what happens after yesterday, I'll always be grateful for the opportunity. It's an experience I'll never forget."

With his help, she happily climbed on his lap, rubbing her still-wet slit along his hard cock. She kissed him, their tongues tangling, tasting herself on him. What she once considered awkward and uncomfortable, she now considered exciting. Everything about her time with Rocco, regardless of what they did, was exciting.

It was as if she'd just been going through life on automatic pilot until they'd met. She supposed in some ways, that was true. And that just reinforced the fact she needed to make some important life decisions about her future. Later. *Now*, she needed him inside of her.

He rummaged through his nightstand and frowned, producing a condom. "Shit. It's the last one." His tired eyes showed disappointment. She should've suggested they get some sleep. He needed it. But he tore the condom wrapper and sheathed his cock before she could get the words out. "Ride me, baby. I'll buy a gross later today."

She giggled. A gross—damn. But what fun they'd have using them. Not wasting any time, she slowly impaled herself on his hard length. Even wet, it took a bit of effort. He stretched her nearly to the point of pain but Hannah didn't mind. Her pulse picked up and heat rushed through her as she seated herself fully.

He sucked a nipple and tugged on the other as she rode him for all she was worth. Each down stroke delivered the most delicious pleasure she'd ever felt. "I'm so glad you weren't angry with me for sharing with Carlo," she panted out.

Rocco gripped her hips tighter, guiding her harder up and down his length the way he wanted her. "I could never be angry with you, *bella*," he said as he switched his attention to her other nipple, sucking hard until her clit throbbed.

She continued riding him, every inch of her body alive with energy. When he started rubbing her clit, she held him close and felt his warm breath against her skin. Thrills ran up and down her body as she came in waves. A few more strokes and she felt him fill the condom in spurts as he groaned her name over and over.

Relaxing in his arms, she sighed in contentment. They sat, embracing while the gentle nature sounds continued to provide a soothing backdrop. When she felt him soften, she carefully lifted herself off of him and groaned.

She leaned back and cupped his cheek, gazing into his exhausted but pleasure-glazed eyes. He smiled up at her and her heart swelled.

"I know you don't quite believe it yet, but I think you're beautiful, Hannah. Talented and amazing. With a giving, compassionate spirit." He stroked her cheek and she felt the warmth his touch.

Rocco was right to a certain degree. He was slowly convincing her. "I'm working on it, I swear. And I wish you saw the beauty I see in *you*. Inside *and* out." She kissed him tenderly and felt his smile against her lips.

"Touché. I'm working on it, baby. I promise," he

whispered back.

Chapter Nine

Rocco smiled, watching Eli and Eason gobble up his latest creation which was now offered at all three Cucina Antonetti's restaurants. Eli sat behind his desk while Eason had taken a spot at the small conference table in Eli's office.

Seated in a guest chair in front of Eli's desk, he was pleased his bosses had been flexible about his schedule. Dixon-Shaw had grown large enough and were still expanding to the point they were able to accommodate the most challenging of associates' schedules with a variety of assignments. If they wanted to employ the best, flexibility was key. He felt honored to be on their staff.

"So, in the two and a half weeks you've been cooking at Antonetti's, this amazing gnocchi with sausage and garlic mushrooms in creamy tomato vodka sauce makes how many of your dishes they've added to their menu?" Eason dipped a piece of focaccia bread in the sauce and moaned after popping it into his mouth.

Eli laughed and shook his head. "Damn, man. Should we leave the room? You fucking your lunch or eating it?"

Eason gave Eli the finger and continued devouring his lunch. It did Rocco's heart and ego good to see his bosses enjoying his cooking, regardless of if they were at the restaurant or not.

"Five dishes and the focaccia bread. I've got a few others I want to share but will wait a little while. Some might work better as weekly or monthly specials rather than regular menu offerings." He was proud to be a part of Antonetti's expansion plans.

He'd been nervous at first, but Carlo's mother had assured him her feelings weren't hurt by the chain's switch to his recipes. She, Carlo, and Uncle Rudy had encouraged him to make suggestions on kitchen and prep process improvements. Just a few small changes they'd implemented had improved the ebb and flow in the kitchen and with the wait staff. To borrow a phrase from Richard the Dick, Rocco *fit* and he loved it. And Hannah for believing in him enough to share his cooking with Carlo. She'd led him to his bliss. He was still undecided on how he should gently nudge her toward what he believed would be hers.

"You can jar some of this vodka sauce for us, right?" Eason asked as he finished up.

Rocco chuckled. "I *should* make you guys go to the restaurant from now on, but sure, I'll jar some for you. No problem."

His spirits lifted when he noticed Hannah's name on his ringing phone's display. He smiled and connected the call. "Hey, baby. What's going on?" He heard commotion over the line and assumed she was coordinating an event but had a minute to touch base. Wait, was that a siren? The hairs on the back of his neck stood up and his muscles tensed. Something was wrong.

Hannah sniffled. "Um … Rocco?" Her full-out sob broke his heart.

"Hannah, what's wrong? Where are you? What's happening?" He stood, heading toward the office door just as his buddy and off-duty firefighter Cole Palmer entered, a concerned look on his face.

Cole and Hannah both spoke but all he heard was the word *accident*. It was enough and he bolted out of Eli's office with him and Cole hot on his heels. Rocco raced to the elevator, blood pounding in his ears. Panic threatened, but he needed to remain calm for Hannah. He jabbed at the down button, willing the doors to open.

"Hannah, baby. Sit tight. I'm on my way. Everything's going to be all right, okay?"

She sniffled as the elevator doors opened and the three men piled in. Cole calmly pressed the lobby button.

"Oh … um … thanks. I love…"

Their call disconnected. "Fuck!" He turned to Cole while they were taken to the lobby. "What the fuck happened? Where?"

Cole ran a hand through his hair and shook his head. Rocco's gut clenched. Shit. "A multiple-car pileup right around the corner. Intersection of 22nd Street and Route 83. From what I can tell on the police scanners, some drunk fuck caused the whole thing. Oh, and they found thirty kilograms of heroin, twenty-five kilograms of cocaine, and ten kilograms of fentanyl in the asshole's SUV. Some bad injuries but no fatalities."

Thank God for small miracles. Before he reached the lobby doors, Eli stopped him.

"Let me drive you there. No arguments." Eli held out his hand, most likely waiting for Rocco to hand over his truck keys.

Rocco's chest rose and fell with rapid breaths. He wanted to argue. He needed to get to his Hannah. She was scared, probably hurt, and needed him. Eli knew his background and training. Knew he was more than capable of getting himself the short distance to the accident location without issue.

"Come on, *compagno*. Let Eli help you so you can be there for your girl." Cole placed an assuring hand on his shoulder and squeezed.

Rocco nodded, blew out a breath, and dug in his jeans pocket for his keys. He tossed them to Eli and shoved out the door. It was only just past the first week in August, but waves of heat and humidity hit hard, stopping him for a second. They needed to hurry. Hannah was most likely sweltering in the heat, in addition to probably being hurt and afraid.

Dixon-Shaw's headquarters were located on Midwest Avenue, a short distance from the accident location. As Eli approached the accident scene, his stomach knotted. What a fucking mess. The area looked like a war zone. After a quick scan, he counted nine damaged vehicles, including Hannah's white BMW. The entire front of the car had been crushed nearly up to the windshield.

"Fuck me," Eli said as he surveyed the scene. Oak Brook police officers were directing and diverting traffic. Rocco recognized many of them. Tow trucks and ambulances littered the area. Local news affiliates were filming and he could hear and see helicopters overhead.

Before he could exit his truck, Eli grabbed him by the arm. "Short leash, Rocco. I mean it."

Fuck that. When he found the asshole who'd hurt Hannah and the rest of innocents being treated, all bets were off. Piece-of-shit, drunk drug dealer had it coming. He knew the law enforcement on the scene would look the other way. Give him a minute with the scumbag responsible for this mess. It was one of the benefits of his association with Dixon-Shaw. He was untouchable.

Rocco didn't respond and set out to first find Hannah and then the motherfucker who would soon have an even worse day. He held out his credentials as he scanned the area, looking for her.

He spotted her sitting up on a gurney, strapped in. Her hair was tousled, her makeup splotchy, and her pretty, flowery summer dress wrinkled, having left her formal pantsuits behind since they'd gotten together. Paramedics were tending to the side of her head, their gloves and gauze stained with her blood.

Her eyes were glazed over but showed with relief when they found his. His stomach twisted in knots. This was un-fucking-acceptable. *No one* hurt his woman and got away with it. No one.

"He's over there," Eli said, standing beside him, pointing to a young Hispanic man covered in poorly done tattoos surrounded by police officers and handcuffed to the back of an ambulance. "Remember. Short leash."

Rocco shoved his ID in his pocket and sprinted toward the soon-to-be-dead man, not saying a word but aware Eli was right behind him. He'd have to pull him off the fucker. To hell with Eli's leash. This was personal. And he knew damn well if it were Eli's woman who'd gotten hurt, he wouldn't hesitate to take the man out.

The young man's eyes widened when he realized Rocco was coming for him. He yanked on the cuffs, as if by some miracle they'd spring open and he could get away. *Not gonna happen, asshole.*

Just as he'd expected, law enforcement and the paramedics stepped aside. "*Te voy a hacer pedazos, cabrón,*" he said before slamming his fist into the man's face so hard, Rocco crushed his nose. The man wailed as blood spurted from his broken nose, but Rocco continued his assault on his face then and slammed his head against the ambulance door several times, rendering him unconscious.

That wasn't enough for him, though. He yanked on one of the asshole's arms, dislocating his shoulder, and felt satisfaction when he felt the cocksucker's arm break.

Rocco focused his attention on the man's other arm, but he felt someone trying to pull him away. Not yet. He wasn't anywhere near finished.

He kneed the man's hand against the ambulance

door, crushing his fingers. "Stand down, soldier! That's an order!" Eli shouted and yanked him away from the unconscious and now badly hurt scumbag.

He stood, ramrod straight, panting with his fists clenched, ready to tell Eli to fuck off, but refrained. His rage was at a full boil, but somehow he kept it together.

"Let the paramedic get you cleaned up so you can get back to Hannah. *She's* what's important right now. This idiot's done. He won't ever hurt anyone again."

Rocco looked down at his blood-covered hands and nodded, slowly getting his bearings. He watched Hannah wipe her eyes and say something to her paramedics as his tended to his hands. They didn't hurt much, but he didn't want to touch her until every last drop of the drug dealer's blood was wiped and cleaned away.

She offered him a weak smile as he approached. He knew she had to be in shock, exhausted, and overheated. It was fucking roasting out, the sun bearing down on them.

"Get the woman some water, she's baking out here," Eli barked out.

Rocco unscrewed the top off the bottle he was given and held it up to her lips. "Small sips, baby."

She nodded, taking a couple of small sips before turning her head away. "Can I go home now?" she whimpered. Her sorrowful eyes were nearly his undoing.

"Ma'am, we're taking you to Elmhurst Memorial Hospital. You need to be examined first." The paramedic looked at Rocco for help when she began crying.

"But my head hurts and I want to go home. And … my car is wrecked." She leaned back on the gurney and whimpered, squeezing her eyes shut as the tears fell.

The other ambulances around them were taking accident victims to nearby hospitals as tow trucks were hauling away the wrecks. "Let's get her inside and to the hospital right now."

"I'll meet you there," Eli told him and left.

As the paramedics got their things packed up, he held Hannah's shaking hands. "I know you want to go home, but first let's let the doctors do a quick once-over to make sure you're all right. Please, *cara*?"

She sighed, nodded, and swiped at her damp eyes. "You'll come with me, right?"

He squeezed her hands, then kissed her knuckles. "I'll ride there with you. I'll be with you every step of the way," he assured her. He wasn't sure how truthful he was being. He wasn't family and the hospital staff would most likely prohibit him from being present during her exam.

As the ambulance left the scene of the accident, sirens blaring, he held on to Hannah's hands with one hand and worked his cell phone with the other. He asked Joe to contact Hannah's parents, assuming they'd prefer to hear from someone who—wasn't him.

Just as he ended his call with Joe, his brother Massimo called. "Jesus Christ. What the fuck happened? You and the accident were all over the news. I'm guessing the guy you beat the shit out of caused the whole mess? Did you kill him?"

Damn. He'd forgotten about the news camera crews. His only focus had been on Hannah and the drug dealer who'd caused the mess. He turned and gazed at her. She was clinging to his hand but appeared to be resting with her eyes closed as they headed to the hospital.

Eli had been right. The asshole was finished. He didn't need to kill him, though he would've loved to do it. Scum like him needed to be eradicated. Period.

"No, he lost consciousness pretty quickly. I didn't

let that stop me until Eli pulled me away and ordered me to stand down. Hannah was among the people hurt in the accident. We're on our way to the hospital now." He kissed her hand softly and her lips curved into a slight smile. It would be all right. He knew that. Thankfully, she was only bruised and shaken up.

The thought of something happening to her pained his soul. Now that he'd found her, he couldn't imagine living without her. He felt the full weight of Richard's words about not fitting in when he'd accompanied her to visit her grandmother, Patty's estranged mother, the week before.

But now wasn't the time to think about that. Rocco hoped he was wrong, but he had a bad feeling about how things would play out now that Hannah was hurt.

"All right. Syd's parents are on standby to watch the kids. I know you've got things under control, because that's you, but know we're here to help if you need us, *va bene*?"

He chuckled. He didn't *feel* like he had everything under control at the moment, but he understood what his brother meant. "*Va bene*. Thanks. I'll call you later."

He'd finished texting Heath just as they pulled into the emergency drop-off at the hospital. Tears stung his eyes when Hannah sobbed because he wasn't allowed into the exam room with her. *Family* only. It didn't matter that she was the love of his life and she'd insisted she needed him with her.

Waiting for word that she was indeed all right, he sat impatiently in an uncomfortable waiting room chair. He was startled out of his thoughts when Hannah's parents, followed by a smug-looking Richard the Dick burst into the waiting room. Patty took one disapproving look at his uncovered arms and he instinctively rubbed them.

Rocco stood when Hannah's father Denton approached him with his hand extended. "I saw the footage on the news, son. Thank you for beating the shit out of the motherfucker who hurt my little girl. Too bad Mr. Dixon intervened, isn't it?"

He shook Denton's hand and nodded. "Yes, sir. I agree."

Richard snorted as if he would have beat the shit out of him, too. There was no reason whatsoever for Richard to be at the hospital. He was just putting on a show for Patty's benefit, but he was fairly certain Hannah would dismiss his little display and Rocco wanted a front-row seat to that.

"I'm sorry, Richard, but they'll only allow Denton and me in Hannah's exam room. We'll come and get you when we get the all-clear," Patty announced, not acknowledging Rocco at all. Not surprising, but it irritated him nonetheless.

Richard kissed her cheek and flashed her a pacifying smile that didn't reach his eyes. Patty went for it, unfortunately, and smiled back. "I'll be right here. Just make sure they take good care of our Hannah."

Rocco nearly laughed out loud when Denton rolled his eyes and frowned in Richard's direction. So … Hannah's father wasn't on Team Richard? He was relieved to know that.

"You're staying, son?" Denton asked him. *Son.* His heart swelled at the endearment. He was grateful to have someone in Hannah's family on *his* side. He believed her brother was as well, but he hadn't arrived yet.

"I gave Hannah my word I'd stay. She was upset when they wouldn't let me join her in the exam room."

Richard's smile dimmed for a second before he plastered it back on. "Well, *we're* all here now, that's what matters. Right, Patty?" Richard wrapped his arm around her shoulders and gave her a quick squeeze. And Richard the Dick had just earned his fourth bullet.

This time Rocco rolled *his* eyes and Denton chuckled. He liked Hannah's father from what he'd seen so far. Richard was a real piece of work.

"Douche," they both whispered and then full-out laughed together. Yes, he liked Denton Hailey very much.

Richard had the surprising but good sense not to speak to Rocco after Patty and Denton were escorted to Hannah's exam room. Rocco's spirits lifted as *his* family, his brothers-in-arms entered the waiting area like they owned the place. He stood to greet Eli, Cole, Heath, and Luke. Right behind them, a panicked-looking Eric came rushing in. Seemingly relieved to see him, he joined his support group, ignoring Richard completely. *That's right, Dick.*

"Sitrep," Eli requested before the others could speak.

Rocco shook his head and ran a hand through his hair. "They wouldn't let me in the exam room with her. No surprise there. She was pretty upset about that. I don't have much to report. They escorted her parents to her exam room a little while ago."

A few waiting onlookers snapped photos of Luke but kept their distance, for which he was grateful.

"I caught the news footage. Thanks for giving that piece of shit what he deserved for the mess he made and hurting my little sister. She's never been in a car accident before." Eric bear-hugged him and Rocco hugged him back. He'd wanted to do *more*, but Eli had stopped him before he could.

"Her car was totaled, but from what I could tell, she only hit her head and will most likely only be sore from the impact. Wouldn't you agree, Rocco?" Eli said as he and Eric broke apart.

He agreed. Hannah was emotionally affected more than physically hurt. He nodded, hoping to offer her brother some comfort. "Completely. Eli's right. I appreciate all of you coming, but it's going to be all right. You don't have to stay. Really."

His family all looked at each other and shrugged. "We'll stay until Hannah gets the all-clear. Right, guys?" Heath received nods from everyone and they all took a seat to wait for the all-clear.

Three hours later, after Hannah insisted she was going home with *him*, rather than her parents, her brother, and most of all Richard, she was tucked inside his truck, dead asleep as he navigated out of the hospital parking lot and headed to his apartment.

He'd felt ten feet tall when Hannah had stood up to her mother, and her father and brother came to his defense. Richard the Dick had been left out in the cold and Patty had been more than a little annoyed. The battle between mother and daughter in reference to Richard didn't appear to be over. He worried about what he saw as the final showdown coming to a head soon.

Seeing Hannah with her family and even Richard made him feel out of place. Just like he had when he and Hannah had visited her grandmother in Town & Country, Missouri. He'd have to worry about that later. First, he needed to get Hannah in a warm bath, then to bed.

"And you're sure she's fine? Just bumps and bruises?" Joe asked in Rocco's Bluetooth.

"Positive. I'm going to get her in a nice warm bath and then to bed. I promise you she's going to be all right." Joe had been beside himself when Rocco had phoned him with updates while they'd waited for Hannah to be sent home.

"I'm sorry. It's just—she's my family. I don't know if she mentioned it, but Patty and Denton became my legal guardians when my folks tossed me out of the house when I was twelve and they caught me kissing a boy. Said they wouldn't tolerate a faggot in their home. Patty and Denton didn't even hesitate taking me in. I know Patty's a lot to take and is especially hard on Hannah, but she's not *all* bad."

Christ. He had no idea. Rocco knew all too well about being discarded. His grandparents had saved him and his brother. No wonder Joe had been so concerned. "I don't care if you're gay." It was the truth. He couldn't care less if Joe preferred men to women. What mattered to Rocco was that he was a true friend to Hannah. He was family.

"I hate labels, but I'm not gay. To me, a person's gender doesn't make a difference in matters of the heart. I'm going to let you go and call her tomorrow. Don't be too bothered by this thing with Patty and Richard. Hannah loves *you*, not Richard."

They said their goodbyes as he continued driving home.

Rocco prayed love was enough as he pulled into his covered space at the Club Envidious complex. She was still sound asleep, hadn't moved the entire drive over. He hated to wake her, but he had no choice.

Kyle appeared at the passenger door, ready to help him get Hannah up to his place. She hadn't protested much as Kyle carried her while Rocco led them through the lobby, past the key-carded door and into the elevator.

"If you need me, just call or text me." Kyle kissed Hannah's cheek and winked.

She yawned and offered Kyle a grin. "Thanks, Kyle. I'm mostly fine. Just tired and sore. A nice hot bath is exactly what I need."

"I'd offer to join you both, but I have a feeling Rocco wouldn't allow it." Kyle chuckled and shook his head. "What a shame."

Hannah's face flushed and Rocco's ire ignited. Kyle wouldn't hesitate to join them in the bathtub. It wouldn't happen as long as Hannah was his woman. "Never going to happen, pal. Thanks for your help, though."

"You know how to reach me if you change your mind." He chuckled again and let himself out.

"Be nice to Kyle. He's your friend, remember?" She undressed as the warm water slowly filled the oversized jetted tub.

He poured in some *Falling in Love*-scented body wash and stripped down himself. This would be his first time using the tub. He wished it were under better circumstances. He guided Hannah into the center and positioned himself behind her. She surprised him by turning around and straddling his lap.

Her warm soft skin felt delicious against his. He scooped up the scented, bubbly tub water, pouring it over them both. He had to admit, it was relaxing, especially with Hannah joining him.

She held him tight and sighed. "Thank you. For—everything," she murmured. "I hope I wasn't too much trouble today."

Gently nudging her away from him so he could look her in the eyes, he cupped her cheek on the side of her face where she had a gauze bandage covering the nasty bump on her head. "You were no trouble at all. I *love* you. I *wanted* to be there for you."

He knew he shouldn't want her, considering what

she'd been through, but his cock reacted to a naked, wet Hannah. Slowly, she stroked his length, her hand feeling like a brand on his skin.

"The moment I knew I would be in a huge accident and probably be killed, all I could think about was you. How I'd never see you again, never hold you, never be able to love you again."

"When you called and Cole came in— all I heard was the word *accident*. I needed to get to you as fast as I could. Cole told me there were no fatalities, but I needed to see for myself." Rocco removed Hannah's hand from his aching cock and slowly lifted her, gently guiding her down his length until he was snuggly inside of her. Perfect. His—for now.

She rode him slowly at first, the warm water sloshing around them, cocooning them. As her pussy stretched to accommodate him, she increased the pace, her luscious tits bouncing and she fucked him. He'd never forget how beautiful she looked all wet and sudsy.

"I'm so lucky to have you," she whispered and continued riding him for all she was worth. Her pussy clenched and rippled around his dick. He knew he wouldn't last long.

"No. I'm the lucky one, *cara*." Rocco rubbed her slippery little clit and moaned as his balls drew tight. Her cunt clamped down on his aching cock even harder and he emptied his balls deep inside her as he shouted her name. She followed him over moments later, grinding her pussy against him.

He startled in her arms after he realized he'd forgotten a condom and had come inside her. "Baby? I'm so sorry. I forgot to wear a condom." He gazed into her tired eyes, looking for signs of panic and didn't find any.

Surprisingly, he wasn't all that panicked anymore either. He'd imagined Hannah pregnant with their baby many times. Under different circumstances. But maybe a baby would stop all this Richard nonsense for good. Patty couldn't continue pushing Richard on Hannah if she were pregnant with another man's child. Could she?

Hannah kissed his cheek and nuzzled him in the cooling bath water. "I think we're good. Past that point in my cycle since it's August eleventh."

He couldn't help but feel disappointed at the prospect of not getting her pregnant as he helped her dry off and get ready for bed. What the fuck was he going to do to ensure Hannah didn't surrender and go along with Patty's plans for her which didn't include him?

****

Hannah took a sip of her chilled orange juice and sighed. She was enjoying another delectable breakfast with Rocco at his place since she'd been in that dreadful car accident the previous Friday afternoon. Aside from her soreness, which had fully passed, and her nervousness about getting behind the wheel again, it had been an amazing five days. For the most part.

Rocco had been an absolute dream. Doting on her more than he needed to, but she'd greedily accepted the attention. How could she not? She was head over heels for the man and had essentially been living with him for the past few days. He'd even had a key-card and apartment key made for her so she could come and go as she needed to. Kyle and Grace had been welcoming and understanding.

While her insurance company had been processing her claim, he'd let her drive his Cadillac. Her totaled, leased BMW had been her mother's idea, insisting it made a good impression for the company. She'd enjoyed driving the Cadillac. Rocco had ridden with her at first, or followed her in his truck, in case she panicked behind the wheel. Another of the many reasons she loved him.

"Thank you for making extra stuffed chicken parmesan for my father and Eric last night. Normally, Eric doesn't like pepperoni, but he sure inhaled your cooking." Hannah shook her head and chuckled.

Dinner the night before with her father, brother, and Rocco had been wonderful. The only downside to the evening had been the absence of her mother. She'd begged off, claiming she had an event-related meeting she couldn't reschedule. Hannah called bullshit but wasn't going to argue the point.

She and her mother had been on the warpath during her entire stay at Rocco's. How many times and in how many ways could she tell her mother she was personally finished with Richard before Patty would let it go? She'd been close to telling her to go to hell a couple of times but had done her best to remain respectful, even though she *and* Rocco were being disrespected.

Rocco grinned but his eyes remained somewhat dimmed. She knew the contentiousness with her mother bothered him. As well it should. It bothered her, too. She'd figure out a way to resolve it once and for all. She had to. Enough was enough.

"That's why I made extra. I didn't want to get in the middle of those two battling for leftovers." Rocco shrugged and finished his breakfast in silence.

Hannah's stomach twisted in knots. Despair stabbed at her like a knife. She couldn't help but believe something awful between her and Rocco was on the horizon and it was because of her mother.

Even with the difficulties her mother had been causing, she'd enjoyed staying with him. They'd gotten on well. The time had come for her to live back at her place full-time, however. If their time together hadn't been marred by her mother's abysmal behavior, Hannah wanted to suggest they try living together. Now she'd have to wait for a better time to broach the subject.

She checked the time on her phone and stood. They needed to get going so she could stop at her place and get ready for her workday. "Let me get my things and I'll help with the dishes before we head out."

Rocco stood and shook his head. "It's no problem. Take your time. There's not much to do here. I'll take care of it," he replied with little emotion.

Not wanting to end their time together on a low note, she smiled as brightly as she could and kissed him on the cheek. "Thanks, I'll just be a minute." She hurried to his bedroom nearly in tears. Shit.

After placing her clothes and toiletries in her travel bag, she took a slow glance around the room as if trying to memorize it all. Her stomach sank at the prospect of never returning to Rocco's place again.

Her ringing phone startled her. She gazed down and frowned, debating whether to answer. After taking a deep fortifying breath, she connected the call. "Hello, Mother."

"Hannah, you really should have let Richard take you back home. He's heartbroken, you know. The way that Marine forbid him from coming to see you while you recuperated from your accident. It's not right." Was her mother fucking kidding?

"I told you not to call him that. And *I* didn't want Richard here. It had nothing to do with Rocco. Dad and Eric were here for dinner last night and we had such a nice time. *You* should've been here too. How do you think that made me feel? Made Rocco feel?" Was her mother this dense or just cold-hearted, mean-spirited, and self-serving to her core? It didn't matter which because she wasn't having any of it.

"This game you've been playing to make Richard

jealous, it's got to stop. You've had your fun, made your point. *Richard's* your future, not some Marine," her mother continued as if they were having this conversation for the first time.

"I told you not to call him that! What the hell is wrong with you? Richard isn't *anything* to me. Just a business associate I have to tolerate and that's it. If you think he's *that* wonderful, *you* fucking marry him then." Hannah disconnected the call and threw her phone against the wall, her blood boiling. She didn't even get the satisfaction of watching it shatter due to the rugged, protective case it was in.

Rocco sighed and shook his head from the bedroom door, obviously having heard her side of the conversation, and her heart sank. She'd been so incensed she hadn't heard him approach.

He picked up her phone from the floor and handed it back to her, his face tight. "Ready?"

No, she wasn't ready. Once she walked out the door, she knew in her heart it would be for the last time. She knew Rocco well enough to know what he was thinking. And even though she hated it with everything she was, she understood his perspective. She didn't blame him, even though she wished things were different.

"Yes," she croaked out, the fight gone.

She followed behind him as he carried her bag. Always the gentleman. They rode the elevator down to the lobby in silence. A first for them since they'd met. The awkward silence made her soul ache.

After making sure she was buckled in securely in the passenger seat of his truck, she endured the grueling short drive to her condo. She breathed deeply, trying to keep her stomach from roiling, her heart from breaking. At least not in front of him. She had her pride.

He turned to her after he parked near her building. Her rental car was in her assigned underground space.

"She's right. You know?"

Hannah shook her head. "No, she's not."

"We started this to make him jealous. It worked. You tried to tell me and Joe it was a stupid idea and we didn't listen. We let things go too far. I blame myself. I should've known better."

"I love you." She sounded pathetic even to herself. "That's all that should matter."

"I love you, too. Honestly, I do. But this situation with your mother, I just can't. I can't be the reason for all the tension and arguments. You can understand that, right?"

Hannah nodded. She understood completely but hated it nonetheless. "I can. But I'll talk to her and Richard and put an end to this. I promise. Just give me a chance to make things right."

"I think you'll see she's right. I don't really fit in your world. Your circle. That became pretty clear when we visited your grandmother."

Was he kidding? "I can't afford the mansions my step-grandfather builds either. It doesn't mean I shouldn't visit them. I thought we all had a nice visit."

He sighed. "We did. That's why I cooked breakfast for everyone during the weekend we were there. I'm in the way. Even if it's not Richard, there's someone who's more appropriate. Someone who fits in with your family. Who doesn't create friction and conflict."

She felt tears well up and unbuckled her seat belt. His mind was made up. She wasn't about to beg him to stay with her. "Well, you've got it all figured out, don't you? Thanks for the ride." She got out, slammed the passenger side door closed, and grabbed her bag from the backseat.

"Hannah, don't be that way," she heard him call out as she walked away, head held high and tears streaming down her face. She felt the weight of his stare behind her as she let herself inside her building.

Hannah tossed her bag on the ground next to her front door after entering her condo unit. She locked up and glanced around. Everything was as she'd left it five days before. Now, though, it felt like a tomb.

Miserable and alone, she threw herself on her couch and let her tears fall unchecked until she had none left. She dialed the one person she'd always been able to count on since she was five years old.

"Hey, hon! Back at your place safe and sound?" Joe's cheery greeting brought back a flood of tears.

"Rocco just broke things off. What do I do now?"

Chapter Ten

A week after Rocco had torn Hannah's heart to shreds, she was busy at Cucina Antonetti's in Barrington, overseeing a corporate dinner and celebration for Abbott Labs. Executives and many of those involved in creating several of their recently FDA-approved antibiotics were in attendance. From what she understood, they were also honoring some of their best salespeople. In her current emotional state, celebrating was the furthest thing from her mind. She'd been on autopilot the last seven days.

She observed the celebration attendees mingle and enjoy passed appetizers. Just because she was miserable didn't mean everyone else had to be. She stood by as Gino Antonetti, Carlo's second younger brother, approached her with Joe right behind him. Chastising herself for her pity party, considering Gino had recently lost his wife and infant son, she plastered on a smile. *My breakup is nothing compared to losing a spouse and child.*

He offered her a slight smile. "Dinner service can begin whenever they're ready."

"I sampled a few bites in the kitchen. Delicious as usual," Joe stated. She needed to get herself together. Joe had been a trouper since her devastating breakup, so she needed to step it up. She was a professional, regardless of the shambles her personal life was in.

"Thank you, Gino. Joe, can you please tell the CEO we'll start dinner service in ten minutes? That'll give everyone a chance to freshen up their drinks and use the restroom." It should be plenty of time for the enthusiastic group.

"Of course, hon." Dutiful as ever, Joe set out to

rally the troops in preparation for dinner.

Gino nodded. "Thanks, Hannah. I'll let the wait staff know. I'll check back shortly to make sure everything is running smoothly."

Gino took his leave and Hannah grinned as Abbott employees scurried around after their CEO informed them they had ten minutes to prepare for dinner. She watched as Joe chuckled and rejoined her at the banquet room's entry doors. They both stepped aside, leaving room for attendees to exit and re-enter easily.

She spotted Richard and his crew filming the frenzy. It would make for some fun viewing later on, she was sure. Luckily for Richard, he'd had the good sense to steer clear of her after she'd told her mother she and Rocco were over and if she *dared* to ever bring up her and Richard getting together again, she'd quit on the spot.

Hannah must've been convincing as she and her mother had barely spoken since that conversation a week ago. The truth was she planned on resigning after Luke Stryker's wedding in two weeks. She wouldn't let Darren Stryker or his family down. He had enough to deal with after his pancreatic cancer diagnosis and surgery.

What would she do *after* Hailey's? She wasn't sure. Throughout her event planning career, she'd been courted by many other firms. She had numerous connections and if she chose to continue in event planning, she doubted it would take long to secure another position. The question was—did she *want* to? *No. I don't.*

She startled when Joe spoke. "Hannah, you with us?"

She laughed at herself and nodded. "Sorry. What did you say?"

"I said we should take our seats for dinner." Joe

made a show of extending his arm to escort her to their table. The same table they would share with Richard and his crew. She'd had no appetite all week, and no desire to sit across from Richard and share a meal.

"Would you mind if I stepped outside for a little bit? I need some fresh air. To clear my head. I won't be long. I promise not to miss dinner." She hoped he didn't give her a hard time. He'd been supportive during the last several days, but she didn't want to push her luck. They were working an event. They were supposed to be a team.

Joe kissed her cheek and smiled warmly at her. She sighed in relief.

"Of course. Take your time. I've got everything under control. If you want to duck out early, go ahead. You know, this is a rather tame event. Having both of us here might be overkill."

While she agreed with Joe's assessment, she wasn't about to shirk her responsibilities. "I'm not going to leave early. I just need a few minutes, that's all."

She gave him a quick hug and ducked outside, taking a seat on one of the guest benches placed around the front of the property, perfectly positioned under a tree. Though it was the third week in August, it wasn't sweltering like it had been the day she'd gotten into the car accident. Shivering at the memories, she rolled her shoulders and tried to put those thoughts aside.

Restaurant customers happily came and went as she took a "time out" from her duties inside. When she spotted her new red, fully loaded Cadillac CT6 sedan Platinum, she smiled. At least she had a ride of her *own* choosing which she loved and felt safe in, even if she was alone now. Rocco had introduced her to the car in the first place, but that didn't matter. This one was *hers*.

Her stomach knotted when Richard sat down on

her bench. Why wouldn't he leave her the hell alone? At least he hadn't sidled up too close. *That* she wouldn't have tolerated for a second.

He'd received plenty of attention from several of the female celebration attendees and restaurant staff. Why he continued to play this game with her, she didn't know.

Her hands clenched and she took a deep cleansing breath. She refused to lose it at an event. "Shouldn't you be inside filming and taking shots?" She didn't have the patience or will to deal with him. She made to stand, but he reached out, not touching her, but gesturing for her to stay.

"My guys have everything covered. Please don't run off. I just want to talk to you. You don't have to say anything, just listen." Richard leaned back on the bench, a casual, non-threatening air about him.

Not sure if she could trust him, she remained on alert. She didn't say anything, hoping he'd move things along so she could return inside. The evening couldn't end soon enough.

"First, I'm so sorry for losing my cool at Grace of God before Jake and Cassie's wedding. You've got to know I'd never intentionally hurt you. I'm a lot of things, but I'm not *that* guy." Richard's shoulders dropped with a sigh and he shook his head unhappily.

Rubbing her eyes, feeling physically drained, she believed him. As upset as she'd been about their altercation that afternoon, she doubted he'd truly meant to hurt her. "I know."

With a relieved expression on his face, he continued. "I should have never encouraged our mothers' ridiculous idea of pushing us together. I'm sorry for not putting a stop to their plan sooner. I knew from the start we didn't have a real future together. Not personally, at least."

She'd known it all along too, but hearing him say it surprisingly stung. "Gee, you really know how to charm a girl don't, you?"

He chuckled. "God, I'm fucking this up. Sorry. Again. Not that you don't deserve love, Hannah, you do. You're an amazing woman. Be honest. There was nothing between us. Not romantically, anyway."

She let out a deep sigh. He was right. There was nothing. Not even the tiniest spark. "I know. You're right."

"Not like with you and Rocco. Damn."

She felt a smile tug at her lips. Even though her heart was battered and bruised, she loved the man. "So, we actually made you jealous?"

He scoffed. "Are you kidding? Hell, yeah you did. Not because I wanted you, no offense, but because I wanted what you both had. It was obvious to whoever saw you together you had something special. You can't just throw it away. Not because of our mothers. Not for *any* reason."

She couldn't believe what she was hearing. Richard was on her and Rocco's side in all of this? "I don't know what to say."

When he placed her hand in his, she didn't pull away. He was offering comfort and friendship, and she needed it. "He was right when he told me to be a man and make my way to Hollywood on my own instead of on your backs. He's not right about letting you go. Patty's a tough one. I get that. She's dealing with what I think is a lot of personal bullshit after too many years, so I can understand him not wanting to get stuck in the middle. But you've got to fight for the two of you."

She squeezed his hand, unsure of what she should do. "He seemed so sure splitting up was the right thing to do."

"Then you have a little work to do. Make him understand what you two have is special and not even Patty is a good enough reason to throw it all away. After I have an honest conversation with my mom, Patty will back off. If they really want to join forces, let the lawyers make sure they're both legally protected."

Hannah gasped. Who was this man? Not the Richard she'd been dealing with for so long. "That's exactly what I thought all along. Let the lawyers hash out all the details. Why are you being so nice?" What was his angle? She wasn't used to this version of him.

He chuckled, kissed her hand tenderly, and let it go. "Because it's the right thing to do and contrary to popular belief, I'm *not* a dick. And after you settle things with Rocco, you can make plans for life *after* Hailey's. I'm guessing you're going to resign after the Stryker wedding, right?"

Hannah's mouth fell open. Was he a mind reader? "Yes, that's my plan. Darren and his family deserve our best and I won't let him down."

Richard's expression turned somber. Darren's cancer diagnosis and retirement from the Cobras' organization had been a shock. It was true what people said, bad things can happen to good people.

"We won't, either. And after the wedding, you're going to buy Blumenthal's and start your own couture bridal gown line. Because it's what you're meant to do." He nodded with certainty and smiled warmly.

"My bliss," she whispered. "But I don't have a clue about starting my own line. All I have are my designs." And more importantly, she was terrified of striking out on her own. Professionally, all she'd ever known was her mother's company. *How pathetic.*

"Let Nora and Cora help you. And what about the

177

connections at design school? You can do this. Don't make excuses. You've got this."

She wanted so much for what Richard was saying to be true. To believe in herself like she should. Like Richard did, and Joe, and her brother—and Rocco who'd pleaded with her to seriously consider Nora and Cora's offer to buy their bridal salon. That conversation seemed like eons ago.

She quickly glanced at her watch. "The Twisted Tea Society meeting starts in a half an hour," she mumbled and stood. Richard followed suit.

"What's the Twisted Tea Society?"

Her hand flew to her mouth. Had she said that out loud? Should she tell him? He looked down at her with a curious but amused expression on his face. He'd been so sweet. So supportive. She supposed it wouldn't hurt to tell him. They were adults, right? Hell, they'd slept together, for Pete's sake.

"It's an erotic book and social club for women." That was the truth. Just not all of it.

Ever the shrewd observer, he studied her for a moment. "And?"

She huffed and rolled her eyes. "And the women are served refreshments from male servers wearing only bowties." Her face heated and she glanced away.

His mouth fell open and then he started laughing. "Is that so? And I'm guessing a certain Italian, badass Marine is a server?"

She scowled at him and narrowed her eyes. Then she began laughing herself. "Maybe." She headed back toward Abbott's banquet room with Richard in tow. She needed to tell Joe she was leaving and try to figure out a game plan on the drive over to Club Envidious's building and a "certain Italian, badass Marine server."

"So, is there a men's version of this club? You

know, with naked women serving the men?" he whispered so guests and wait staff couldn't overhear them.

She shrugged and grinned up at him. "Sorry. You'll have look to Club Envidious for that. And I'll tell you all about it tomorrow."

After a quick conversation with Joe and Abbott's CEO, Richard escorted her to her car. He hugged her quickly before opening her car door for her. "It's going to be fine. You can make him see reason."

She sure as hell hoped so. If she couldn't, she'd still resign from Hailey's after the Stryker wedding and regroup. *I'm down, but not out.*

"Thanks, Richard. I appreciate it."

He closed the car door once she was comfortably seated inside. "I like us much better as friends and not enemies, don't you?" His smile was warm and seemed sincere.

She couldn't agree more. "Absolutely. Here goes nothing."

Pulling into the Club Envidious parking about forty-five minutes later, Hannah's stomach did flips. Not having formed a true game plan for what she believed would be a confrontation with Rocco, she wondered if she should wait until she felt more confident about facing him about their future.

Needing a little courage, she called Joe, hoping he could spare a minute to talk to her. Just to give her a little nudge in the right direction.

"No second-guessing yourself. Get in there and talk to him," Richard said into her ear, the sneak.

"That's right. There's no turning back now," Joe added in the background.

"Come on, Hannah. You've got his." Grateful for the new direction her relationship with Richard had taken, she smiled to herself and nodded. She did. This conversation would most likely be the first of several she'd have with Rocco. She'd make him understand they were worth fighting for. That Patty wasn't an issue. Not one that mattered. She'd gone too far, meddling in their relationship and wouldn't be allowed to do it again.

"You're right. I do. Thanks." Feeling hopeful, but cautiously optimistic, she exited the car and took a deep breath. She squared her shoulders and strode to the lobby door with a renewed sense of purpose. Dressed in one of her favorite pink dresses, a form-fitting, button-down bodycon with a flirty amount cleavage, she knew she looked attractive. She'd take whatever advantage she could to get him to at least *listen* to reason.

A bundle of nerves and emotions, she strode to the Twisted Tea Society's meeting room. Praying the right words would come to her when she finally saw Rocco, she entered the meeting room and sought him out.

It took her but a moment to spot Rocco preparing a member's plate in the kitchenette area. Her heart skipped a beat even though they weren't together. She watched in fascination as his pecs and biceps flexed while performing his server duties. Wearing only a burgundy bowtie, he was much too distracting this way and her body reacted as it always did. He needed to be dressed for their conversation so they could be on equal footing.

"Hey, Hannah." Leah was seated in her usual spot with her feet soaking in what she knew was a warm, lavender-scented footbath.

Everyone in the room turned and looked at her, but she was only interested in one person taking notice. When their eyes met, his widened in surprise, then turned lustful as his gaze boldly flicked to her breasts and swept down her body to her pretty, open-toed pink heels.

A thrill pulsed through her and her nipples tingled in response. She chastised herself for feeling aroused. Now wasn't the time. Ignoring Leah and everyone else, with her head held high, Hannah sauntered to her target. One stubborn, too handsome for his own good, Italian Marine.

"We need to talk." She placed her clutch on the granite countertop and folded her arms under her chest, with Rocco watching intently.

He lifted a brow, studying her as if contemplating what she might do next. *Good. Let him wonder.* The way she felt, she wasn't sure what she might do. He had her that out of sorts.

"There isn't anything left to say. You shouldn't have come here tonight." He crossed his arms and stood firm.

Hannah stood her ground, well aware they were now the center of attention in the room. She didn't care, this was too important.

"I disagree, since you did most of the talking a week ago. I have some things *I* need to say. *Now.*" Did he have to be so difficult?

She panicked when he came around the counter to face her directly. A smug look on his face. So, he wanted to play dirty? It would be the most daring thing she'd ever done, but she could play dirty, too. Their relationship, their future was worth it.

"Go ahead. Talk," he said with a smirk.

Her traitorous body trembled with arousal. Her pulse raced and she went hot and slick. Mindless with lust for a moment, she forced herself to focus on the reason for her visit.

"Please put something on," she pleaded.

Rocco shrugged with a knowing smile. "I'm comfortable just the way I am. Something wrong?"

That was enough. He asked for it. "Not at all." She quickly undressed before she lost her nerve.

"What the hell are you doing?" he asked as he nervously glanced at the other servers.

She heard some of the members snicker and felt the servers' stares but she couldn't let that deter her. Her body trembled as she stood in front of a now-panicked Rocco. To her surprise, she felt free and empowered.

"There. Now we're on equal footing." She stood tall and proud while he seemed ready to have a panic attack.

"Hey, honey, I'll wear whatever you want and talk with you all night long." That came from Brody Dobbs, the mountain man. The same man she knew Rocco was jealous of, though he needn't be.

"You stay the fuck away from her, Brody," Rocco snapped.

Brody's eyes narrowed and she took a step back. "Or what?"

Someone cleared their throat, loudly, and she turned in the direction it came from. *Shit.* Kyle Asher stood in the doorway, with a grimace on his face and fury in his eyes. She couldn't help but feel desirable when he gave her a quick, but lustful once-over. She thought she may have heard Rocco growl. *Good.*

"Or not a fucking thing. Rocco, Hannah—in my office. *Now.*"

"Damn it, Hannah. Put your clothes back on. You're being ridiculous." Rocco picked her clothes and shoes up off the floor and handed them to her.

"*You* don't get to tell me what to do. I'll get dressed when *I* want to and not a minute sooner." She poked him in his warm, solid chest and took her clothes from him. Adding her clutch to the pile of clothes, she turned and headed toward the conference room door. She was met with cheers and applause from the ladies in the room and whistles from the men. Her heart raced as she followed Kyle to his office down the hall. She was angry and exhilarated at the same time.

"God damn it, Hannah," Rocco called out behind her.

She entered a rather ordinary-looking office with a cherry executive desk and dark-brown leather accent furniture. After dropping her clothing on the floor, she took a seat in a comfortable chair in front of Kyle's desk, crossing her legs at the knee. She sat up proudly, placing her hands on the chair's armrests.

Rocco stormed in behind her and slammed the office door closed. "Kyle, will you tell her to put her fucking clothes on?" He took a seat in the guest chair beside her and ran a hand through his thick, dark brown hair. He had such soft hair, she'd missed running her own hands through it.

Kyle smiled wide, showing off his dimples and white teeth. He was such a handsome man and she felt absolutely nothing, romantically speaking, toward him at all.

Kyle winked at her and she giggled. "And why the hell would I do that? I happen to like the view from this side of my desk—very much."

She noticed Rocco clench his hands and lean forward in his chair, glaring at Kyle.

"Stop looking at her, Kyle. I mean it."

"Like Hannah already told you, you don't get to tell me what to do. This is *my* fucking building and I can do or say whatever the fuck I want. Got it? Now, what the fuck is going on?"

Kyle folded his arms and waited for one of them to say something.

Rocco threw his hands up and then turned to her

with a softer, gentler expression on his distressed face. "Please put your clothes on," he pleaded calmly.

Hannah shrugged, having a little fun at Rocco's expense. He deserved it for putting her through hell the last several days. "Why? *You're* not dressed. No big deal, right?"

"That's different," he blurted out.

She gasped. Now, *she* was pissed. "If you dare say something as sexist as it's different because I'm a woman, you'll be sorry."

Rocco sighed and his shoulders slumped. "Damn it. And Kyle, will you stop looking at her, for shit's sake?"

Kyle narrowed his eyes and clasped his hands together on his desk. That gave Hannah a moment of pause. "How about I do this instead? The Twisted Tea Society is a place for the women to relax and feel comfortable. To be pampered. What I just walked in on was neither relaxing nor comfortable. So I'm going to revoke Hannah's membership and fire you as a server if you don't tell me what the fuck is going on. *Now*."

Hannah didn't want either of those two things to happen. She needed to get the situation under control and fast. "Rocco broke things off last week and I came by because I wanted to say a few things I should have said last week. He was being a stubborn jerk and I'm sorry things escalated the way they did."

Kyle's eyes widened as he glanced at Rocco. "You *dumped* Hannah? You're shitting me, right?" Rocco remained silent, staring Kyle down. "Idiot." Kyle sighed and rubbed his eyes. "Hannah, tell this idiot what you came to say. I had no idea he let you go."

So, he hadn't said anything? She wondered if that meant something. She'd much rather have their conversation in private, but at this point, she'd take what she could get and didn't want to press her luck with the Texas Dom and club owner. He seemed angry and frustrated enough.

Taking a deep breath, she hoped she could make Rocco see reason, or at least reconsider breaking things off for good. "When you dropped me off last week, you said a lot of things. I was too heartbroken to respond like I should have, but I'm settled now. A lot of what you said was just plain wrong."

Rocco made to speak, but Kyle put his hand up. "Don't say a fucking word."

She smiled and nodded. "First, I understand your feelings in regard to my mother. I don't blame you, but it's partially my fault. I should have stood up to her a long time ago. That's on me. She's got issues she needs to work on that she hasn't—and that's on *her*. I'm leaving the firm after Luke and Abbey's wedding."

"Hannah," Rocco said.

She put a hand up this time. "No. The firm is *her* dream, not mine. You were right about that. *Only* that. All your talk about fitting in and circles."

Closing her eyes a moment to gather her thoughts, she prayed for the words that would resonate with him. Aware she had an audience with Kyle, she wanted to have her say and let Rocco think about what he truly wanted. She was certain about where she stood in all this.

"The circle you don't think you fit in isn't even mine. It belongs to my family. I just maneuver around in it. The circle I felt most a part of was—ours. The circle that includes Joe. That has you and your brother in a constant debate over which one of you is better looking. I've got news for you. The two of you are like bookends. You're a little rougher around the edges but that's not surprising. Your life experiences have been much different than Max's."

Kyle leaned back in his executive chair and gestured for her to continue, an approving smile on his face. She smiled back, grateful for his understanding and support.

"The circle that includes that enormous family of yours. They were so wonderful a few days after my accident when we went to your *Zia* Alba's for the coq au vin throw-down."

"How they were able to choose Max's version over yours, I don't know since both of your dishes were exceptional. Since Antonetti's wants him joining you at the restaurant some days, I think the cooking debate is settled too." She turned to Kyle and shook her head. "You really dropped the ball on that one, Kyle. You know that right?"

Kyle glanced at Rocco and then back at her. He sighed and shrugged. "I know," he finally admitted.

"I fit with *your* family. *We* fit with them. I know you think so, too. And your American family—Heath, Leah, Luke, and the rest of them. And especially Beverly and Ruth." She giggled, thinking back to their first date at Jake and Cassie's and the condoms Grandma Ruth had given her. The ones Rocco refused to use.

"And yes, this all started as the 'make Richard jealous plan,' but it turned into something amazing. At least for me it did. I thought it had for you, too. Did you tell your therapist you broke things off with me?"

He shook his head. Having Rocco sitting so close but closed off was awkward and uncomfortable. Maybe confronting him hadn't been a good idea after all. Maybe he'd been looking for a way out all along and had used her mother as an excuse. The thought had her stomach knotting.

Feeling self-conscious now, she gathered her

things and stood, her dress partially covering her front. "Life is full of conflicts. Even with my mother out of the equation. Maybe our relationship meant more to me than it did to you. Maybe I love you more than you love me. If that's the case, I'll have to live with it. But if I'm wrong and you care—then stop being such a coward. Get your shit together, *Italiano*. *Marine*. Get your head out of your ass. And don't take too long. Not because I'm going back to Richard. That will *never* happen. But because I deserve someone who recognizes how amazing I am and doesn't have to think about or decide whether or not they want to be with me. They know with certainty."
****

Rocco sat in silence after Hannah walked out the door, softly clicking it closed. He'd expected her to slam it, but she'd maintained her cool. As mortified and jealous as he'd been that the men had seen her luscious body, he was so fucking proud that she'd had the courage and confidence to strip bare in the first place. *He'd* helped her feel comfortable in her own skin.

His own stubbornness had brought her here. He'd been miserable the past week without her but believed he'd been justified in breaking things off, although it tore at his heart.

When someone knocked at Kyle's door, hope bloomed it was Hannah, while he was still at odds about what to do next. Or if he should do anything at all.

"Hey, it's Heath. Can I come in?"

"Come on in," Kyle answered.

"Is there a reason Hannah's walking around carrying her clothes instead of wearing them?" He sat in the chair Hannah had just vacated and waited for an answer.

Jealousy bubbled up again and his temper simmered. "Did you look at her?"

He and Kyle both chuckled, but Rocco didn't find his question funny in the slightest. He didn't like other men looking at her. As stupid as it sounded, there it was. She was a precious treasure that until a week ago had been his. Only his.

"She saw me and said 'Hello,' right before she ducked into the ladies' room. What was I supposed to do? She was mostly covered in front." He shrugged. "Can't say that about the back though. Sorry, brother."

Rocco growled, ready for a fight but decided it wasn't worth it. Heath was his brother-in-arms. Had saved his life. Hand-to-hand combat with him was no way to express his gratitude.

"What's going on? Leah came and got me in the lounge. Said there was some sort of naked showdown." Heath glanced between him and Kyle, confusion etched on his face.

Kyle typed something on his cell phone and smiled. "*Idiota* or *stupido* over here dumped Hannah last week and she came by to try and talk some sense to his sorry…" Kyle typed something else into his phone and nodded when he'd found what he was looking for. "*Culo.*"

Heath laughed and joined in Kyle's lame attempts to insult him in Italian, typing away on his phone. After a beat, seemingly stunned, he looked up and at Rocco. "What? You dumped Hannah? When the fuck did *that* happen? Why didn't you say something?"

Shit. He wasn't out to hurt Heath's feelings. They were incredibly close. Confronting the enemy together in battle did that. Surviving combat together did that.

Rocco raked his hand through his hair. He'd barely slept in the last week since ending things. He was exhausted and confused. "Because. That's why. Fuck. I didn't know what to say, all right? This shit with her mother came to a head last week as I was getting ready to bring her back to her place after she'd spent a few days with me after the car accident. I didn't want to bother you with my shit since everything with Leah was going so well."

Heath scoffed. "I have no clue how things are going to turn out with Leah. If things go to shit, I don't care what anyone says—my friendship with Jake and his family will probably be ruined. But I can't let her go. I can't believe you were able to let Hannah go, brother."

"I didn't fucking want to! Her mother doesn't want me around and maybe she's right." Hell, his own mother hadn't thought much of him either and had just abandoned him and his baby brother. Even after he'd suffered through all the physical abuse trying to protect her from his father's wrath while she was pregnant with Massimo.

"That's just a bullshit excuse. What did she mean about the 'make Richard jealous plan'? Who the fuck is Richard?" Kyle asked.

"Hannah's asshole or *stronzo* of an ex. Richard Hayes of Hayes Studios. The mothers want them together and they were for a little while, but he treated her like shit. Then he hurt her the day of Jake's wedding—"

"Hurt her how?" Kyle and Heath demanded.

He grabbed his arm and demonstrated. "They got into an argument in Fellowship Hall and he grabbed her. *Hard.* Left finger-shaped bruises on her arm."

"Fuck. Is he still able to walk?" Kyle asked in disgust. Knowing how protective the men of Envy and Rapture, Texas, were of their women, Kyle's response wasn't surprising.

"Did you shoot the fucker?" Heath felt for his small folding tactical knife over his pants. He'd carried it with him since being discharged from the service. It served as a comfort for him.

"Hannah wouldn't let me. Begged me not to hurt him. So Joe and I came up with the idea of acting like she was my date to the wedding. Pretending to be into each other and shit to make him jealous for being such a dick to her. A lame revenge plan. It was stupid, I know."

"But you weren't acting, were you? You wanted her from the get-go." Heath knew him better than anyone. In some ways, better than his own family.

Rocco nodded, defeated. "No. I wasn't acting at all. Brody called me out on it. About being jealous over her. I've felt in over my head with her sometimes. Probably like you do with Leah."

They all sat silently for a moment, each seeming lost in their own thoughts. He wasn't sure what the hell to do. Should he have mentioned their breakup to his therapist? Probably. Why hadn't he? Because he didn't want to be convinced to reconcile with her. Because he believed he might not be the best choice for her in the long run.

"She's right. You better figure your shit out. Fast. You can't let her get away." Kyle looked at Heath for affirmation.

"Kyle's right, brother. Jealousy plan or not, you're lucky to have found her. You can't just throw it away so easily, can you? As unsure as I am about Leah, I know *I* can't."

Rocco hadn't wanted to. He'd never felt more content or satisfied in his life. Overall, he was managing his PTSD much better, using some of the non-medical treatments his brother had emailed to him. He was grateful the frequency of his nightmares had been significantly reduced. Although it was early on, he believed therapy would be beneficial but was unsure it would make a difference where Hannah was concerned.

"I didn't *want* to give her up. It was one of the hardest things I've ever done and I've felt like shit since I did."

"What *do* you want, then?" Heath asked in all seriousness.

"I want to feel confident we should be together. That it's the right thing. For Hannah especially." Rocco wanted guarantees but knew that was impossible. Life didn't come with guarantees. You did the best you could and hoped it was enough.

Kyle grunted. "I suggest you get your shit together, just like she told you before she left. And don't take too long. She's too special to be left alone for long."

He blew out a frustrated breath. He hated the thought of Hannah with someone else. Didn't know how he'd survive if Hannah truly moved on. Wasn't sure he wanted to.

"I know. You're both right." At a loss for further conversation about the mess his personal life was in, he left Kyle's office and returned to his apartment.

Standing alone in his kitchen, still only wearing his bowtie, he sighed at the stark loneliness that consumed him. His place felt lifeless without Hannah there. Everything was less without her. Nodding to himself, he acknowledged it was time to figure his shit out. Fast.

Chapter Eleven

The Saturday after Hannah's visit to the Twisted Tea Society, Rocco sat at his brother's deck table while Max grilled up lunch for them. It was a gorgeous afternoon, closing in on the end of August, but Rocco was too lost in his own thoughts to pay much attention.

He glanced down at his sleeping nephew in his portable carrier and smiled. Not for the first time, jealousy gnawed at his gut. Regretting he hadn't apparently gotten Hannah pregnant the night of her accident. In his mind, it would have made things a lot simpler for him.

Sydney stepped outside carrying burger buns and other condiments with a frowning Adrianna following closely behind. His niece wore the cutest little pink cartoon-adorned leggings and a matching t-shirt. His heart ached. Pink. Hannah's favorite color which he'd grown so fond of himself. She took a seat beside him and pouted.

"I like it when Anna sits next to me too, *Zio*." She looked up at him with watery eyes and his gut clenched. It was *his* fault Hannah wasn't joining them and *his* fault his niece was on the verge of tears.

Max placed a platter of grilled cheeseburgers on the center of the table and sighed as he sat down. Sydney sat down beside him and took ahold of his hand and squeezed.

"Sweetie, *Zio* already told you Hannah had to work, remember?" And it was also because of *him* his brother was now lying for him to his daughter.

Adrianna nodded sadly and slumped her shoulders. "Maybe she could come next Saturday?"

Adrianna's hopeful expression nearly did Rocco in.

"I'm sure *Zio* will check with her and see if she can, okay? Roc, you mind preparing a plate for her?"

That he could do, with pleasure and without guilt. "Of course." He busied himself preparing Adrianna's burger with a slice of tomato the way she liked it and cut it in half. He added some potato salad, corn and avocado salad, minus the avocado chunks and set it down in front of his niece, hoping she'd perk up a bit.

Her sparkling blue eyes greeted his and he sighed in relief. Her precious little girl's grin tugged at his heart. "Thanks, *Zio*."

"You're welcome. *Mangia* before your burger gets cold, all right?" She nodded and began eating after he removed the other half of her burger and took a huge animated bite, causing her to giggle. *She's going to be fine.*

As they all settled down to lunch, Rocco felt a bit more settled, but not much. He'd spoken to his therapist since seeing Hannah. Explained to him what had happened the morning he'd brought her back to her place and her subsequent visit to the Twisted Tea Society last Wednesday.

Logically, he understood the physical abuse he'd endured as a boy hadn't been his fault. He'd been an innocent thrust into an untenable situation before his grandparents had intervened. The verbal abuse his mother had inflicted had been more difficult to move past.

He understood his mother had also been abused and traumatized by his father, causing her to lash out at him. But being repeatedly called useless and worthless, even knowing that, still hurt and had stayed with him. Obviously for far too long. The friction with Hannah's mother had brought his past hurts to the forefront. None of it Hannah's fault, just like it wasn't his. *What a fucking mess.*

"So, babe, when do you think you'll cook with Rocco again at Antonetti's?" Sydney's gracious smile brought him out of his momentary funk. He needed to get his head back in the game. Enjoy the afternoon with the people who meant the most to him, other than Hannah. Christ, he missed her.

He'd wondered that himself. He'd called Max as a last resort when Chef Rudy hadn't been feeling well and Max had come right over. To say the Moretti brothers had been a hit as a cooking duo would have been an understatement. They'd worked together like a well-oiled machine even with frequent trips to the dining room for pictures with happy, well-fed diners. Eli and Eason included. They'd kidded about being the co-Presidents of their fan club.

Max's frown had Rocco wondering what the hell was troubling his normally good-natured, upbeat baby brother.

"Yeah, Daddy? You looked so good in your cook's hat!" Adrianna giggled as she finished her lunch, seemingly over missing Hannah for the moment. He, however, was not.

Max gazed at his wife with such affection it made Rocco's heart clench. He'd shared those kinds of looks with Hannah so many times. Max turned to him and shrugged. What the hell?

"I don't know. Are you sure they want me back? I wouldn't be stepping on any toes?"

Was his brother serious? They were anxious to have Max back, in fact. He couldn't imagine why he was hesitant. He'd seemed in his element cooking and working beside him that night.

Just then, his nephew let out a wail the entire

neighborhood could probably hear. "Hey, little man, it's all right," Rocco cooed to the baby, to no avail.

"He needs Mommy, don't you, MJ?" Sydney lifted the unhappy infant out of his carrier and headed inside the house with Adrianna close behind.

"Hey, Syd, no need to rush back out. We'll take care of cleaning up," Max called out.

Rocco sighed and blew out a frustrated breath. That was code for he wanted to talk in private. *Shit*. He may as well get it over with.

"What?"

Max sighed and shook his head. The disappointment on his brother's face racked him with guilt.

"Really? Like you don't know what," Max snapped.

"I know," Rocco conceded.

Max scoffed at him. "Do you? Do you *really*? I had to lie to my baby girl because of you. Because of your bullshit issues."

Rocco bolted out of his chair, ready to get the fuck out of there. His brother was pushing his luck. He'd lived a charmed life compared to him. Not that he resented him for it. But their lives were completely different, in almost every way.

"No, you don't, man," Max said, getting out of his own chair. "Don't you fucking leave. We're having this out, once and for all." He got right up in his personal space and shot him a venomous look.

Rocco felt overheated. His breaths came short and fast. His brother didn't know what he was doing. This was a bad idea. A very bad idea.

"Don't push me, Massimo." Rocco growled and poked him in the chest. His brother shook and took a step back but held his ground. Rocco respected that. He wouldn't be so easily intimidated.

"You won't hurt me," his brother said, voice cracking.

"You sure about that?" Rocco stepped up so close to Max their noses nearly touched. "Because you're really pissing me the fuck off right now."

"I—I'm sure. You've been protecting me since before I was born. I know everything, Rocco. And it's time for you to stop doing for everyone else and start doing for yourself."

Rocco backed away as if he'd been burned. How did his brother know he'd protected him before he was born? What the fuck was going on?

"It took a lot of pestering, but *Nonno* finally told me how we came to live him and *Nonna*. How he cried the night they came and got us when he gave you a bath after seeing your arms covered in bruises."

Instinctively, he rubbed his arms. He'd tried so hard that night to comfort his grandfather. Lying. Telling him he wasn't hurting. He'd endured endless beatings protecting his pregnant mother and unborn brother. He'd do it again in a heartbeat.

"That's why you got your arms completely inked, isn't it? So you wouldn't see the bruises?"

Rocco nodded. There were times his mind played tricks on him and he saw bruises instead of the magnificent artwork that decorated his arms now, but that didn't happen as often anymore. He leaned against the deck railing, putting much-needed distance between them.

"As decent as they were, you insisted on sleeping next to me those first few months, just to make sure they wouldn't hurt me." Max's tone was now calm and comforting.

"I was scared. I couldn't let anything happen to

you. You were a baby. Innocent." Didn't he understand?

Max threw his hands up and glanced up at the sky. "So were *you*! You weren't much older than Adrianna is now. You were an innocent in everything that went down as much as I was. Only worse, because you can remember. I carried around such guilt for a long time after *Nonno* told me."

Rocco sighed and rubbed his eyes, feeling emotionally drained. Why did his brother feel the need to revisit their shitty beginning? Especially now.

"Look, Matteo was a piece-of-shit drunk and Allegra was abused and traumatized by him, but she could have and should have done better than to just verbally abuse you and then bail on us. You've let the first shitty six years of your life dictate the last thirty, trying to prove you're good enough. Worthy."

Max was right to a certain degree, he supposed. He was working on that in therapy. He loved his family and would always be there for them, no matter what. That would never change. Therapy or not.

"You didn't need to give Syd's parents money for the wedding. You didn't need to send so much money home while you served. I was the one who told *Nonna* to save it all for when you were discharged."

"You're my family. I take care of my family."

"They raised me too, and I take care of mine. And you're mine. So for once, let *me* take care of *you*. Can you do that?"

This was uncharted territory for Rocco. "Why don't you want to come back to the restaurant? Why don't you ever want to hang out with me and Heath and the rest of them? I think Sydney would like the women."

Max shrugged and frowned. "I felt like you should have something that's just yours. Without me tagging along."

His brother really didn't understand him at all. He'd have to help him. "You don't get it. I'm *proud* to have you with me."

Max's eye's widened and glistened. He finally understood. "Okay, then."

"So, how exactly are you going to take care of me?"

Max gestured to the patio table chairs. Rocco waited after they were both seated.

"Just talk to me. Brother to brother. Friend to friend. Can you do that?" Max's hopeful expression made Rocco smile. His brother was a good man. Maybe he'd been unfair all these years. Maybe this conversion was long overdue.

For the next hour, they talked, brother to brother. Friend to friend. That hour proved to be more therapeutic than all the hours of counseling he'd clocked to this point. He'd learned things about his brother he hadn't known and shared things he'd kept close to the vest for years.

Max had felt out of place with Sydney at first, being a computer geek. She'd been a popular cheerleader with jocks pining over her, but in Rocco's opinion, she'd chosen wisely. She was no dumb blonde and Max had fought for his woman, like he was encouraging Rocco to do.

Although his family had been incredibly proud Rocco had decided to serve their country, they'd also been scared to death of losing him in combat. If it hadn't been for Heath, they might have.

"I need to get to know Heath better since he's the reason I still have a brother. Let's set something up soon."

Rocco shared how the first six years of his life had affected him deeply. His self-worth had taken a beating and contributed to his decision to join the Marines. Had he had a death wish? Possibly. But in those moments in Sangin when he believed he might not make it out alive, he knew then he wanted a life worth living. He had that now and Hannah had been the icing on the cake.

He explained how the shit with Richard and Hannah's mother had brought up old insecurities and it had messed with his head. In reality, Hannah's mother had been traumatized as a young girl and could benefit from therapy herself, as well as reuniting with her sober mother after decades of estrangement.

"If Hannah thinks you two fit, that's what matters," Max assured him.

"I know. She told me to get my shit together and to get my head out of my ass. She called me *Italiano* and *Marine*. Really pissed off and naked in Kyle's office."

Max raised a brow.

"Yeah. I didn't like the way Kyle was eyeing her, but I couldn't help but be proud of her, though. She was so shy when we first met. But last week, when she bitched me out, she was confident, fierce ... and angry. It was all my fault, but still."

Max chuckled and shook his head. "I'm sorry, man. I don't understand BDSM."

Rocco waved a hand dismissively. "It doesn't matter. BDSM had nothing to do with her getting undressed. I was being an ass. She asked me to get dressed but I wouldn't."

Max furrowed his brow, presumably contemplating his dilemma with Hannah and what he should do next. "Syd mentioned the bridal gown sketches you showed her that Hannah had drawn. Were you planning something? If you were, now's the time."

Max was right. Rocco pulled his cell phone out of

his jeans pocket and forwarded the sketches to Kyle and fired off a quick text.

Rocco: **Hannah drew these. I could use your help. You know who to send them to. Thx.**

Kyle: **On it. Idiota. Stupido.**

Rocco grunted. Kyle was having a little too much fun with Google Translate at his expense. He glanced at his brother, ready for additional advice.

Max narrowed his eyes, glancing over his face. "What's up with your face? Too lazy to shave?"

Rocco rubbed his stubbled jaw and sighed. "Hannah kind of liked me scruffy, as she calls it. Not shaving for a couple days made me feel closer to her." He knew it sounded lame, but that was how he felt.

His brother seemed to think on it but shook his head. "Save it for the winter. You're getting her back, anyway. Come on, I've got extra razors."

He followed Max to the guest bathroom where he was set up with a razor, shaving cream, and a towel. The house was peaceful, so he assumed Sydney had MJ in hand in the nursery with Adrianna as her attentive little helper.

"What's next after this?" Rocco was surprised he enjoyed being the recipient of advice and assistance for a change. He trusted his brother completely. He knew without a doubt Max had his best interests at heart.

Max leaned against the wall and crossed his arms. "You're not gonna like it, but tough shit. You're gonna confront Patty and claim your woman."

Rocco paused mid-stroke to prevent from nicking himself. Max was right. He didn't like it but knew it was necessary. His future happiness and Hannah's depended on it.

His phone chimed with a text message from the vanity. Max leaned over and read it with a smile on his face.

"It's from Kyle. It says 'Bellatoni's in town Wednesday August 30th, meet at Blumenthal's 10am, don't fuck it up, *idiota*.' That's amazing, it's only a few days away."

"Let's hope Hannah thinks so too." Rocco wiped his clean-shaven face down and examined himself in the mirror. He was presentable.

He gave Joe a quick call and learned Patty and Denton were at Hailey's corporate offices. Joe would meet him there and join him for moral support.

"All right, I'm going to run home and change shirts real quick before I go over there," he said, heading toward the front door.

"Wait a minute. Why?" Max asked, a disapproving look on his face.

Rocco rubbed his arms, hoping his answer was obvious.

Max rolled his eyes. "Does Hannah like your ink?"

Rocco's lips twitched and he nodded. "Yes, a lot. She's always looking at and touching my arms."

Max nodded with satisfaction. "There you go. That's all that matters. You go over there just the way you are. The way *Hannah* likes you."

Not knowing how to express his gratitude, he hugged his little brother until he heard him sniffle. Well, damn. He'd made the man cry. He hadn't meant to do that.

Max laughed nervously and wiped his eyes. "Go on. You've got this."
****

A short while later, Rocco parked at the Regency Towers building in Oak Brook across the street from the Oak Brook Mall. He wanted to collect his thoughts before seeking out Joe and ultimately Patty.

Exiting his truck, he looked up at the white stone building and took a deep breath. This was it. He'd confront Patty and then would be well on his way to getting Hannah back.

He rode the elevator up to the top floor, his stomach in knots. Once he got through the next few stressful minutes, he'd be home free.

Relief flowed through him when the elevator doors opened and a cheerful-looking Joe greeted him. He was dressed in khakis and a white dress shirt, making Rocco feel not so self-conscious.

"Ready?" Joe asked.

Fuck yeah, he was. Hannah had made her feelings clear in Kyle's office. There was nothing left to discuss. He was here to give Patty the memo.

Rocco gestured to Joe. "Lead the way."

He followed Joe with his head held high, passing employees and who he assumed were clients or potential clients on their way to Patty's office. Anxious instead of nervous, he was looking forward to putting this meeting behind him so he could focus his attention on Hannah and their plans for the future.

Joe stopped in front of a door with Patty's name on it and knocked three times. "Patty. It's Joe—and Rocco."

Rocco heard muffled voices from behind the door. "Come on in." He smiled at Denton's invitation to enter. This was going to be interesting.

Joe led them inside Patty's domain. A sense of surprising calm washed over him. He had nothing to fear. He was where he needed to be. Things would work out the way they were supposed to. He'd survived his difficult childhood and Afghanistan for a reason. That reason was Hannah and their future. With a renewed sense of certainty and determination, he shook Denton's extended hand.

Patty's office was as he'd imagined it. Soft pastels, impeccably tidy, with everything from invitation sample books, to silk flowers and favor samples stowed in their proper place. Denton gestured for them to sit.

Patty appeared stunned and tongue-tied. Denton amused. "Good to see you, Rocco. Although I see you're empty-handed. I wouldn't have minded some stuffed chicken parmesan." Denton winked and Rocco chuckled.

"Yes, sir. Message received."

After getting her bearings, Patty cleared her throat. She gave him a quick once-over, lingering over his arms before looking him directly in the eyes. "Did we have an appointment? Are you planning an event?"

His brother was right. The woman needed help. Rather than feel anger toward her, he felt pity. She'd been struggling emotionally for far too long and had taken her issues out on Hannah the most.

"Patty, the reason Rocco is here—" Joe began.

Rocco placed a hand on Joe's shoulder, stopping him. He took a deep breath and glanced at Denton, who nodded and winked. "No, ma'am. I know you don't like me, but Hannah loves me. And as long as she does, I'm not going anywhere."

Patty's mouth fell open and she quickly closed it. "I don't not like you, Rocco. You misunderstand me."

"You just prefer Richard for Hannah. Am I right?"

Joe and Denton both snorted. Patty had the nerve to appear offended. "What? Richard's…"

"An asshole, Trish," Denton snapped while Joe nodded in agreement.

"With all due respect, he's right. Richard's an amazing photographer and videographer, but he has an ugly soul. He's been homophobic toward Joe and physically hurt Hannah."

"What?" Denton and Patty exclaimed.

Damn. He hadn't meant to dredge up those particular details. Only to stake his claim and lay out his plans.

Joe turned to him and nodded. "It's all right, Rocco. Richard's been incredibly insulting to me, *many* times, but it's all right. I've dealt with it."

"It most certainly is *not* all right. You're our second son. That fucker has no right insulting you. *None.* And what the fuck did he do to Hannah? When? Why weren't we told?" Denton was breathing heavily and Patty dabbed at her eyes with a tissue.

Shit. "Apparently, they got into an argument before Jake and Cassie's wedding. She stood up for herself against him and he grabbed her. Hard. Bruised up her arm," Rocco explained as briefly as he could while still providing the essential details.

The color drained from Patty's face and she began shaking. Denton wrapped a comforting arm around her shoulders and held her tight. "And why didn't you put a bullet in the man's skull?"

"What good would Rocco do for Hannah in prison?" Patty asked.

Denton scoffed. "Rocco wouldn't go to prison. You saw the accident footage. Didn't you wonder why everyone stepped aside when he went to the scum that caused the accident and beat the shit out of him?"

She glanced between her husband and him with a furrowed brow. "I never really thought about it. I know I didn't say it at the time, but I was grateful you did something to the jerk who hurt her and everyone else involved in the accident."

"Trish, Rocco's with Dixon-Shaw Security.

They're former CIA. He could shoot up our entire building and walk away scot-free."

Patty smiled at him warmly. It was something. He'd take it. "Oh."

"Hannah begged me not to hurt Richard. But I told him if he ever hurt her again, he was a dead man. You have my word on that."

"Thank you, Rocco. I never liked him. I never liked the idea of them together. If we want to merge with Hayes Studios, we'll do it contractually. Though I'm not in favor of that idea now."

Patty shook her head. "No. I'm not either. And I'm so sorry. I should have been smarter. More perceptive when it came to Richard."

Rocco needed to steer their conversation back in the right direction though he wasn't sorry Patty wasn't on Team Richard any longer. "Richard had me believing I didn't fit in. That I didn't belong with Hannah. I know you feel that way, too. And for a minute I believed it. Especially when we went to visit your mother in Town & Country, Missouri."

Patty gasped. Her muscles quivered and her body tensed. "You don't know what it's fucking like to—"

"No, ma'am. I don't know what it's like to be shuffled around from family member to family member because my teen, drunk mother would rather spend time screwing whoever showed her some attention than with me."

Denton did his best to wipe away his wife's tears and nodded for him to continue.

"All I know is mine left after I suffered through beatings trying to protect her while she was pregnant with my brother. She abandoned us when I was six and my brother was three weeks old, but not before telling me what a useless piece of shit I was, just like my father, before she walked out the door. My father hadn't been home in three days. I never saw either of them again."

Patty sobbed, yanking several tissues from the box on her desk and Rocco felt like shit. He hoped they emerged from this conversation stronger, closer.

"Rocco, I'm so sorry, son." Denton appeared ready to cry himself but kept it together. Joe wiped his eyes with the back of his hand but didn't say a word, having known his fair share of heartache.

He shrugged. It was ancient history now. He wasn't looking for pity. "You don't have to be sorry. Despite a rough start, I'm proud of the man I've become. I've served this country honorably. I wanted you to know in case you thought I intended on sponging off your daughter, I support myself well between my salary at Dixon-Shaw and now because of Hannah, my part-time income from Cucina Antonetti's. I've invested all the money I sent home while I was in the Marines and added the inheritance I received when my grandparents passed away. I knew Hannah was mine the minute I saw her in her boring navy pantsuit with her hair up in a messy bun. I'll do right by her. Always."

Patty offered him a weak smile and nodded. "You must think I'm such an awful person, don't you?"

"No. I think you've been badly hurt and instead of getting the help you needed, you took it out on your little girl." Rocco knew this from personal experience himself, only recently getting the emotional help he so desperately needed.

She squeezed her eyes shut, a few tears leaking out the sides. "And Janice?"

He glanced at Denton, not sure which of them should answer. Denton nodded, giving Rocco the go ahead. "Clean and sober for the last twenty years. Your stepfather's name is Gerald Mason. He designs and builds luxury estates in the Town & Country and Chesterfield, Missouri area. Your stepbrother's name is Paul. He's a project manager for Gerald's firm. She's so proud of you and everything you've accomplished. And heartbroken because you haven't had a relationship in so many years."

After taking a shaky breath and squaring her shoulders, Patty glanced at all the men in turn. With a genuine smile on her face, she returned her focus to Rocco and nodded. "What now?"

Feeling like they'd reached a turning point, Rocco smiled back. He retrieved his cell phone and swiped until he found the pictures he needed to show her. Placing his phone in front of her on her desk, he leaned back in his chair. "Take a look at those. What do you think?"

He watched on as Denton and Patty gazed in amazement at Hannah's bridal gown renderings. His woman had a gift. He couldn't wait until she shared it with the world.

"Oh my God. You drew these? They're magnificent." Patty's bright blue eyes were wide with disbelief and wonder.

"No, ma'am. Hannah did."

Denton leaned back in his chair and full-out laughed. "We did send her to design school and she graduated with honors."

She shook her head and handed his phone back. "Amazing. You showed us these for a reason? I'm guessing you have a plan of some sort?"

"Yes, ma'am, I do."

It didn't take long to explain what he had in mind and the part they would all play. He'd spoken to Nora and Cora on the drive over and learned they already had a contract ready and waiting for signatures. A copy was faxed over to Patty's and Jake's office. Jake and Mel at Cobras' HQ would be the second and third set of legal eyes. When the time came, Denton, Mel, and Jake would review the future Bellatoni contract.

Patty frowned, turning her attention to Joe. "Joseph, I assume you'll leave me as well?"

Joe's shoulders slumped and he blew out a breath. "I'm sorry, Patty. If Hannah agrees to Rocco's plan and she asks me, I will."

She shrugged but didn't appear upset. "I know. The two of you work so well together. Of course, you should go."

"Have we covered everything?" Denton asked Rocco.

"There is one other thing. I have an idea for a yearly Veteran's Day wedding event. It would be great PR for Hailey's and the wedding vendors you work with. You'd be surprised at how little the military pays. I was thinking you could hold a contest. Select ten from the best how-we-met entries and donate the entire wedding from the dress to the venue, food, flowers, music, and provide seating for maybe twenty of the couple's family and friends. A joint wedding for ten couples."

Rocco knew he was asking a lot. Event planning and weddings were a big business, not a charity, but it was worth a shot. His heart sank when everyone remained silent.

The smile that suddenly graced Patty's face lit up the room and hope bloomed. "That's an amazing idea. Why haven't we considered this before now?"

"Because we never had a veteran in the family before," Denton answered.

Rocco's heart skipped a beat at the thought Hannah's father considered him family. It meant the world to him. More than Denton could ever know.

"I'm on it, Patty," Joe said when she turned to him, already busy on his cell phone. "And we need to at least provide the winning couples a two-night stay at a fancy hotel like the Drake or the Fairchild."

"Hailey's has organized dozens of destination weddings. We'll be able to get some wonderful honeymoon spots donated if you think the couples would have the time. I'm not sure what you call it in military terms. I'm sorry." Patty glanced at him apologetically. It was a look he wasn't used to coming from her.

"It's called leave. Depending on the winner's status, you can provide them with option choices for a honeymoon. You're going to receive a lot of entries, though. What about the couples who don't win?" He hated the thought of his deserving brothers and sisters in uniform missing out. Maybe this wasn't such a good idea after all. He didn't like the idea of losers as part of the event.

"Since Hailey's is spearheading this event, all participating vendors have to offer substantial discounts for their services to the couples who aren't selected. It's the right thing to do, don't you agree?"

He'd misjudged Patty as much as she'd misjudged him. "Yes, ma'am."

"Excellent idea. I'll get the ball rolling," Joe said as he dashed out of Patty's office.

They couldn't possibly mean what he thought they did. "But Veteran's Day is about two and a half months away. I thought maybe you'd consider this for *next* year."

Patty laughed, though not in a condescending way. "Oh, Rocco. You don't know who you're dealing with, do you? Did you think pulling this off in two and a half months would be difficult?" She turned to Denton and scoffed. "This event is nothing. We can handle it in our sleep, and it will be spectacular. No problem. Give me something that's actually difficult."

He sighed and ran his fingers through his hair. She would regret saying that. He hated what he was about to say next, but it needed to be said. For all their sakes.

"You won't like it, but tomorrow morning I should bring you to see your … Janice. If for nothing else, closure."

Patty winced and clenched her jaw. Various emotions played out on her sorrowful face.

"I'll come along, too," Denton offered.

"And I'll prepare breakfast paninis and cappuccinos for the drive down," Rocco said, hoping to sweeten the deal.

Patty raised a hand and chuckled. "All right, all right. I'll go. But I can't guarantee anything after this trip tomorrow. That's my condition."

"Understood," he and Denton replied in unison.

"Thank you, Rocco. For everything. I'd like for us to consider all of the plans we're making here today a new beginning for us, as a family, if that's all right with you?" It was as if Patty held her heart in her hands and offered it to him on a silver platter. She was vulnerable and asking for forgiveness. Because he loved Hannah so much, he'd be gracious and give it. If things went his way, the woman before him would become his mother-in-law in the not-too-distant future and family meant more to him than anything.

"Yes, ma'am. That's fine with me."

Chapter Twelve

Hannah silently observed the exchange between Abbey Jayne and the owner of Shamrock Garden Florist. It was just after nine in the morning. Abbey and Luke were getting married in one week, the following Wednesday, and the meeting today was a final review of their flower selections.

Later on that day, Abbey and Luke were having a housewarming-slash-bachelorette-and-bachelor party at their new home located in the exclusive gated community Paradise Oaks Country Club in Oak Brook. Instead of paying closer attention to the conversation at hand, Hannah was trying to conjure up a plausible excuse not to attend.

She'd been planning on attending with Rocco. It had been a week since she'd confronted him at the Twisted Tea Society meeting and then in Kyle's office. She'd never felt more terrified but empowered and emboldened, pleading her case for their future—naked. Never before meeting Rocco would she have ever considered doing something like that.

After she'd left Kyle's office that evening, she'd hoped to find Rocco waiting outside the ladies' room door when she emerged dressed. She was disappointed but not surprised when he wasn't. The man had his pride.

But now, a week later and still not having heard from him, she had to move forward, acknowledging he obviously didn't love her as much as she loved him and their relationship wasn't as important to him as it had been to her. She'd have to live with that sad fact like she'd told him she would.

Her resignation letter was already prepared and

would be on her mother's desk the evening of Abbey and Luke's wedding. Then Hannah would decide what to do with the rest of her life—without her job at Hailey's *and* Rocco.

"This is perfect," Abbey exclaimed with a huge smile on her face. "Thank you so much, Linda, Hannah."

Startled out of her depressing thoughts, Hannah smiled back and nodded. "Good, I'm glad. There's a reason Shamrock Garden is one of our preferred vendors."

Linda, the owner, blushed and waved her hand. "We've been working together a long time. It's always a pleasure. I haven't seen or heard any buzz. I think everyone still believes you're getting married in the spring."

Abbey held up her hands and crossed her fingers. "Yes. So far so good. And thank you for helping us keep our secret."

"We're happy to help. I can't even imagine what it must be like for you."

Hannah half listened as Abbey explained some of what her life was like now that she was with a former professional athlete and major league baseball team owner. She nearly jumped out of her chair when her cell phone rang.

Every muscle went rigid when Rocco's name flashed on the display. She took in a deep breath and her heart rate kicked up a notch. She was about to let it go to voicemail but picked it up, needing to hear his voice. *I'm pathetic.*

"Hello," she said after clearing her throat and rubbing a hand down her black linen pant leg.

"*Buongiorno*, Hannah," Rocco said in that sexy timbre that had butterflies taking flight in her stomach.

God, how she loved it when he spoke to her in

Italian. Even if it was just a few words. Not knowing why he was calling, she did her best to appear calm. What she *wanted* to do was tell him how much she missed him, but she had her pride, too.

"Good morning. What's up?" she asked awkwardly, feeling lame. *What's up?*

"I need for you to meet me at Blumenthal's as soon as you can ... *please*."

A chill ran through her blood. "Oh my God. Is something wrong with Nora or Cora?"

"No, no. They're fine. I promise you. Can you come over, though? Quickly?"

What kind of game was he playing? She didn't have time for this. "What for? I don't have any appointments there today."

She sighed and rubbed her eyes, aware Abbey and Linda were watching and listening. "Why, Rocco? What's so important that I need to rush over there? I'm with Abbey at the florist." Hannah waved a hand after Abbey and Linda mouthed, *Go ahead.*

"I'll tell you when you get here," he replied.

She took a deep breath and held it in as her anger simmered just below the surface. "I don't know what's going on here, but—"

"This Marine has gotten his shit together, that's what's going on. He's gotten his head out of his ass. Did I take too long? Am I too late, baby?"

Tears welled up and she shook her head as Abbey and Linda continued to watch on in silence. "No. Not too late," she whispered. A week was nothing, although it had felt much longer.

He sighed on the other end of the line. "Thank you, *bella*. Thank you so much. Can you stop at home and get all your gown sketchbooks before you come to the salon? Please? I'll explain everything as soon as you get here."

Abbey and Linda smiled and nodded enthusiastically, having obviously overheard. What did her sketchbooks have to do with the two of them? None of this made any sense. Anxious to see him again and curious as hell, she relented.

"Sure. But no games, okay? You'll tell me what's going on as soon as I get there, agreed?"

"Agreed. I can't wait to see you, *cara*. I've missed you so much," Rocco said in a low, sensual tone.

A tear ran down Hannah's cheek and she quickly wiped it away. "I've missed you, too."

"I'll see you soon, baby," Rocco said and disconnected the call.

"Get going!" Abbey and Linda nearly shouted at her.

Hannah giggled and got her things together, feeling lighter emotionally. She speedily said her goodbyes, promised to see Abbey later at the housewarming, and raced home to get her sketchbooks. *What do my sketches have to do with anything?*

It was nearly ten o'clock by the time she hurried through the front doors of Blumenthal's Discount Bridal salon with her sketch pads in her arms. She was excited, nervous, and not sure what the hell to expect. Rocco had her all tied up in knots. He'd better have a good reason for his request. They needed to sit down in private and have a heart-to-heart, not meet up at the salon for whatever the hell this was.

The reception desk wasn't occupied. *That's strange.* She took a few steps into the salon and found a dashing-looking Rocco striding toward her in what she knew were custom-tailored, navy-blue Armani suit pants and a white silk shirt with a small-point collar. He'd rolled up the sleeves to his elbows, showing off his extraordinary tattoos.

She cringed, looking down at herself briefly. Though she hadn't reverted back to those matronly pantsuits she'd been pressured into wearing for so long, she had on black linen pants and a pink short-sleeved silk blouse.

When he smiled at her, Hannah nearly melted on the spot. A low and pleasant hum warmed her blood and her skin tingled. She was ready to toss her sketchbooks aside and jump the man.

With a gleam in his eyes, as if he'd read her mind, he extracted the sketch pads from her arms. "It's so good to see you, baby," he said and kissed her gently on the lips. Then he proceeded down the hall toward the salon's conference room. *What the hell?*

Hannah followed closely behind, confused as hell. "What's going on? You said you'd tell me once I got here. Where are Nora and Cora?"

Rocco stacked her sketch pads in front of three chairs at the conference room table and turned to her. He checked his watch and grinned that smirky grin that made her body react every time. Now was not the time. She needed answers.

"And I'll tell you. Just give me one minute." He brushed his lips against hers all too briefly and was out of the conference room door in a flash.

She paced the room that seated ten for a moment before she became impatient. Just as she decided she was going to find Rocco and give him a piece of her mind, she was stunned when three people she never expected to meet entered the room. *Holy shit.*

Rocco took his place beside her and held her hand. She gripped his tight, unsure of what the hell was going on.

"Hannah, this is—"

"Enzo, Stacey, and Heather Bellatoni. I know. What's going on, Rocco?" Hannah began shaking and felt lightheaded.

Enzo stepped forward, rubbed her arms in a comforting gesture, and kissed her on both cheeks, followed quickly by Stacey and Heather. "We're here to see *you*, of course, lovely Hannah," Enzo announced.

Lovely? *Her?* Was he serious? She was a complete frump compared to the three of them. Enzo in his stylish Bellatoni navy suit. Stacey in her chic, sleeveless red pencil dress that ended just above the knee, and Heather in her pretty, white floral spaghetti-strapped mini dress. Mother and daughter looked more like sisters with their flowing blonde hair and sparkling blue eyes. Heather's complexion matched Enzo's and Rocco's Mediterranean skin tone, giving the semi-retired supermodel a more exotic look than her mother.

"You're here to see *me*? Why?" Hannah glanced between them, confused as shit, still not any closer to understanding what the hell was going on than she was when she walked in the door.

Enzo swiped the screen on his cell phone until he was satisfied and held it out to her. "*This* is why."

Hannah gasped when she glanced down at one of her gown sketches. "How did you get this?"

"I sent it to him. And several other amazing sketches you drew," Heather answered happily.

"How?" None of this made any sense to her. How did Heather get ahold of her designs?

"Why don't you take a seat and start reviewing these? That's everything," Rocco said to the Bellatonis, gesturing to the three stacks he'd placed on the conference room table earlier.

Before she knew it, he'd led her to the furthest end of the room, allowing for a little privacy while the

Bellatonis reviewed her designs. He held her hands tight and kissed her forehead.

"Don't be upset, baby. I took a few pictures of your designs when you were getting ready for our first date. I always intended on passing them to Kyle who knew the Bellatonis much better than me."

"You did? Shouldn't you have asked me first?" She'd only shared a few of her designs with Joe. She hadn't been confident enough in her own abilities. She shook her head. It was more than likely because of her mother. She was glad she was leaving Hailey's in a week. She needed some distance from Patty desperately.

"What would you have said if I had?"

She glanced over at Enzo, Stacey, and Heather. "Shouldn't they be smiling if my designs are so good?"

"Hannah, look at me." Rocco gently guided her chin until she faced him.

"If they don't like them, we'll present them to other designers. It'll be the Bellatoni's loss. Just like it was Kyle's loss he didn't want me to cook for him, right?"

Her heart fluttered. "*We'll* present them to other designers?"

He wrapped his arms around her and held on tight. She'd missed him so much and clung to him greedily, unconcerned they weren't alone.

"Yes, *we'll*. If you want me with you. I talked some shit out with Massimo last Saturday. I know I messed up and I'm so sorry. If I get scared or unsure, I won't bail on you again. I'll talk it through with you, I promise."

Hannah's heartbeat quickened and she felt herself smile. It was what she needed to hear, and all she could ask for. She pulled out of their embrace and gazed into Rocco's deep brown eyes.

"I have your word on that?" she asked.

He smiled down at her with such love and tenderness her eyes welled up.

"You have my word. Absolutely," he said with certainty she didn't doubt.

"Hannah, you have many bridesmaid dress sketches here as well," Heather called out.

"Answer her confidently. Like the talented designer you are, baby." Rocco nodded and kissed her forehead.

Hannah squared her shoulders and stood tall. "Yes. I wanted the bridesmaids to feel special, too. Some designs have sweep trains. Some have court-length trains."

Heather smiled at her and nodded enthusiastically. "They're so pretty," she said and resumed flipping through the pages of her sketchbooks.

For the next few minutes, Hannah held Rocco's hand while Enzo, Stacey, and Heather appraised her designs, comparing notes in Italian, unfortunately. Rocco wasn't offering insights, the rat.

Her stomach was in knots by the time they concluded their review and stacked up her sketch pads into a neat pile. Enzo waved her over. When she didn't move because she was afraid, Rocco gently dragged her over to the Bellatonis and they all stood.

"Thank you for letting us take a look your designs," Stacey said.

"It was truly an honor," Enzo added.

"Rocco told us the owners of the salon have been trying to convince you to buy it and that you had some ideas for a renovation." Heather looked at Hannah expectantly.

Hannah's face heated. Renovation was putting it mildly, but Nora and Cora were her friends.

"What if the salon was owned by someone you didn't know and considered a friend? A stranger? Someone named Marie Johnson? Take us through each floor of the building and tell us *your* vision," Rocco said.

Hannah considered Rocco's suggestion. There was no harm in that, although she was curious to know what the Bellatonis thought of her designs. She had discussed the basics of her ideas with Nora and Cora several times before and had been met with nothing but encouragement from both of them.

The fact that she felt like she was betraying the sisters was really on her and no one else. She'd need to get over it. Nora and Cora wanted to retire and were offering her the opportunity of a lifetime. She needed to have the courage to take it.

"As you know, Blumenthal's is a budget salon and there's nothing wrong with that. But my vision is for a couture salon, ideally including my designs," Hannah began. She led them from the conference room to the main area of the salon where brides were admiring themselves in potential gowns with their entourages.

It didn't take but a moment before Stacey, Heather, Enzo, and even Chef Rocco were spotted and were asked to pose for pictures with brides and their families and friends.

"I'd put in plush carpeting and overstuffed white couches and chairs, serve champagne and light refreshments. I'm going for an upscale experience for the bride and her entourage."

"Very nice. Similar to what we offer in *our* salons," Stacey said.

"The gown storage area is enormous and I have ideas on how to organize the new inventory that would fill the space," Hannah said. She led them to the elevators and the second floor.

The hum of sewing machines could be heard as they stepped off onto the second floor. She knew all the seamstresses and gave them a quick wave before leading everyone away toward the small kitchen area.

She whispered so she wouldn't be overheard. "The sewing machines need to be replaced along with some of the seamstresses, for starters. I'd probably hire on a few more."

Hannah brought everyone to the third floor. Before the Blumenthal brothers passed away, they'd finished the space, but it was empty. Baron. It had bathrooms and a kitchenette.

"I'm not sure what I'd do with this space, to be honest," she admitted.

"We'd manufacture your gowns, of course," Enzo said as he moved around in the space. "We're near capacity at our New York factory, and this would be perfect."

Hannah felt a lightness in her chest and giggled. "What are you saying?" Were they suggesting they liked her designs?

"What do you think?" Stacey asked. "We love your designs, Hannah. We want them ... and you. We'll call the line 'Hannah by Bellatoni.'"

Hannah's heart raced so fast she thought she might faint. Rocco wrapped an arm around her waist for support. "I'm thrilled. Honored."

"I'd like to be the face of the line—if that's all right with you," Heather said, almost hesitantly, as if she were afraid Hannah would refuse.

"That would be amazing. And Stacey, too?" The Bellatoni mother and daughter debuting her line would be more than a dream come true.

"Before you say no, Mom, how about we select one of the grandest designs and we end the show with you, Dad, and *Zio* Paolo walking down the runway together?" Heather suggested.

Hannah gasped she was so excited. "That would be amazing. What a way to end the show."

Stacey glanced at Enzo, who gave her a sexy wink and she sighed. "Fine. I'll do it."

Hannah hugged each of them in turn, ending with Enzo.

"House of Bellatoni will pay for any renovations needed to create a state-of-the-art bridal gown factory on this floor. This is not up for negotiation," Enzo stated firmly.

"And so you understand I meant what I said downstairs, I want to help you realize your bliss, like you helped you me realize mine at Antonetti's. I want to be your silent partner. I'd like to invest in your new salon with you," Rocco said as he took her hand and kissed her knuckles tenderly.

Hannah's heart felt full as tears of joy streamed down her cheeks. She liked that idea very much.

"Oh my gosh! Bliss Bridals would be a wonderful name for your new salon," Heather exclaimed.

"*Perfetto!* We're in town for a few days, then you must return to Milan with us to see our operations," Enzo said. Stacey and Heather nodded in agreement.

"So, baby, are we all in agreement?" Rocco asked with a hopeful expression on his handsome face.
****

Rocco gazed at the love of his life and seemingly overwhelmed potential business partner as she contemplated the opportunity presented to her. He hoped like hell she took a chance on herself. On living her bliss. She deserved all of it, and more.

He checked his watch—again. Where the fuck was Trish? Patty had asked him to call her that now that she considered him family. After their trip to visit her mother Janice, which had gone surprisingly better than anyone could have possibly expected, he *felt* more like family.

Trish had a part to play in executing his plans for Hannah and she was MIA. How could he have misjudged her so badly? Damn it all to hell. She'd played him. *Fuck.* He hadn't seen that coming and he should have.

It would be all right. Trish didn't matter in the grand scheme of things. If Hannah agreed, the salon and her gown line would be more than enough. Trish's part of his plan had been more like the cherry on top.

Hannah smiled brightly at all of them and he sensed she'd decided to move ahead with their plans. He was so incredibly proud of her.

They all turned in the direction of clicking heels on the tile floor to find Trish rushing toward them, elegant as always in a baby-blue, short-sleeve sheath dress. Rocco sighed in relief as she hadn't fucked him and Hannah over after all.

"I'm so sorry I'm late, everyone," she announced.

"No, Mother. I don't know what you're doing here, but no." Hannah glared at Trish without blinking and clenched her fists.

"Don't be upset. Rocco invited me. You see—"

"What?" Hannah exclaimed. "Explain." She glared at him with fire in her eyes. Why the hell did Trish have to be late? Everything had gone so well up to now. He was grateful the Bellatonis let them play out their family drama without butting in. He imagined they'd experienced their fair share over the years. They were Italian, and tempers tended to flare.

Trish held a hand up and shook her head. "Hannah, I'm sorry. For so many things. But mostly for not treating you like the amazing, talented, wonderful woman you are."

Hannah's shoulders slumped as tears streamed down her face. "I tried so hard to be perfect so you'd love me. Nothing was ever good enough for you." She whimpered.

Trish wrapped her arms around a sobbing Hannah as the rest of them stood by, giving mother and daughter their space. Rocco's heart ached for her. He knew she'd suffered emotionally for years. None of it her fault. Just as Trish had suffered, no fault of her own. Healing had begun in Missouri a few days ago, and he hoped it was beginning right here and now.

Trish held on tight and rocked Hannah back and forth where they stood. He heard Stacey and Heather sniffle. "You *are* perfect, Hannah. And I love you so much. You are more than good enough. *Too* good. My issues have screwed everything up and I'm working on that. I'd like a new beginning for us, if you'd allow it. Please?" Trish's cheeks were covered in tears, but she didn't let Hannah go.

Hannah ended their embrace and wiped her face with the back of her hands. She offered them all a small smile, seemingly embarrassed for her emotional outburst, and nodded. "I'd like that, if you're serious."

Trish sighed in obvious relief and smiled. "Yes, dead serious. Thank you for giving me a chance to make it up to you."

Feeling like things had taken a turn in the right direction, Rocco wanted to take control of the conversation. "Trish, why are you late?"

Hannah raised a brow and he shrugged. There would be time to explain that later. He held her hand while they waited on Trish to enlighten them.

"Right. The producers at WGN were running late." She turned to face the Bellatonis. "Are you going to carry my daughter's designs? We can offer them to Allure, Oleg Cassini, Ines Di Santo, Badgley Mischka, or a host of others."

"You most certainly will *not*. Hannah and her designs belong with House of Bellatoni," Enzo exclaimed.

Trish nodded with determination. "All right then. WGN accepted my pitch with one condition."

Hannah's brow furrowed. "What pitch? What the heck is going on?"

Rocco chuckled and kissed her hand. "Nothing to worry about. Your mother pitched them an idea for a Chicago-based *Say Yes to the Dress*-type show from your new salon. But what's the condition, Trish?"

"You," Trish said.

Him? That made no sense. He was just a silent partner. He was inconsequential.

Trish shrugged and offered a coy grin. "They want the tattooed, Italian Marine chef on camera. Not *every* episode, but many of them. You're making a name for yourself, Rocco. And since you're featured on an upcoming episode of *Chicago's Best*, I can see their point. I couldn't offer a valid argument against it. The salon is a woman- and Veteran-owned business, after all."

It wasn't right. The focus needed to be on Hannah. He would just be in the way.

"I love the idea. You should see this one when we watch episodes of *Say Yes to the Dress*. He has quite the fashion sense," Hannah announced to everyone.

Everyone chuckled and Rocco's face heated. That was supposed to be *their* little secret.

"But you never answered my question before your mother got here. Are we in agreement? With everything? The salon? Your bridal gown line? The show, with me as a part of it since you and WGN insist? All of it?" He so wanted this for her. She deserved all of it and more. Even it if meant he'd have to participate in ways he hadn't anticipated. Working beside her wouldn't be a hardship. He looked forward to it.

Hannah wrapped her arms around his waist and looked up him, her beautiful brown eyes bright and joyful. The smile on her face lit up the empty space that would hopefully house her bridal gown factory. "Let me ask *you* something. Why did you do all of this?"

That was a simple question to answer. "Because the day I met you, my soul recognized yours as belonging to him. You became my family and I take care of my family. I love you, Hannah. *Sei il mio cuore.* You are my heart."

He wiped away the tears that streamed down her cheeks, mindful of sniffles from the other women present. Hannah giggled. "Good answer. You're my heart, too. My family. So I say yes. Or rather, *sì*. I'm in agreement with everything."

The room broke out in applause and he couldn't have been more pleased. He checked his watch. They needed to get moving if they wanted to finish up their business and make it to Luke and Abbey's housewarming party on time.

"Let's head downstairs. Hannah has contracts to sign. Nora, Cora, and your father should be in the conference room." Rocco led her by the hand to the elevator with everyone else following closely behind.

"Kids, I know the Blumenthals are selling this place at a steal considering what real estate goes for in Lombard, but Denton and I want to purchase it for you, no strings attached, so you can put your funds toward the renovations and inventory. Please let us do this for you. It would mean so much to us. To *me*." Trish glanced between him and Hannah with a hopeful gleam in her sparkling blue eyes. He hated to refuse. He knew she was trying to make amends for years of horrid treatment toward her daughter. Not wanting to get in the middle of mother and daughter, he remained quiet and let Hannah decide.

The elevator dinged and they all stepped inside, Hannah still silent. As they descended to the first floor, he waited, holding her delicate hand in his, wondering what she was thinking. She nodded, facing her mother.

"Thank you, Mom. That's incredibly generous of you both. It'll help our money go a lot further." She hugged her mother and he exhaled a breath he hadn't realized he'd been holding.

"Don't be upset, but I'm asking Joe to come work for us. Probably as salon manager."

"I'd expect nothing less. He'll do an amazing job for you," Trish said as they all proceeded to the conference room.

Denton sat with the contracts awaiting Hannah's signature. Rocco had already signed where appropriate. Nora and Cora were pouring champagne and the delicious aroma of appetizers or *antipasti* from Cucina Antonetti's filled the room. Rocco had borrowed from Jake and Cassie's wedding, selecting mozzarella-stuffed bacon-wrapped shrimp, Italian sausage-stuffed mushrooms, and mini Italian meatballs. He'd bet the cost of renovations Hannah hadn't been eating properly since they'd broken up.

Hannah made a beeline to Cora and Nora and they group-hugged, swaying back and forth together. He couldn't help but smile. This was a huge step for her, but he believed she was ready. He was so proud of her.

They broke apart and she took a seat next to her father. Everyone eagerly filled their plates while he prepared one for himself and his woman. He sat down beside her and placed her plate down in front of her.

"Just because I can't always text you and remind you to eat, it doesn't mean I'm not thinking about you, *cara*. I'm *always* thinking about you. Things are about to change in a big way. We need to be at our best," he said to Hannah as she dug in.

She wiped her mouth and nodded. "I know, you're right. I'll take better care of myself. I promise. How about some days I text *you* and let you know I'm eating and what I'm up to?"

He nodded. "Sounds like a great idea." He liked knowing she was thinking about him, too. This was all new territory for him but he was man enough to admit he liked it.

Nora and Cora held up their champagne glasses and everyone joined them. "To the end of an era and the beginning of a new one. To Hannah and Rocco and Bliss Bridals," Cora toasted.

"And to Bellatoni's new bridal gown line— Hannah," Enzo added.

After everyone sipped their champagne and resumed eating, Hannah leaned in close and whispered in his ear, "You're drinking champagne?"

Luke had been nice enough to supply the good stuff. He was turning them all into champagne snobs and that was fine with him. "Max helped me realize having a little champagne or a couple beers during a game doesn't make me my father. I'll never be Matteo, no matter what."

She squeezed his hand and nodded. "Max is absolutely right. I'm proud of you."

"Hey, everyone, I was thinking about a name for the show. What do you think about Blissfully Ever After?" It had just popped into his head and by everyone's lack of response, he should have kept his mouth shut. He knew he was better off as a silent partner. *Damn it.*

Everyone began speaking at once and he couldn't keep it all straight.

"*Perfetto!*"

"Oh my God!"

"That's it!"

"Brilliant!"

Rocco turned to Hannah because her opinion mattered to him most. "Baby, what do *you* think?"

She beamed. "I think it's perfect. Just like all of this."

"I was thinking, I know we're going to be busy when we go to Milan, but would you want to take a day and visit my family in Catania?" They were going to be exhausted, but he wanted to show Hannah off. They could sleep on the flight back home if she agreed.

Her eyes widened and she nodded enthusiastically. He was one lucky fucker.

"What about for the show tagline you ask the bride 'does this dress scream wedded bliss' and the bride yells out 'yes'?" That came from Trish. He had to hand it to her. She was coming around. It was a fantastic suggestion. It would make for great TV.

Everyone around the table nodded in agreement. "Thanks, Mom. I like that. It'll be a lot of fun."

"And Hannah, dear, Nora and I will stay until the grand opening and the launch of your new line. We'll handle all the orders that are in progress so you can focus on Bliss Bridals. Blumenthal's no longer exists as of tomorrow. No new orders, not even for shoes."

Rocco listened as they discussed their transition plans, but Enzo caught his attention. "Thank you for letting my family be a part of what you're doing for

Hannah. My brother Paolo and everyone in Milan are looking forward to meeting you both."

"I'm glad you recognized the talent I did in her designs."

Enzo scoffed. "Your woman's talent is obvious. During your visit, we need to measure you. When you're on camera for the show you need to wear Bellatoni menswear. Don't you agree?"

Rocco chuckled. He should've seen that coming. He didn't mind. They were investing in Hannah. The least he could do was wear the designer's clothing. They were exceptional.

"Of course. I'd be honored."

Hannah leaned over so Enzo could hear her. "You should take some shots of Rocco for your men's line. Especially after he hasn't shaved for a couple of days."

Rocco laughed. The idea was absurd. "Hannah, no one would want to see that."

"Yes, we would," Heather and Stacey said in unison.

Enzo slapped his hand on the table and nodded. "Excellent, I was thinking the same thing. Then we are all in agreement."
****

Rocco keyed in the security code, locking them inside the new Bliss Bridals later that evening. He and Hannah had spent a nice time at Luke and Abbey's, even visited with Darren some, but now it was *their* time, and he needed her. Badly.

"Are you sure you don't mind stopping by for a little while?" Hannah asked for the third time. She stepped further into the salon and slowly spun around, taking it all in.

He began unbuttoning his shirt, not able to wait any longer. "Of course not. It's your salon."

"*Our* salon," she corrected him.

Right. He was a business owner now. It would take some getting used to. He observed her gaze around in awe and wonder. Once this place was renovated and truly theirs, it would be amazing. He had no doubt.

She turned to face him and eyed him curiously. "Why is your shirt off?"

"The better question is why is yours still on? We have a verbal agreement, don't we?" He strode toward her while he unbuckled his belt and unzipped his pants. His cock was already hard, making it difficult.

Hannah glanced around nervously as if someone would jump out from behind a mannequin and surprise them. That wouldn't happen, they were alone.

"Here?" she asked.

"Yes, here. You just said it's our salon. We can do whatever the fuck we want. Now either you take your clothes off or I tear them off and you go home wearing one of these gowns. You have five seconds to decide, baby." He toed off his shoes and removed his pants after grabbing a condom from his wallet first.

Hannah took off running toward the back where the offices were, giggling and unbuttoning her blouse. He followed her into what used to be Nora or Cora's office and closed the door. She surprised him by running her arm across the desk, sending its contents crashing to the floor. Her joyful laugh made his heart swell.

"I've always wanted to do something like that." She quickly undressed and sat on the edge of the desk. She spread her legs, her pussy glistening.

He quickly sheathed his aching dick with shaky hands and positioned himself at her entrance. He claimed her mouth with a savage kiss. Her luscious tits crushed against the hardness of his chest as she held him tight against her.

"I've been waiting all day for you, baby," he said, panting. Hannah wrapped her legs around his waist and he thrust into her snug pussy. They both cried out in ecstasy.

"I ... know. Me too," she breathed.

Rocco pistoned in and out of Hannah's tight cunt hard and fast, loving the feel of her wrapped around his dick. She belonged to him. Always would. When he felt his spine tingle and his balls draw up, he rubbed her hard little clit in tiny circles. He pounded into her like an animal. After she came, he followed her over, emptying his balls into the condom, biting her between her neck and shoulder, as if he were marking his mate.

She slumped against him, breathing heavily, and sighed. He kissed her sweat-dampened forehead, carefully pulled out, and discarded the condom. One day soon, he'd stop using them and they'd start a family. Something just a short time ago he didn't think was in the cards for him. They had such a bright future ahead of them it nearly brought him to tears.

Chapter Thirteen

Rocco finished dressing, trying to ignore the men who were *supposed* to be his best friends while they fucked with him. He should have known better and kept his big mouth shut. He double-checked his charcoal-gray tails and turned around to face Luke, Heath, and Jake.

"What the fuck did you expect me to do, huh? One minute Enzo Bellatoni's asking me to wear from his product line when we're filming *Blissfully Ever After.* Then Hannah's telling him they should take some modeling shots of me in Milan after I haven't shaved for a couple of days. I started laughing, but Heather, Stacey, *and* Enzo thought it was a great idea." Surely, they'd understand after he'd explained. Instead, they all laughed at him. "Assholes."

"Don't mind them," Luke said as he clapped him on the back. "They're just jealous you're prettier than they are."

Rocco shoved him away. "Fuck you, pretty boy. *You're* the one with all the endorsement deals," Rocco reminded Luke.

"He's got you there," Jake teased from across the room where he was zipping up his tuxedo pants.

Heath remained conspicuously silent. Something had been *off* with his brother-in-arms since Luke and Abbey's housewarming party the week before. He'd left the party after only an hour of poker, claiming he hadn't been feeling well. He knew Heath and knew he wasn't sick, but he hadn't called him out on his bullshit.

Luke nodded. "Yeah, and there's a damn good reason for that. I earned far more from my endorsement deals than I ever did from my pitching salary."

"How hard could it be? You put on some suits, they snap some pictures," Heath said. A lot of fucking help he was, finally opening his mouth.

"Yeah. Let the photographers do all the work," Jake added.

"Look. House of Bellatoni is one of the premier designers in the world. Now you and Hannah are a part of their family. If it turns out you end up doing more than just the one shoot, you invest the extra income back into the salon. Just have them fax over any contracts to Jake. We'll look them over. I've signed dozens of endorsement deals. We'll help you. It'll be all right," Luke assured him.

Rocco was burning up. It was only September sixth, much too early to turn on the furnace. Why wasn't the air conditioning on? He removed his tuxedo jacket and tossed it on a nearby chair. "But I can't go back and forth to Milan. I've got to be in town for the salon and the expansion at Cucina Antonetti's. I want to see that through."

"You won't have to. They can send you the clothes and you'll already have seamstresses at the salon to do alterations. You settled shit with Richard, so he can take the shots and film footage if they want it. It'll be a piece of cake. But something else is bothering you, man. What is it?" Luke looked at him with a concerned expression on his face.

The office in Grace of God Lutheran Church was where he'd met Hannah back in June on Jake and Cassie's wedding day. It had seemed enormous back then. Today, it seemed like the walls were closing in on him.

He felt like he was choking and tugged on his shirt collar while he paced the room. His chest rose and fell with rapid breaths. He glanced around the room at his friends. They looked like quadruplets in their gray tails. Jake was wearing the matching gray top hat. His heart raced and he thought it might burst through his chest.

"I can't do this," he said and threaded a hand through his hair. He couldn't go through with it. No. It was a bad idea. He was such an idiot for thinking otherwise.

"Shit," he heard Jake whisper.

"Wait. What can't you do, exactly?" Luke asked.

Rocco shoved his hands in his pockets and shook his head. "Everything. All of it. It's not a good idea. I was wrong."

Luke stepped right up into his personal space. "No, man. That's fucked up. We've got everything and everyone in place. My jeweler hooked you up with an awesome ring. What's the problem?"

Of course, Luke wouldn't understand. He wouldn't expect the retired star pitcher and MLB team owner to. Not that his life had been perfect, but he'd lived a rather charmed life, all things considered.

He shook his head again. "No. Not now. We leave for Milan on Saturday. She's meeting my family in Catania. After we get back. That's safer."

"Holy shit. You think she's gonna say no?" Luke asked, incredulous.

Rocco didn't answer. He didn't know what she'd say. That was the point. He wasn't sure about anything right now.

"So, she went against her mother *because* of you and went into business *with* you, but won't *marry* you? Have I got that right?" Luke crossed his arms in front of his chest and looked down at him disapprovingly.

Rocco felt like shit when Luke put it that way, but he couldn't help how he felt. "I don't know, all right? Plus, there'll be a ton of professional athletes and celebrities at your wedding, Luke. If she says no, I'll look like a total fool."

Luke stood there glaring at him, seemingly unconvinced. "Heath," he called out behind him.

"On it," Heath said as he set his phone on speaker and made a call. It rang twice and then connected.

"Rocco, what the fuck, man?" Massimo's voice blared out from the small cell phone's speaker.

Rocco's mouth fell open. "You called my little brother on me? What the hell?"

"Yes. We needed a backup plan in case you pussied out.

Rocco shoved Luke and he stumbled back. "Watch it. It would be a shame to walk down the aisle with a black eye. I'm no pussy."

Luke shoved him back. "Don't threaten me, asshole."

"Stop it! Both of you," Max called out.

Jake took a position behind Luke and Heath behind him while still holding his cell phone. What a clusterfuck.

"Everyone calm down. If Abbey found out you guys almost came to blows, she'd be pissed. Don't you think?"

The last thing Rocco wanted to do was ruin Luke's wedding over his own personal shit. Luke needed to respect his wishes and back the fuck off. Max did too.

"You don't actually think now that she's got a contract in place with the Bellatonis and she has her own salon she's going to toss you to the curb, do you?" Max asked him.

Shit. He hadn't considered that. That she'd just used him to advance her career. *Fuck*.

"She wouldn't do that to you, Rocco," Heath assured him. Jake and Luke both nodded.

"Listen, she didn't even know you had any association with the Bellatonis until recently, right?" Max asked.

Rocco felt crowded in by all of them and extricated himself from their tight formation. He paced around the room, rubbing the back of his neck. "That's true, I suppose." He didn't know what to believe.

"Rocco, it's just you and me. *Parlami.*"

At least they'd have privacy in Italian with the guys in the room. "I promised Hannah if I got nervous or unsure about something, I'd talk through it with her. How can I when what I'm worried about is asking her to marry me?"

"It's okay to be a little nervous. I nearly pissed myself when I asked Syd," Max said.

Rocco had no idea. It was the first he was hearing about it.

"Other than Luke, I think most of us are nervous when we ask our girl. We're putting ourselves out there. It's scary shit. Hannah loves you. You know she does."

He did. So much was happening sometimes it was hard to believe it was his life and not someone else's. "It's a lot, Max. You know? I can't wrap my head around it sometimes."

His brother sighed over the speaker. He hated dumping his issues on him. He had his own to deal with. "I know. What did your therapist say about today?"

"I had to cancel with everything going on. I should have called him. I will next time." Their office counseled active-duty military and did telephone sessions. Rocco wouldn't make the mistake of canceling again. His sessions had been beneficial and he wanted to continue his progress.

"Just know this. I mean, really understand it. This is *your* time. You deserve to be happy. You've earned it.

All of it. Now celebrate Luke and Abbey. Eat some good food. Dance with your girl. And when the time is right, like we planned, you propose—then later tonight, celebrate in private," Max said with a smile in his voice.

Rocco smiled himself. Luke had booked them all private luxury suites at the Fairchild Hotel again and he had plans for Hannah. He prayed there would be something to celebrate. He was being paranoid. She loved him. He had to have faith.

"You're right, Max. Thanks. I got a little freaked out. I'm sorry. I'm good now."

"All right. Adrianna's so excited. She picked out a pretty party dress and matching tights. She wants to call her *Zia* Anna right away."

Rocco chuckled. He supposed one of these days they needed to correct her pronunciation of Hannah's name. It didn't seem to bother Hannah though, and it was cute.

"I think she'd like that a lot," Rocco said.

"And if God forbid, Hannah does say no, me and the guys in the room you're in, your *family*, we'll figure it out. We'll help you through it. But that's not going to happen. She'll say yes. So you should start having kids right away unless your dick is broken."

Rocco threw his hands up. His asshole of a brother ruined the moment by switching back to English with his dick insult. It didn't help that the guys were all now laughing.

"Okay, I didn't understand any of what you guys said except for a few names and *familia*. I think that means family. Who is Anna? Great dick joke, by the way," Luke kidded.

"If Max said we'll have your back as a family if Hannah says no, he's right, we will." Heath placed a hand on his shoulder and squeezed. Rocco needed to speak to him privately after the wedding and find out what was going on with him. Something wasn't right. He could tell in Heath's eyes.

"And you don't think Abbey will be upset? It's her wedding day." Rocco didn't want to upstage the bride.

Luke scoffed and shook his head. "You kidding? She'll love it. You know women. She'll think we'll share an anniversary or some shit. It'll be all right. You'll see."

That was good enough for him. "And there's nothing wrong with my dick. Heath, you can hang up the phone," Rocco told him.

"Are you sure? Because as of right now the score is Max two, Rocco zero." Max had the nerve to laugh.

"I'm positive. I think we're done here. Hang up, Heath."

"Okay, okay. I'm sorry. Before I see you later though, one thing. Adrianna's German is really good. I think you can move on to the next language," Max said.

Rocco froze. Shit. How did Max find out? Adrianna promised she wouldn't tell anyone he was teaching her German. Heath mouthed the word *busted*.

"Don't worry. Adrianna didn't rat you out. I overheard her when she was playing tea party with her dolls and MJ, although he was sleeping. I think she's ready for the next language. I want to encourage her while she's interested in learning, if you don't mind teaching her."

Rocco grinned and nodded, even though Max couldn't see him. "I don't mind. It's kind of become our special thing. I could bring her to Dixon-Shaw, if that's all right. I was thinking Mandarin or Russian, but I'm not fluent enough. There are associates there who are, who can help us."

"That's cool. I know she'll be safe there with

you."

Of course, she would be. He'd protect her with his life.

****

Rocco sipped from a bottle of water standing near the bar, wanting to remain clear-headed. The day had been nearly perfect after the incident in the church's dressing room, and the broken-dick jokes. He snorted. As if. Luke and Abbey's guest list was star-studded with so many professional athletes and celebrities it made his head spin. Eli, Eason, and their best associates were working the event. They were all in good hands. So far, the paparazzi was still in the dark. He hoped it stayed that way.

Rocco had taken Max's advice and relaxed as best as he could. He'd enjoyed the ceremony. Abbey had looked like a princess, as Luke always referred to her in a Bellatoni gown, covered and draped in diamonds, courtesy of Luke, and topped off with a diamond tiara. In a private moment with his groomsmen, he'd shared Abbey was expecting. It had been a blessed day.

Luke's Uncle Darren had been feeling well enough to attend the ceremony and the reception. Despite his surgery and cancer treatment, he was doing fairly well. The family was cautiously optimistic.

They'd all feasted on delicious Cucina Antonetti's Italian specialties, but he'd been forbidden from going into the kitchen. It hadn't been easy, but he'd followed orders and stayed away.

And Hannah. His lovely, sweet Hannah. She'd been worried since she'd chosen a lacey, form-fitting, kelly-green, off-the-shoulder, tea-length cocktail dress, rather than something pink. He didn't know why she worried. She was gorgeous no matter what color she wore. Didn't she know that?

He was nervous but tried to have a good time. He danced and celebrated along with everyone else. Joe and another event planner from Hailey's took up the slack so Hannah could enjoy the day more as a guest rather than an employee. From what he could tell, they were doing a wonderful job for Luke and Abbey.

His cell phone vibrated in his pants with a text message.

Eason: **Everyone's here. Waiting for the green light when you're ready.**

Rocco: **OK. Thanks.**

Rocco scanned the room in search of Luke. When their eyes met, he nodded. This was it. His stomach churched as he watched Luke kiss Abbey's forehead and excuse himself from his bride and the guests they were speaking to. Luke had a few quick words with the DJ and then winked in his direction.

Rocco headed toward Hannah, who was chatting with Abbey's mother and Abbey's friend Karla who he stood up with. Hannah beamed when he approached, calming him slightly.

"All right, everyone, we're going to slow things down a bit, so grab that special someone and bring them to the dancefloor," the DJ bellowed out over the room's speaker system.

He held out his hand. "Dance with me, baby?"

Hannah nodded enthusiastically and placed her delicate hand in his. "Of course. We'll talk later, ladies," she said as he led her onto the dancefloor.

Rocco held Hannah tight as "All of Me" by John Legend began to play. He'd left it to Luke to select the song, too nervous to do it himself. Who knew Luke was so sentimental? He'd nailed it.

As he swayed with the love of his life while John Legend sang, he acknowledged he loved all of her. Her curves, edges, imperfections, and all. He inhaled the perfect scent of her own natural musk, *Falling in Love*, and sighed. If she didn't want to marry him, he didn't know what he'd do.

"Are you all right? You've seemed a bit distracted today," she whispered in his ear.

The DJ slowly turned the volume down. His heart raced. That was everyone's cue to get off the dancefloor.

"I have been a little distracted today, baby. You're right," he said. She knew him so well.

"Why? Hey, what happened to the music?" Hannah ended their embrace and looked up at him, a confused expression on her beautiful face.
****

What the hell was going on? They'd checked. Double-checked everything for Luke and Abbey's wedding. Everything needed to be perfect. And it had been. Until now. And something had been slightly off with Rocco all day. Something had him distracted, but she didn't know what.

As she glanced around them, she noticed they were now alone on the dancefloor. She did a double-take. "Grandma?" Her grandmother stood at the edge of the dancefloor with the other guests but was holding her mother's hand. Both of them were smiling. Her father and brother were beside them. Hannah stood frozen. Stunned.

"Hi, Anna!" Adrianna shouted from Max's arms, waving at her. Hannah waved back. Adrianna looked adorable in her pretty party dress and white tights. But why were they all here? None of this made any sense. She knew none of them had been invited to the wedding. Especially her family and her *grandmother*?

"Shush, honey. *Zio* Rocco has something to ask Hannah, remember?" Sydney gently scolded the little girl.

He did? She turned back to Rocco and gasped. Her skin tingled and her heart raced. He was on bended knee in front of her, holding a sparkling engagement ring in one hand and tugging on his shirt collar with the other.

Her Marine warrior was shaking. She felt for him. Why he'd chosen to propose in front of a crowd of celebrities and professional athletes, she didn't know, but she admired his courage nonetheless. She'd organized her fair share of high-profile events but even *she* was overwhelmed by Luke and Abbey's guest list.

Hannah quickly wiped a tear before it slid down her cheek. "Oh my God, Rocco," she whispered.

He cleared his throat and smiled up at her tentatively. "Hannah, baby. What started off as a joke became all too real very quickly," he began.

She looked over Rocco's shoulder to find Richard filming their moment with a smile on his face. Nodding and smiling back, she turned her attention back to her nervous Marine.

"And like John Legend said, right from the start, my head was spinning because of you. I love everything about you. Especially the parts of you that you think aren't perfect. I'll give all of myself to you if you'll agree to be my wife. Will you marry me?"

Her breath hitched as tears streamed down her face. The guests remained silent as they and Rocco awaited her answer.

"Say yes, Anna, so I can call you *Zia*!"

"Baby, shhh…" Max said to his excited little girl.

"Give him a break! Make an honest man out of him!" Luke called out.

She and the guests laughed, but Rocco remained serious. Poor guy. Was he worried she'd say no?

Hannah shook her head and took a deep breath. "I

suppose since we just went into business together it makes sense to marry you."

Rocco's mouth fell open. He quickly closed it and his shoulders sagged.

"Hey, come on. Get up." Hannah helped him up and held his free hand once he was standing.

"You want to marry me just because of Bliss Bridals?" he whispered.

She sighed and tried again. "No, of course not. I want to marry you because I love you so much my heart hurts. I went along with that stupid plan to make Richard jealous because I didn't think I'd have a shot with you otherwise."

He squeezed her hand and brought it to his lips, kissing her knuckles softly. "How could you think that, *bella*?"

"I wasn't the only one with insecurities, though, was I?" she asked.

"No," Rocco admitted after a brief pause.

"But you showed me otherwise. I like who I am with you. I like who we are together, regardless of Bliss Bridals or my contract with House of Bellatoni. You're an amazing man. And I'm guessing you're the reason my grandmother is here, standing beside my mother after decades of estrangement."

He grinned and shrugged. "Maybe."

"And it's for those reasons and so many others that I'd be honored to marry you. Just try and stop me."

Rocco sighed in relief and slipped the stunning platinum oval engagement ring with trillion accent stones on her finger. He must have used Luke's jeweler, it sparkled so brightly. The guests erupted in cheers and applause around them as he kissed her all too briefly.

Abbey was the first to offer their congratulations. "Oh my God. We have the same anniversary, sort of.

How fun," she said as she hugged Hannah.

"Told you," Luke told Rocco as he shook his hand and clapped him on the back.

They spent the next several minutes receiving well wishes from friends, family, and celebrities alike. It was surreal. She never would've imagined a proposal like this and from someone like Rocco. She was grateful. Her heart was full and she was ecstatic.

"We're going to work with Adrianna, I promise," Sydney said.

"We're so sorry, Hannah. We'll get her to start pronouncing your name correctly," Max assured her.

Hannah waved her newly bejeweled hand dismissively. "It's all right. I think it's sweet. She'll learn it eventually. For now, it can be our special thing."

Rocco grazed his lips along her bare shoulder and her body warmed. The evening was winding down. She looked forward to celebrating privately in their suite at the Fairchild Hotel.

"You're sweet to be so patient with her. She adores you, baby," Rocco commented.

She beamed up at him. "I adore her, too. I'm thrilled to be her *Zia*. And MJ's, too."

Max shook his head and gestured to their right. "Would you look at those three? They're going to be trouble."

They all turned. Her grandmother, Janice, Grandma Beverly, and Grandma Ruth were deep in discussion. Uh oh. That couldn't be good. Now that she thought about it, they'd been thick as thieves since Rocco had proposed. She wondered what they were up to.

When the three grandmothers noticed they were being watched, they all smiled brightly and Hannah knew they were in trouble. She wasn't sure if she should be afraid or pleased Janice seemed to get on well with Ruth and Beverly despite Janice's age difference.

Hannah's stomach coiled as the three grandmothers approached them, although they were all smiling. Rocco must've been nervous as well because he squeezed her hand.

"The three of you seem to be having a nice visit," Hannah said tentatively. She wasn't sure what to expect and wanted to tread lightly.

"Bev and Ruth are wonderful. I'm enjoying getting to know them," Grandmother Janice chirped happily.

Rocco glanced at Hannah and raised a curious brow. "That's wonderful," he commented cautiously.

"Ruth and I are thrilled for you both," Beverly said. "You two are going to make such beautiful Italian grandbabies!"

And there it was. Baby talk. Only a little while into their engagement. She should've known.

"I know!" Sydney chimed in. "Can't you picture it? Little Roccos running around? So adorable."

The four women giggled among themselves. Hannah shook her head, mildly amused but Rocco glared at his brother. That was strange.

Rocco scoffed and pointed at Max. "Not according to Max over here. He thinks my dick is broken. So, I'm sorry. No Italian grandbabies for you."

Max's mouth fell open and the color drained from his face. "Oh my God, Max!" Sydney gasped.

"How could you say something like that about our Rocco?" Grandma Beverly scolded.

"How dare you? Rocco's dick isn't broken. It's perfect," Grandma Ruth added.

"Ruth's right. His dick is just fine. Hell, if he'd met Hannah sooner, they'd had three or four children by now," Grandma Janice said.

Max held his hands up as if in surrender. "Ladies, please calm down. I was just kidding when I told Rocco that. Rocco, tell them I was kidding, will you?"

"You know? I'd love a dance with my new fiancée. See you later, Max. Ladies." Rocco laughed and led Hannah by the hand to the dancefloor, joining the other guests dancing to "Just The Way You Are" by Bruno Mars.

"Do I even want to know why the two of you were discussing your dick?" She smiled at guests dancing near them and glanced back toward Max as he tried to calm his wife and three angry grandmothers down.

Rocco shrugged and twirled her around the dancefloor. "I got nervous about proposing while we were getting dressed for the ceremony and Heath called him. We actually had a nice brother moment, then he fucked it up with a broken-dick joke. Serves him right."

They both watched on as Sydney and the grandmothers each hugged Max. He must've said something that satisfied the irate women. Hannah and Rocco both laughed. "Maybe next time, he'll watch his mouth before he says something stupid where you're concerned," Hannah said.

"He better. Or he'll have three angry *nonne* on his ass if he doesn't," Rocco remarked. He checked his watch and sent her a steamy glance. "It's just about time for the wedding festivities to end and our *private* festivities to begin, *cara*."

Rocco captured her hand and lifted it to his lips, pressing her knuckles with soft kisses. The heat from his lips burned her skin. Her nipples puckered and her core slickened. She liked the sound of private festivities very much. Even before he'd proposed, she'd been itching to get her hands on him.

After semi-rushing through their goodbyes, Rocco helped her into their waiting limousine. Her form-fitting dress made it difficult, she but managed and slid across the supple leather seat, making room for him.

As the chauffeur began their forty-minute drive to the Fairchild Hotel in Oak Brook from Barrington, Rocco laid her down on the seat and claimed her lips in a searing kiss. It was possessive and greedy. He ground his erection into her belly and groaned.

"I need you, baby. Right now." Rocco struggled with the hem of her dress, trying to pull it up. She knew he'd be unsuccessful and sighed. "Damn it. It's too form-fitting to pull up."

She pushed him until they were both sitting up. In the dim limousine lighting, she was saddened by the disappointed expression on his handsome face. She needed him too.

It was awkward, but she was able to position herself on the floor between his legs. When she went to unbutton his tuxedo pants, he tried to stop her.

"What are you doing, baby?" he asked.

"What do you think? We've got time before we get to the hotel. I'm going to take care of you." Reluctantly, he let go of her hands and she unzipped him, freeing his hard cock from his pants and boxer briefs. A drop of pre-cum glistened at the tip and her mouth watered for a taste.

"But I wanted to fuck you *before* we got there."

Hannah leaned forward and licked the tip, savoring the flavor of Rocco's unique essence. He hissed and she smiled. "How about I suck *you* now and you fuck *me* later?" she whispered.

Rather than wait for an answer, Hannah ran her tongue from root to tip. He drew in a breath and lifted his ass off the seat. She took his hot, thrusting cock into her mouth and sucked hard, nearly choking on it.

He'd been so stressed today, she wanted to do something just for him. He was still getting used to the idea of people doing for him rather always being the person doing for others.

His fingers threaded through her hair, working her head up and down his hard dick the way he wanted her to. She was more than happy to oblige. "I love your mouth on me, baby." He groaned.

"Mmm."

His body bucked as she sucked him. She deep-throated him and looked up, loving his reaction. His eyes were squeezed closed. He panted and the tendons in his neck were strained. As she cupped his balls, they drew tight in her hand.

"God, Hannah!" He held her head in place as he came in her mouth, and Hannah greedily swallowed every drop.

****

Rocco startled awake, unsure of where he was. He rubbed his eyes, slowly getting his bearings.

"We're almost at the hotel," Hannah whispered and gently squeezed his hand.

He leaned his head against the seat and sighed. *Fuck.* He'd fallen asleep after Hannah had blown him. Damn it.

"I'm so sorry, baby." He brought Hannah's wrist to his lips and kissed her fluttering pulse.

"It's all right. I dozed off a bit myself," Hannah assured him.

The limo came to a stop and Hannah smiled dreamily up at him. He'd make sure she'd never regret choosing him. Rocco was blessed. He still wasn't sure he deserved her, but he wasn't letting her go. Ever.

"We've arrived at the Fairchild Hotel, Mr.

Moretti," the driver announced through the car's speakers.

Finally. Rocco allowed the driver to help his woman out of the car before taking her hand once he exited himself. Leading Hannah toward the hotel lobby doors, he stopped when his name was called.

"Hey, guys, wait up," Jake called out.

Jake and an exhausted-looking Cassie were right behind them. Cassie held a plastic container with wedding cake. He chuckled at the mommy-to-be. Poor thing. She needed her rest, and apparently—cake.

"Is everything all right?" Hannah asked, obviously concerned.

Cassie yawned and they all stepped inside the quiet hotel lobby heading toward the gold elevator banks. Two associates from Dixon-Shaw were stationed there, already awaiting Luke and Abbey's arrival.

"No, not really. Cassie's beat. We ducked out of the reception just after you did. Our car was behind yours most of the way back to the hotel," Jake replied as they stepped inside the empty elevator car.

"Brenna Sinclair's treating us all to breakfast around ten-thirty to make up for what happened after our wedding brunch. She'll be in disguise and everything," Cassie informed them happily.

"I missed your brunch fiasco so I'm looking forward to breakfast. What could go wrong, right?" Hannah asked straight-faced.

The four of them looked at each other, waited a beat, and laughed. So many things, *that* was what could go wrong. But between the associates from Dixon-Shaw, their family, and *especially* their three sassy grandmothers, whatever chaos ensued, they'd handle it.

Rocco quickly led Hannah down the hallway toward their room on the Fairchild's top floor after saying goodnight to Jake and Cassie. Several Dixon-Shaw associates lining the hallway congratulated them on their engagement, but Rocco didn't linger. He was on a mission.

He needed to get Hannah out of her dress ASAP.

"Fuck!" The red light flashed for the third time, preventing him from entering their room and getting his hands on his woman. He jammed the room card in the door again only to be taunted by the red light yet again.

"Hey. Calm down. Give me the card," Hannah said in a soft, calm tone.

"One of you call down to the front desk. They fucked up our room key-card," Rocco called out behind him.

"No need to do that, guys. We're fine." She turned the card around, clicked it in place, and they were thankfully green-lighted into their room. Shit, he hadn't had the card facing in the correct direction.

Once they were both inside, he took a moment to gaze at the beauty before him. Hannah was everything he'd ever dreamed of and thought he'd never have. Believed he didn't deserve. Today, in front of their family, friends, and celebrities no less, she'd said she'd be *honored* to marry him. He still couldn't wrap his head around it all, but he'd take it—and he'd work on it.

He cupped her face with his hands. Her skin felt warm and soft. She gazed up at him, all her love reflected back at him. Love wasn't a strong enough word to describe how he felt. He not only loved Hannah, but he respected her, cherished her, valued her, was amazed by her, and was in complete awe of her.

He smiled down at her, willing her to understand what she meant to him. "We're getting married," she whispered, as if she didn't quite believe it.

"Hell yeah, we are." Rocco showered kisses

around her mouth and along her jaw. He placed tiny tantalizing kisses along her neck and shoulder until she swayed and clung to him.

His cock ached. He couldn't wait much longer.

He shrugged out of his tuxedo jacket and tossed it aside. Unbuttoning his vest, he noticed Hannah just standing there, not undressing. "Did you forget our verbal agreement, *bella*? We're alone. You're supposed to be naked," he reminded her. He took her by the hand and led them to the luxury suite's bedroom.

He kicked off his shoes and removed his vest, hurling it on a nearby accent chair. Hannah turned her back to him. Didn't she want him? She'd just agreed to marry him.

"I need a little help getting out of my dress," she said.

He chuckled. Ah, so that was it. "Aside from Abbey, you were the prettiest girl at the wedding. How the hell did you get *into* this thing?" He handily unzipped her, revealing a lacy pink strapless bra and matching pink panties. Because of her, he'd grown quite fond of the color pink. His dick throbbed in his pants as she shimmied out of her dress, revealing her luscious curves. His mouth watered for a taste.

"Joe had to help me," she said and giggled.

"Did he?" Rocco wasn't jealous. He knew Joe was just a friend. No. He was family. He trusted him with Hannah completely. After unhooking her bra and hurling it toward his vest, he turned her around to face him.

"Yes," she moaned after he suckled on one pebbled peak and then laved the other one. He loved how responsive she was. "You're way overdressed," she whispered and unbuttoned his shirt and yanked it out of his pants.

"I'll take care of this. Get in bed, *cara*."

Hannah hurried through pulling the extravagant bedspread and sheets down and climbed onto the comfortable bed after slipping out of her pretty pink panties. His dick throbbed at the sight of her glistening pussy.

Finally undressed except for his bowtie, he grabbed a couple of condoms from the nightstand drawer and tossed them on the bed. He was wide awake and ready to claim his bride-to-be.

He positioned himself on top of her and took possession of Hannah's lips. Hers were warm and sweet on his. She wrapped her arms and legs around him, holding him close. He forced her lips open with his thrusting tongue and devoured her until they were both panting.

Nibbling on her succulent flesh, Rocco did his best not to rush and was rewarded with a throaty moan when ran his tongue along her wet slit. She scraped her fingernails along his scalp and he nearly lost it. He needed to hold on a little longer, though.

Rocco slid his fingers inside her tight heat, aching to get inside of her himself. He explored her with his tongue, drowning in her exquisite taste. As he pumped his fingers inside of her while he teased and flicked her clit, it didn't take long before he felt his love's orgasm ripple through her. He smiled, feeling pride like he'd never known with a woman before, while he stroked and petted the inside of Hannah's thighs.

Rocco licked his lips and fingers clean. Once he had the condom on, he looked into her pleasure-glazed eyes. "I love you so fucking much," he whispered and buried himself inside of her with one thrust. "You're mine. All mine. Forever."

"Yes."

Hannah's breath was warm against his neck as he fucked her. Her pussy was still snug even though she'd just come. He drove in and out of her, he needed her so desperately. There would be time for finesse later. Hell, they'd have the rest of their lives.

She lifted her hips, matching him thrust for thrust. "Harder. Please," she pleaded.

"Anything for you, baby." He pistoned in and out of her so hard the headboard banged against the wall. Her pussy clamped around his dick and he groaned. He was close. Slipping a hand between them, he rubbed her swollen little clit. When she screamed out his name, he felt his balls draw up and he followed her over, filling the condom.

They held on to each other, hearts racing and breathing heavily. It was only when he felt himself soften he got up to discard of the condom.

When he returned, he found Hannah sitting up against the pillows with the bright white sheets tucked up under her arms, covering her gorgeous tits. That was a shame. He'd allow it, for now. She was smiling, admiring her engagement ring, but then a frown marred her lovely face.

He got into bed beside her, snuggling up close. It would always be this way, he thought. No more lonely days or nights. She'd be by his side from now on.

"What's the matter? We can exchange the ring for something you like better. Don't worry," Rocco assured her.

Hannah's eyes widened and she shook her head. "No. I love my ring. I was just thinking about when the grandmothers were talking about Italian grandbabies. It got me to thinking about when we had unprotected sex the day of my accident. I was sort of disappointed I didn't get pregnant. The timing wouldn't have been so great, but still."

It warmed Rocco's heart to know Hannah had wanted a family with him. He looked forward to that himself, though he agreed about the timing. "True, but it would have been a blessing, even so."

"So, you're looking forward to a few little Roccos running around?" Her smile lit up the room. Her hair was messy and her skin was flushed, but he thought she was stunning.

Clasping her hand in his, he shook his head. "Actually, I envisioned beautiful little Hannahs."

"Awww. You're so sweet. I'd be happy with either."

"Me too, honestly. But *after* we get the business side of things taken care of first. Let's be smart. This is a major project we've just started."

Hannah nodded and he was relieved. They would be under a lot of pressure as it was.

"Listen, Jake made Cassie wait seven years to get married. Luke and Abbey ended up waiting for more than ten. I don't want a long engagement. I want to make it official as soon as we can. I hope you don't mind, but I spoke with Enzo. Pick your favorite from your designs. Enzo will have a team in place to create it for us so it doesn't take months but maybe a few weeks. It'll be the first in your line. *Yours*. So we can get married after its ready. What do you think?"

He hoped like hell she wasn't upset. But he'd waited his whole life for her and he didn't want to wait another minute. He'd have to wait for her gown, but that was it. Trish was going to lend a hand in organizing the wedding but he'd let her work out the details with Hannah. He just wanted to get to the "I do's".

When Hannah started crying, he thought he'd totally fucked up. Shit. He'd tell her to forget it. They'd plan the wedding according to *her* timetable. *Her* happiness was what mattered to him most.

"Wow. That's amazing. You'd do that for me?" she asked as she wiped the tears from her cheeks.

"Of course. Like I told you. You're my family. I take care of my family. Let's say I'm promising you a blissfully ever after."

"You are?"

Rocco nodded. "I am," he assured Hannah and sealed his promise with a kiss.

Epilogue

Five years later

Rocco dried his hands in his and Hannah's private bathroom at Bliss Bridals Chicago. He shook his head. What a difference five years made. They referred to their salons by city name now, the Chicago salon being their flagship and headquarters.

He doubled-checked his appearance in the mirror. Not bad for forty-one. It was early September, so he'd let his beard grow out a little for Hannah in the coming weeks as the temperature cooled down. He had a little gray at the temples, which he rather liked and Hannah claimed she found sexy.

Rocco remained on the roster at Dixon-Shaw, taking on the occasional assignment when his schedule allowed, so he'd kept up his workout regime. He was as fit as he had been when he'd met her. Maybe even more so now that they had a three-year-old toddler to chase after.

Speaking of little Rocco, he chuckled. His son bore his name. He'd resisted the idea at first, not wanting to appear arrogant or egotistical. But his aunts had brought his baby pictures to the hospital the day their son had been born. Hannah had taken one look and insisted. It'd been impossible to tell them apart, so Rocco, Jr. it was.

Rocco checked his watch and winced. It was an hour past his boy's naptime. It was also thirty minutes before LA Chef Justina Rizzo was due for a consult.

He wasn't sure why she was coming to Chicago. They had a salon in LA. They occasionally filmed

Blissfully Ever After from there. They did their best to include all five of their locations in the filming. Was she trying to make some kind of point? Taunting him? He didn't like it, but he and Hannah had agreed to hear Justina out before making a final decision about having her on the show.

He made his way around the salon, greeting brides and their friends and families until he stumbled upon Richard holding his video camera, looking forward. From his vantage point, he couldn't tell what Richard was looking at so intently. Rocco was fairly certain they weren't filming today.

Once he was standing beside him, he rolled his eyes. He should've known.

"Little Zoolander over there has been keeping the ladies entertained for a few minutes now," Richard quipped happily.

"I would appreciate it if you didn't refer to my son as little Zoolander. He's going to college and will graduate with honors."

"What if he wants to serve?" Richard asked.

"He won't be a grunt like I was. He's going to college first then he'll apply to Officer Candidacy School."

"Hey. Be proud of your time in the Marines. You served honorably," Richard said in all sincerity.

Rocco hadn't meant it that way. He was proud of his time in the military. If he had it to do over again, he would. His time in the Marines meant something to him. It made him the man he was today. In a way, it had brought him to Hannah. To his son. "I am. I just meant getting a degree first would give little Rocco opportunities I didn't have."

He couldn't help it, but he thought his son was so fucking cute. He was wearing the little boy's version of what he was wearing today. Black Bellatoni wool slacks, a white dress shirt with sleeves rolled up to the elbow, and black leather loafers.

"See? I have tattoos just like my daddy." Little Rocco showed off his forearms with the temporary tattoos Enzo, Jr. and Michael Bellatoni had designed that replicated the actual tattoos Rocco had on his arms. The ladies oohed and ahhed, nodding to his little boy and smiling. They were sweet to indulge him.

"That was a stroke of genius, those temporaries," Richard commented.

Rocco hadn't had much choice. RJ, as they sometimes called and referred to little Rocco, had cried so many times, wanted tattoos so he could look more like him. He'd called Enzo, Jr. and Michael, not sure of what to do. The Bellatoni brothers already created temporary designs, so they'd provided several sheets replicating Rocco's for his son. For now, little Rocco was pacified.

"And I help my daddy at the restaurant, too! I have a black chef uniform and a hat, just like him," little Rocco bragged.

"You do? That's amazing," one of the women said.

"Yeah, I know! I help him a lot. And Mommy, too." He beamed, nodding.

"You're such a good boy," another woman said.

"Yes. I'm a big boy now," he informed them all.

"Did you take a look at the proofs and footage I shot? Tell me your boy isn't the cutest for the boy's line. Even more than Max's son," Richard said.

Rocco had already reviewed everything. Enzo and Paolo were lucky to have Richard on their staff now. He had a gift. "It's not a competition. Rocco and Max are first cousins and they look a lot alike."

"It's just you and me. Be honest," Richard said,

egging him on.

They were family. He loved his nephew. The boys were not only cousins, but good friends. Fuck it. "Yes. I think Rocco was the cutest. You satisfied? Don't say a fucking word. I'll deny I said it."

Richard watched on with a smug look on his face. Asshole.

"And so if RJ wants to model or act? What then?" Richard asked.

"Are you not hearing me? He's going to college. If Luke can be a professional athlete and get an MBA, then little Rocco can act, model, or do whatever the fuck he wants and *still* get a college degree. One that means something, like an MBA or a degree in finance like Heath and Leah got, or a computer science degree like Abbey got." What didn't Richard understand? RJ was bright and inquisitive. He would do well in school. Rocco had no doubt.

"There are so many people with advanced degrees that don't do shit with them. Look at what you've accomplished *without* one. That's all I'm saying."

Huh. Point taken. This so-called meeting with Justina was just that. He had nothing to prove. "All right. But I'm going to encourage little Rocco to go to college and that's that. Don't make me shoot you. At my last count, you were up to four bullets."

Richard put his free hand up in surrender and shut the hell up. Good.

His son chatted up and flirted with the ladies for a few more minutes.

"Your aunts tell me you were just like him when you were his age," Richard commented.

Rocco scoffed. "Bullshit. I was not."

Richard shrugged. "You're right. You weren't. They said you were an even *bigger* flirt."

Little Rocco yawned and rubbed his eyes. That was Daddy's cue. The women glanced up at him and mouthed, *Naptime*. He nodded back at them.

Rocco held out a hand. "Rocco. *Vieni qui*," he called out to his son, who was way past his naptime.

His son stood at attention. "I have to go. My daddy needs me." Little Rocco raced to him and placed his tiny hand in his. Although clearly exhausted, his smile never dimmed. He turned back to the ladies he'd been chatting up and waved. "*Ciao*," he called out.

"*Ciao*, Rocco!" the ladies called back and waved to them both before making their way back to their bride.

"Did new dresses come? Do you need me? Where's Mommy?"

He wondered that himself. Where *was* Hannah? Justina was due soon. He wished Hannah were here. His son found it difficult to argue with his mother. Not so much with him, unfortunately.

Rocco bent down so he was on little Rocco's level. He noticed Richard had started filming. That was odd. It would make for embarrassing footage once RJ was older, though. That could be fun. "Mommy's around here somewhere, I'm sure. Look, buddy, it's time for your nap." He braced himself.

Little Rocco's eyes glistened and he shook his head. "No. I'm big now. I don't want a nap."

Rocco sighed. "Come on. You were just yawning when you were talking to the nice ladies before. Just for a little while. We've got your cool Ferrari bed in Mommy and Daddy's office, right?" It was a gift from Enzo and Paulo Bellatoni, given to them shortly after little Rocco had been born.

His son wasn't convinced and shook his head. "I'm not tired."

Damn it. He didn't want a toddler temper tantrum

in the middle of the salon just before Justina arrived. "You know how you eat good food and vegetables so you'll grow up to be big and strong?"

His son nodded, his eyes drooping. Why was he fighting a nap he so clearly needed? "Like you. Right, Daddy?"

His heart constricted. His little boy wanted to be just like him. He wasn't sure how to deal with such adoration at times. He hoped he never let RJ down.

"Yes, like me. But you also need good sleep and rest to be at your best. Getting enough rest is just as important as food. So you can help Mommy and Daddy like you do. That's why you need your nap."

****

Hannah sped into the parking lot of Bliss Bridals Chicago and smiled. It was like coming home. Big Rocco and little Rocco were there and she couldn't wait to see them. She checked her watch and frowned. Little Rocco would be napping. It'd be all right. She'd share the news with him after he woke up. She hoped he'd take the news well.

After exiting her car, she hurried into the salon. Justina Rizzo, up-and-coming LA chef, was due to arrive soon for a consultation. The woman was full of herself, insisting on a personal meeting when she could easily go to the LA salon.

Just because she and Rocco had agreed to meet with her didn't guarantee Justina would appear on an episode of *Blissfully Ever After*. And if Justina thought she was going to intimidate her man, she had another thing coming. Whatever game the bitch was playing, she would lose.

Hannah frowned when she spotted her men in deep in discussion. If she had to guess, big Rocco was most likely trying to convince little Rocco to take his nap. Good thing she was here. Her little man tended not to argue with her. Not like he did with his father. She didn't look forward to little Rocco's older years in that regard, the arguments between father and son that would certainly arise. For some reason, Richard was filming their tense moment.

Hannah inhaled deeply, prepared to help big Rocco out and get their boy into his Ferrari bed for his nap. The relieved expression on her husband's face when he noticed her caused her to giggle. He must have been at his wit's end.

She took a few steps toward the loves of her life and suddenly felt lightheaded. She stumbled, her head spinning. Her ears rang and she felt herself falling.

"Hannah!"

"Mommy!"

Rocco lifted her into his arms before she hit the ground and gently placed her on the nearest white overstuffed couch. She inhaled deeply, slowly regaining her equilibrium.

"Richard, put the fucking camera down and call 911," Rocco barked out.

Her little boy sat down beside her and held her hand, tears streaming down his face. "What's wrong, Mommy?"

"I'm fine. It's all right." Hannah tried to assure everyone. Joe had now joined them, taking his place beside Richard.

"You're *not* fine," Rocco insisted.

"But Mommy, you almost fell." Little Rocco sobbed.

"I'll be fine in seven months," she told everyone, hoping they caught on and calmed down.

Joe gasped, obviously the first to get it.

"What are you talking about, seven months?"

Rocco asked.

"Oh," Richard said as he continued filming them.

"Daddy?"

Hannah took her son's and husband's hands and gently placed them on her stomach. "Yes, seven more months. I was running late from my OB/GYN appointment."

Rocco showered her face with kisses before turning to little Rocco. "Mommy's growing a little baby in her tummy. That means you're going to be a big brother. That's a very important job in our family. I'm your *Zio* Max's big brother, right? What do you think about that?"

RJ's eyes grew wide and she held her breath. "Really? Mommy's making me a baby brother?" he asked excitedly. What a relief. He didn't seem upset, although she wouldn't know the gender for a few more weeks.

She squeezed little Rocco's hand and smiled down at his sweet face. "We won't know for a little while if it's a boy."

"But it might be a girl. Wouldn't it be nice to have a little sister who looks just like Mommy?" Rocco asked their son.

Hannah's heart swelled. She knew Rocco was praying for a daughter.

Their little boy didn't miss a beat and nodded happily. "Yeah. Mommy's so pretty. Little sister!" he shouted.

"It's going to be a few weeks before we know for sure. Then we'll make plans, okay?" she asked.

"Okay, Mommy." He kissed her cheek, scooted off the couch, and raced straight to Joe, taking ahold of his hand. Her little boy whispered something up to his *Zio* Joe. Joe nodded and led them away.

"Hey. Where are you two going?" she called out.

"I have to take my nap, so I can be the best. Like Daddy said. He's smart, like me." Joe and little Rocco rounded the corner toward their shared office, and she and big Rocco couldn't help but laugh.

"The next seven months will be interesting, that's for sure," Hannah said. She cupped Rocco's face and kissed him tenderly, well aware they will still being filmed. "Are you happy about the baby?"

His bright smile soothed her soul. "Boy or girl, I'm thrilled. Are *you* happy, *bella*?" he asked.

"The night we got engaged, you promised me a blissfully ever after," she reminded him.

He looked concerned, as if she was implying she wasn't happy. "Have I delivered so far?"

"You certainly have. I hope I've done the same for you," she said.

"More than you could ever know, baby," he replied.

She waved Richard off and for the next few minutes, their obligations and responsibilities fell away. They snuggled on the couch together, enjoying a rare moment of solitude before the world demanded their attention again.

Rocco had more than delivered on his promise of a blissfully ever after. She looked forward to what the future had in store for them. If it was anything like their first five years together, she knew she wouldn't be disappointed.

The End

www.daniavoss.com

EVERNIGHT PUBLISHING ®

www.evernightpublishing.com

www.ingramcontent.com/pod-product-compliance
Lightning Source LLC
Chambersburg PA
CBHW030245200626
46816CB00002BA/514